His voice was hoarse.

'When you touch me like that it tips me over the edge of madness. I want you so much it hurts beyond endurance. I'm cautioning you—if you carry on touching me that way I'll take you here and now. I won't be able to stop.'

Joanna licked her lips and swallowed. She slid her hand down between their bodies, feeling the proof of his words. She brushed her hand against the hardness she felt and lifted her face. Hal was watching her intently. She recognised in his expression the desire that filled her.

'Then don't stop,' she murmured.

Author Note

This story takes place in and around my home town of York and the North York Moors, an area I consider one of the most beautiful and dramatic in Britain. I'd urge everyone to visit—especially when the heather is in bloom and there is purple in every direction.

All but two of the locations mentioned in the book are real. Around a third of the way through writing I was delighted to find a female blacksmith named Johane on the lists of guild members working from St Andrewgate. Ravenscrag and Wharram Danby are my creations, but owe a lot to the centuries-old villages on the moors, including Wharram Percy which is managed by English Heritage and can be visited.

Sir Terry Pratchett died while I was writing this book, saddening me more than I can articulate here. When Joanna decided to adopt a dog—nothing to do with me…I didn't know she was going to!—he became my tribute to Gaspode the Wonder Dog. There's also another of his characters I've borrowed. Please let me know if you spot him.

The dog belongs to a friend who agrees with me that dogs with human names are extremely funny, and that Simon is by far the best example. His name was an unplanned but amusing coincidence—I love it when completely unrelated areas of my life collide.

As with all my stories, a particular song acted as a focus for my writing. This time it was *Every Day* by Stevie Nicks.

THE BLACKSMITH'S WIFE

Elisabeth Hobbes

First published in Great Britain 2016
By Mills & Boon, an imprint of HarperCollins*Publishers*
1 London Bridge Street, London, SE1 9GF

Large Print edition 2016

ISBN: 978-0-263-26315-2

Our policy is to use papers that are natural, renewable and recyclable
products and made from wood grown in sustainable forests.
The logging and manufacturing processes conform to the legal
environmental regulations of the country of origin.

Printed and bound in Great Britain
by CPI Antony Rowe, Chippenham, Wiltshire

Elisabeth Hobbes grew up in York, where she spent most of her teenage years wandering around the city looking for a handsome Roman or Viking to sweep her off her feet. Elisabeth's hobbies include skiing, Arabic dance and fencing—none of which has made it into a story yet. When she isn't writing she spends her time reading, and is a pro at cooking while holding a book! Elisabeth lives in Cheshire with her husband, two children, and three cats with ridiculous names.

Books by Elisabeth Hobbes

Mills & Boon Historical Romance

Falling for Her Captor
A Wager for the Widow
The Blacksmith's Wife

Visit the Author Profile page at millsandboon.co.uk.

To Jenni, Paul and Fredi.
Thanks for the entertaining conversation
about vellum and parchment.
And the accompanying caipirinhas.

Chapter One

Hooves thundered on the ground as the horses charged. Lances met armour, splintering on impact and sending shards of wood cascading across the lists. The riders wheeled their mounts round to face each other once more. The crowd roared, stamping feet, pounding fists against the wooden fences that separated them from the contestants. In the stands the women gasped in alarm, clutching each other's hands in excitement and suspense. To watch was agonising, but not a watcher, high- or low-born, could bear to tear his or her eyes from the spectacle before them.

None more so than Joanna Sollers.

'Sir Roger leads. Sir Godfrey must unseat him or deliver a strike to the head to win,' muttered a man to Joanna's left.

'Sir Godfrey will win,' his companion replied. 'He has twice the experience of Sir Roger.'

Roger Danby *would* win the joust; Joanna's certainty was iron hard. It was true that today's encounters were between knights untried in battle but Sir Roger was the best and brightest. His skill on horseback was the talk of Yorkshire. He told Joanna so whenever she mentioned her fears for his safety, laughing at her protests as he silenced her with clandestine kisses, more forward and demanding each time they met.

Joanna forced her eyes back to the arena. At either end of the tilt the knights wiped sweat from their brows, as squires brought them fresh lances. Sir Roger's chestnut stallion pounded the dirt fiercely, tossing its head, as eager to be off as its master.

Trumpets sounded and the knights lowered their visors once more, hefting their lances in readiness for the final encounter. A hush descended as the flag was raised. Joanna bit her lip anxiously. For three years she had known Sir Roger and could not remember him ever becoming unseated. Even so her hands twisted the linen scarf she held in her lap, tightening it around her fist until the blood pooled in her fingers.

The flag dropped and the knights charged, roaring. Sir Godfrey's lance smashed into Sir Roger's chest. The younger knight rolled his shoulder back and the lance remained unbroken. At the same time Sir Roger's weapon caught his opponent square in the chest, shattering on impact. The crowd surged *en masse* to its feet in a deafening roar. Joanna let out a breath she had not even been aware she was holding.

Sir Roger was victorious, winning a purse of silver and his place in the following day's competition.

The knights trotted back along the tilt, hands raised in salute to Sir Bartholomew Clifford, Sheriff of York. Sir Roger raised himself in his saddle, his eyes sweeping the crowd. Joanna leaned forward on the low wooden bench, desperate to catch his eye but knowing he was unlikely to spot her at the rear of the stands.

She craned her neck to see the central stand where noble ladies sat, dressed in a dazzling rainbow of silks and velvets and she felt a pang of longing. Perhaps this would be the year Sir Roger finally asked for her hand in marriage. If he continued to win tournaments he would soon have the riches he insisted were all that had prevented him asking so far.

The thought of becoming Lady Danby brought a smile to Joanna's lips. She could scarcely believe that the niece of a merchant blacksmith had caught the eye of a nobleman. Roger had come to her uncle's workshop seeking a new helmet and in Simon Vernon's absence Joanna had taken the order. When her uncle had returned the young knight had been in no hurry to depart, his interest in the seventeen-year-old Joanna abundantly clear. Simon had strutted around St Andrewgate boasting to the other guild members for weeks of his niece's skill at attracting such a prestigious suitor. For Joanna the matter was clearer. She loved Sir Roger. The months he was absent from York were grey and cheerless. She lived for the day he returned and her life once again was filled with warmth.

Lost in her reverie she almost missed the riders leaving the lists to loud cheers. Joanna sat back, her mind wandering as the next bout took place. Only one man claimed her interest and he would not be competing again until tomorrow. When the sun began to sink below the stands she left, threading her way through the rows of stalls, past trinket sellers, food vendors and entertainers.

Joanna crossed the river, then hesitated. Spread around the walls of the castle were the pavilions where the knights were camped. In her bag was a gift she had meant to leave for Sir Roger, but why not deliver it herself? He would have returned to the camp by now. She would see him at the banquet in the Common Hall that evening but she knew from sad experience they would scarcely get a moment alone. Other knights—and other women—would surround Roger.

Instead of taking the road that led back to the city, Joanna made her way among the throng of people heading towards the mass of brightly coloured tents.

'What is your business in camp?'

Two guards stood with pikes crossed, admitting some visitors, refusing others. They gazed stony faced as they barred Joanna's progress but she was prepared for that. She indicated the bulky leather bag tucked under her arm.

'I have a delivery for Sir Roger Danby.'

'I bet you do,' the left guard said with a leer to his companion. 'It's a little early in the afternoon for that sort of delivery, isn't it?'

A blush started prickling around the back of Joanna's neck. She glared at him. 'I come from the establishment of Simon Vernon, of the Smiths' Guild. You dare to suggest...'

The guard held out a hand. 'I'll see it gets passed on.'

Joanna raised her chin. 'I think not! I have promised to deliver it to Sir Roger myself.'

The guards rolled their eyes but let her pass. Their suggestive comments echoed in her ears and her cheeks coloured. She should not have come. Of course there would be women of dubious morals trying to gain access to the camp, but to be considered one of them was mortifying.

As soon as she was out of sight she smoothed her honey-blonde hair back behind her ears, sighing at the unruly single wave that refused to be suppressed by her plaits. She pulled at the sleeves of her thick woollen dress until her wrists were covered and checked the neckline was sufficiently demure so as not to cause comment. It was a surprisingly mild day for late February and she wished she had not worn such a heavy cloak. With a final adjustment of her cloak buckle she was satisfied. The guard's insinuations had been unfair and unfounded. She looked exactly what she was: a respectable member of a merchant's household, not some cheap doxy.

Joanna continued on her way, hefting the bag higher under her arm. Her mood lifted and she hid a smile. She hadn't exactly lied to the guards. She *was* from Simon Vernon's establishment; though it was unlikely her uncle would claim knowledge of her presence if he were questioned. And she *had* promised to deliver the package to

Sir Roger's own hands, even if the promise was only to herself.

Once inside no one paid Joanna any attention. The camp was as busy as the tournament ground had been and everyone was far too busy with their own affairs to notice one more person engaged on an errand. She found Sir Roger's tent towards the back of the encampment, flying his blue pennant emblazoned with a green boar but it was empty save for Sir Roger's page, a dull-witted boy of eight who sat in the corner playing jacks.

Joanna made her way to the courtyard where makeshift stables and workshops had been assembled. She had given up hope of finding Sir Roger when, through a sudden parting in the crowd, she saw familiar black curls and glimpsed the line of his jaw just as he turned away.

A thrill of anticipation rippled through Joanna as she eased her way towards him. It had been six months since Sir Roger had last been in York. Despite the urge to run to his arms Joanna stood back and watched in admiration.

Sir Roger was facing away from her, sharpening a sword with slow, sure strokes. He had removed his armour and padded woollen tunic, but instead of the customary fitted doublet of fine wool he favoured, he was dressed in britches and a shapeless tunic drawn in at the waist with a thick belt. As Joanna watched he laid the sword on a trestle table, rolled his head from side to side and stretched his arms high.

Intending to surprise him Joanna crept behind him. She reached on tiptoe to whisper in his ear, her lips close enough to brush against his hair.

'Greetings, my lord, I've been searching for you.'

He stiffened and turned to face her. Joanna found herself gazing up into Sir Roger's eyes.

In the face of a stranger.

Her mouth fell open and she stumbled backwards away from the man, dropping her bag. Explanations and apologies tumbled unintelligibly from her lips.

'I didn't know…I thought you were…I mean… I'm sorry!'

The man folded his arms across his broad chest. His lips curled into an amused smile. Joanna took another step back, her mind whirling with confusion and embarrassment. Her voice tailed off. Her heart was pounding so loudly she would swear it must be audible. She covered her face with her hands in an attempt to conceal the blush that was turning her pale complexion scarlet and peered through her fingers.

It was little wonder she had mistaken the man for Sir Roger. From behind they shared the same build and unruly curls. Facing her there was still a resemblance. She noticed for the first time that what she had taken for a belt was a long leather apron tied about his waist. Whoever he was, the stranger was no knight.

'I beg your forgiveness!' Joanna said, wincing with embarrassment.

The man ran a hand through the tangle of black curls that fell to just below his ears. He eyed Joanna with an open interest that made her heart thump.

'No forgiveness needed. I thought Lady Fortune was finally smiling on me but alas it seems not,' he said with an exaggerated note of regret. 'It's been so long since I have had such a greeting that I believe I should be thanking you for the experience! Perhaps I will do as a companion?' he suggested.

The guards' earlier comments flooded back. Another flush of shame heated Joanna's cheeks, spreading across her chest to a neckline that suddenly felt much lower than before. Did this man also take her for a whore? Given her immodest greeting it would not be unlikely he had come to such a conclusion. 'I don't know what sort of woman you think I am but I can assure you that you are mistaken,' she said stiffly, folding her arms defensively across her breasts. 'I was looking for someone in particular.'

'I gathered that. Now, I wonder who you're searching for,' the man mused, running a thumb across the stubble that peppered his jaw. His voice was deep, with a slight trace of accent, though Joanna could not say where it was from. 'Would you care to wager a cup of wine that I can guess the identity of your quarry?'

'I would not!' Joanna said firmly. With as much dignity as she could muster under the circumstances she dropped a brief curtsy. 'Once again I beg your pardon. Good day.' She picked up her bag and spun on her heel before her heart pushed itself from her chest.

'Try the alehouse,' the man called after her as she fled. 'Jousting gives a man more than one kind of thirst after all.'

Joanna wrinkled her nose in annoyance. She ran back through the camp, past Sir Roger's tent towards the gate. She paid no attention to her direction and collided roughly with someone. Hands gripped her shoulders and she gave a cry of alarm, twisting to free herself.

'Joanna?'

She jerked her head upwards to look at her captor and found herself looking into Sir Roger's face. She let out a sigh of relief.

Sir Roger frowned.

'What are you doing in the camp? I did not expect to see you until tonight at the earliest.' His face relaxed into a smile as he drew her arm under his and led her back towards his tent, regaling her with an account of the tournament she had just witnessed. She pushed her thoughts of the stranger to the back of her mind.

Sir Roger pushed back the curtain covering his tent doorway and ushered Joanna inside. He tossed his page a coin.

'Go buy yourself some sweetmeats.'

The boy ambled off, leaving them alone. Sir Roger pulled Joanna to him, his hands at either side of her waist.

'I'm surprised at you coming here alone.' His voice was stern but the glint in his eye told Joanna he was far from disapproving. His eyes took on a hungry expression. 'You're usually so modest, too.'

Joanna glanced at the doorway but Sir Roger did not appear to notice her uneasiness. He lunged to kiss her. His lips scraped against hers and his hands began to slide from her waist downwards to spread across her hips. Joanna stiffened. This was the first time they had been completely alone and Sir Roger's behaviour was more forceful than she had expected. The guards' mocking words whispered in Joanna's mind.

She wriggled from Sir Roger's arms.

'I brought you a gift,' she said hastily to hide her unease. She rummaged into her bag until she produced a cloth-wrapped bundle. Sir Roger unwrapped it eagerly, revealing an ornately decorated belt buckle.

'Your uncle made this?' he asked, holding it to the light.

Joanna nodded and rubbed her fingers lovingly over the incised leaves. 'Though I chased the pattern myself.'

Sir Roger took her hands and drew her close. 'It's beautiful. You'll be a worthy heir to your uncle's business.'

Joanna blushed with pleasure at the compliment but laughed. 'His heir? Not I. He has a son now. But of course, it's been months since you were in York. You wouldn't know my aunt's child was a boy.'

'What good fortune for your uncle,' Roger said. 'Perhaps you might congratulate him in person tonight and speak to him about other matters,' Joanna began shyly.

'That could be time I spend in your company instead,' Sir Roger murmured. 'There's no rush, is there?' His hands began moving over her body, one down towards her buttocks, the other sliding towards her breast. He kissed her, his tongue attempting to part her lips. Joanna's brow wrinkled. This was the very limit of acceptable behaviour before they were married. She began to shift away from his reach, turning so she stood between him and the doorway.

A cold draught blew around her neck and a deep, familiar voice spoke.

'Roger, it strikes me...'

Sir Roger released her abruptly and stepped back. Joanna turned slowly around to face the speaker, heart sinking as she saw who stood behind her.

The man she had met before stood in the doorway, his hands outstretched in apology. 'I'm sorry. I saw your boy wandering off. I didn't know you would have company.'

He did not sound contrite in the least. When his eyes fell on Joanna they held her gaze and his lips twitched. Sir Roger gave a long sigh of annoyance. Joanna's eyes flickered from man to man.

'Mistress Sollers, permit me to introduce my brother, Henry Danby,' Sir Roger said in a clipped tone.

Joanna's jaw dropped. 'You never told me you had a brother!' she said.

'Half-brother,' the man said curtly, glancing at Sir Roger.

'Did I never mention Hal?' Roger said carelessly. 'I suppose not. He's been travelling around the country. Our paths have barely crossed in the past three years,'

Joanna stared in wonder from Sir Roger to his brother and back again. Conscious she was staring at the new arrival, Joanna curtsied. 'Good day to you, Sir Henry.'

'Just Hal if you please. I'm no sir.'

'Hal and I share the same father but we have different mothers,' Sir Roger explained.

Half-brothers. That made sense. They were too close in age to make any other explanation possible.

'What Roger means is I'm a bastard,' Henry added with a humourless smile. He lifted his jaw and crossed his arms, as though daring Joanna to confront him. 'Though my father did me the kindness of acknowledging me as his. Many would not.'

Taken aback at the harshness of his voice, Joanna stared at him. When they had met before he had seemed good-humoured, for all his mocking words, but his sudden fierceness was unnerving. His brow was knotted and his eyes dark. For a moment silence hung awkwardly between them as all three stood motionless saying nothing.

Side by side the brothers were not so alike after all. They were of equal height and stature and both had hair the colour of a crow's wing but Sir Roger's was swept back and tied neatly at his nape. He wore a short, neatly trimmed beard while his brother's hair fell forward in careless tangles to a jaw rough with stubble.

The resemblance was strongest about the eyes: deep brown, flecked with green and ringed with long lashes set into faces tanned from a life spent outside, but the expressions in them were markedly different. Sir Roger gazed on Joanna with fondness but Henry appraised her with a dark humour, seemingly enjoying her discomposure.

'I have to go. I am expected home,' Joanna mumbled, reaching for her bag. She smiled at Sir Roger, hoping he would offer to escort her through the camp but he merely smiled stiffly and bade her farewell. Hiding her disappointment, Joanna held her hand out for him to kiss, nodded towards Henry and fled from the tent. She reached the gateway in a rush but stopped as she neared the guards.

One of them smirked at her, his eyes roving up and down her body.

'Finished your delivery quickly, didn't you? Is your load lighter now?'

'I'll bet someone's is,' the other sniggered, nudging his companion in the ribs.

Joanna's eyes prickled with shame. She took a deep breath, determined to walk past with dignity.

'If you don't keep your mouths civil in the presence of women I'll have a word in the right ear and you'll be guarding the middens until the tournament ends!'

Joanna spun round to find Henry Danby striding towards her.

'Mistress Sollers, allow me to escort you back to the city.' He held out an arm for her. Surprised, she took it and let him lead her through the gateway.

'If you are as virtuous as you claim to be you shouldn't visit the camp again,' he muttered as they passed by the guards. 'Those oafs won't be the only ones casting slights on you.'

'What do you mean *claim*?' Joanna pulled her arm free and rounded on him angrily. 'My reputation is no concern of yours and I have done nothing to incite gossip.' She flushed slightly as she thought of the kisses she had permitted Sir Roger to take that were far from fitting for an unmarried woman. 'Sir Roger and I were doing nothing wrong,' she said indignantly. She stopped short. If she had spoken in such a tone to Sir Roger he would have been angry or turned cold but Master Danby simply laughed.

'What you and my brother do in private is none of my business, but I wasn't referring to that. He leaned closer and murmured in her ear. 'When we meet next you can buy me some wine.'

'Why?' Joanna asked in confusion.

'Because I was right in guessing who you were searching for when you whispered so temptingly in my ear.'

Joanna snorted angrily. 'Goodbye, Master Danby. I can make my own way back,' she said. She turned and walked away, his soft laughter ringing in her ears.

Chapter Two

By the time Joanna passed through the gate into the city her face was no longer red though she still shook with indignation whenever she thought of the guards' words.

Visiting the camp had been a mistake and her indiscretions with Sir Roger had been the biggest error of all. His kisses had been more intense than ever before and the way he had touched her more than a little alarming. Such intimacies should wait for their wedding night. Little wonder Henry Danby had cast doubts on her virtue after he had found them together.

Horror flooded through Joanna and she stopped abruptly as his laughing face flashed before her eyes. What if he told Sir Roger of their earlier encounter? How would the knight view such behaviour? She could try finding Master Danby again and pleading for him to keep her secret, but she could not face the trial of talking her way past the guards again, or the scathing expression she was sure she would see in Master Danby's eyes. Whatever happened she would have to deal with it.

She returned home and pushed the front door open cautiously. Even her short interlude had made her later than she would be expected. With luck Uncle Simon would still be at his foundry or the Guild Hall and she could slip in unnoticed. Two girls aged seven and four hurled themselves towards her, squealing with delight. Their older sister, ten and too dignified to show such affection, nodded from the corner and returned to her sewing.

Joanna hugged her cousins, answering the questions that tumbled from them. Yes, she had seen the jousting. Yes, Sir Roger won. No, she did not know which knight had triumphed in the mêlée.

'Joanna, come in here!'

The laughter ceased at the sound of the gruff voice. Joanna walked through to the kitchen, her stomach fluttering.

'You're late.' Simon Vernon folded his burly arms across his chest and frowned at his niece. 'Where have you been? Watching the tournament while I work to feed you all?'

Joanna forced herself to look contrite.

'I beg your pardon,' she said. 'I delivered the buckle to Sir Roger in person.'

Simon's brows knotted. 'You visited him unchaperoned! Do you care nothing for your reputation? Or mine?'

'I do care.' She pushed away the insinuations of the guards and Henry Danby's similar warning. 'Sir Roger sends his thanks for your gift.'

A thin smile cracked Simon's stern face. 'So, you pleased him?'

Joanna blushed, remembering his caresses. 'I hope he will speak to you tonight.'

Simon pushed himself from his stool, towering above Joanna. 'He had better. Even the most charitable uncle is not obliged to keep you forever. For three years I've waited for you to catch him as your husband. The hours I've spent entertaining him have cost me dearly but he still delays. I'm beginning to doubt his feelings for you are as strong as they first appeared to be.'

'Sir Roger will marry me,' Joanna insisted. Of course he must love her, to be so direct and forceful with his embraces.

'I hope so,' Simon growled. 'You will be twenty-one before the summer is over. You should have been married long before this. I have enough mouths of my own to feed, with all the expense that entails.'

Joanna glanced around. Richly embroidered tapestries hung from every wall. Heavy oak chests stood either side of the door and half-a-dozen hams hung above the large fireplace. Simon Vernon was not approaching poverty by any means. In the nine years since the Great Pestilence had claimed her family, Joanna had worked hard to ensure Simon had not regretted taking in his sister's only surviving child, however grudgingly the act of charity had been committed. She closed her eyes to prevent her uncle seeing the grief in them.

Simon came behind her and put his hands on her shoulders. 'If my family is connected to the nobility imagine the doors that will open for me,' he said hungrily.

'I had better go prepare for tonight,' Joanna said frostily.

'Mind your tongue,' Simon growled. 'Remember Sir Roger is used to obedient, well-brought-up ladies. You won't catch a husband of any sort if you can't keep your thoughts to yourself.'

Joanna climbed the stairs to the attic room she shared with the serving girl. She removed her grey dress and sponged herself down with cold water from the jug by the window. Clad in her shift, she shivered as the cold February air whipped around her bare flesh. She changed into a dress of red linen and began to lace the threads of her bodice. She closed her eyes, imagining it was Sir Roger's hands that were deftly working at the cloth, but Henry's sardonic eyes flashed in Joanna's mind and a shudder rippled through her body. She finished lacing her dress and brushed her hair until it fell in a cascade down her back, affixed a fine veil to her hair and wound her finest silk scarf around her neck.

Tonight she must be her most beautiful if she had any hope of winning Sir Roger's hand. And if she failed to do that, well, she didn't want to think about her uncle's reaction.

When Joanna descended the staircase Aunt Mary glanced up and gave her a smile before returning her attention to the infant she was nursing. Little Elizabeth squealed with delight and even Uncle Simon nodded with approval.

'Thomas Gruffydd's wife died birthing her latest boy,' Simon remarked as they walked through the city. 'He returns to Montgomery soon and I know he'd gladly take a new wife with him.'

Joanna's stomach clenched. 'He's more than twice my age.'

'What does that matter?' Simon scoffed. 'I'd rather you brought better connections but if Sir Roger does not ask for your hand a man with the land Gruffydd owns would do just as well. I expect you to consider him.'

They made their way to the Common Hall where lights blazed in the doorway and windows. The heady scent of herbs and rushes on the floor assailed them as they removed their cloaks and entered the hall. Uncle Simon excused himself and joined the huddle of guildsmen by the table laden with food. Old men with paunched bellies and greasy chins and fingers from the meat they ate. Thomas Gruffydd was among them.

Joanna wrinkled her nose in disgust and stared around the room, searching anxiously for Sir Roger. The knights were grandly dressed in the colours of their houses, walking among the other guests gathering admiring glances. The dancing was already underway and her foot began to tap. She finally spotted him standing in an alcove at the far end of the hall. Her heart sank. He was not alone.

She watched enviously as Sir Roger kissed the hand of a young woman, taller than herself with shining black curls. Their eyes never parted as Sir Roger led her to thread seamlessly into the dance.

'I hope you don't intend to spend your evening watching others having fun rather than joining in!'

Joanna jumped as a voice spoke in deep, low tones in her ear. She turned on Henry Danby and glared into his brown eyes, so similar to Sir Roger's that her heart instinctively skipped a beat.

'Is it a habit of yours to creep up behind people?' she snapped, unsettled by her body's infidelity.

Henry laughed, his dark eyes gleaming wickedly. He took two goblets of wine from a passing servant and handed one to Joanna.

'You were the first to try that approach if my memory serves me rightly,' he said, lifting his goblet in salute and drinking deeply.

Icy fingers ran across Joanna's scalp. Simon's warning about her reputation rose in her mind. Was that why Sir Roger had taken another partner rather than wait for her arrival?

'Did you tell your brother what I did?' she demanded, gripping her goblet tightly.

Henry fixed Joanna with a stare that sent a shiver down her spine.

'So you didn't tell Roger yourself. I wondered if you would. Why did you keep it a secret?' he asked, moving closer to her. 'What did you fear he would say?'

'I feared nothing,' Joanna lied. 'You interrupted us before we had chance to speak properly.'

Henry smirked. Remembering what he had interrupted, Joanna blushed.

'Tell me, does he know?' she insisted.

Henry studied her in silence, eyes narrowed. Whereas with Roger she would have instinctively cast her eyes down modestly, she held Henry's gaze boldly, refusing to be cowed. With his dark eyes and curls he was handsome in the same way as his brother, but the expression in his eyes was sharper, reminding her of a fox watching its prey.

'No, he doesn't,' he admitted finally with a shrug.

'Thank you,' Joanna breathed. She took a mouthful of the warm wine, the sharpness burning her throat. 'I am in your debt.'

Henry extended his arm towards her. 'I will relieve you of your obligation if you dance with me now.'

Joanna's eyes slid to the centre of the room where Sir Roger still danced with the dark-haired woman. Surely he would finish soon and seek her out. He could not have forgotten she would be there.

Hal's eyes followed hers. 'Do you fear his disapproval so much that you will not dance with me?'

'Of course not!' Joanna said. 'I just don't want to dance yet.'

He snorted. 'I don't believe you. You were jigging up and down like a fiddle player on a carthorse.'

The image was so comical that despite herself Joanna smiled.

'I have my reputation to think of.'

Henry raised his goblet to her once more, a gleam in his eye. 'You would risk your reputation to visit my brother alone but will not chance a dance in public?' His eyes blazed. 'A dance means nothing. If anything it will protect your reputation: to refuse other offers and dance with him alone would invite talk, wouldn't it? Even my brother could not censure you for that.' He held his arm out again but when Joanna shook her head he did not press the point.

The music came to an end. Joanna attempted to catch Sir Roger's eye, but to her dismay Sir Bartholomew presented another young lady who curtsied demurely and they returned to the dance immediately. Joanna's mouth twisted downwards and she gave a small sigh of disappointment.

Henry was watching her closely, an odd mix of pity and scorn on his face. Joanna dropped her head, the expression in his eyes searing her heart.

'What did you expect to happen?' he asked archly. 'This evening is to honour the knights. You aren't the only woman to have her heart turned by the glamour of the pageant, or intending to catch a husband.'

'My head hasn't been turned by glamour!' Joanna snapped. 'That isn't why I love him.'

Henry smirked disbelievingly. 'Do you mean you would marry my brother if he was penniless and not a knight?'

Joanna gazed at Sir Roger, trying to imagine him as anything other than himself but could not picture him without his armour or velvet robes.

As she watched Roger laughed enthusiastically at something his partner whispered. He led her off the floor in the opposite direction with the vitality he displayed at the tilt. Joanna's eyes began to burn. No other man of her acquaintance, few as they were, made her heart turn over with a single glance.

'I would love him whatever he was,' she insisted.

'You hesitated though,' Henry said, raising an eyebrow. 'Now, are you content to wait all night for Roger to notice you or will you dance with me?'

Joanna tossed her head. 'I'd rather stand here

alone than dance with you. You've mocked me and been nothing but rude to me since you joined me. I know why too. I think you're jealous because you are not a knight yourself.'

She made to turn away but caught the expression on Henry's face and paused. His eyes were blazing and his jaw thrust forward angrily. When he spoke next his voice was clipped.

'As it happens you're wrong. I made my peace with my fate long ago.'

He began to walk away. Shame flooded Joanna. He was a bastard. Of course he could never hope to be a knight.

'Master Danby,' she called. 'Wait!'

He paused. Suspicion flickered across his face though it softened as he returned to her, never letting his eyes slip from hers. Her heart beat oddly in her throat.

'Call me Hal,' he said shortly.

'I didn't mean to offend you,' Joanna said, twisting her hands in embarrassment. 'It must be hard knowing you cannot be what your brother is.'

'I have no desire to be what he is,' Hal replied so curtly Joanna stepped back in alarm. His eyes hardened as he waved his hand across the room, shadows flickering across his face as he obliterated the candlelight. 'What sensible man would want this gaudy pageantry?'

Now it was Joanna's turn to feel sceptical. 'How could anyone not wish to be a part of such excitement?'

'Quite easily. When it's over what is left of the opulence beyond empty lists? I prefer things that last.'

Joanna considered his words. When the fairs and tournaments were gone York felt empty and she spent her time dreaming of their return.

'Why are you here if you hold it in such contempt?' she asked.

Hal's jaw tightened. 'I would much rather not be. I have my own reasons for being in York, which will be poorly served by standing with you. If you are determined to wait until my brother notices you I shall leave you to your solitude. Good evening.'

He bowed briefly and strode past her, skirting around the edge of the room towards the entrance hall. Impulsively Joanna turned after Hal to follow after him but at that point the music ceased. She glanced to the dancers and saw Sir Roger dancing with yet another woman. As he bowed to his partner he turned and saw Joanna. She beamed at him, her heart beginning to race.

Sir Roger sauntered to where she stood. He lifted her hand to his lips. 'I had given up hope of you coming,' he said.

Joanna's stomach fluttered with satisfaction. Of course he had not seen her or he would have come sooner. He held out an arm and she slipped hers into it. She moved towards the centre of the room but Sir Roger tightened his grip and tugged her in the opposite direction.

'I've been dancing long enough,' he muttered.

Sighing with regret, Joanna allowed him to lead her outside. She shivered, wishing she had brought her cloak. 'It's cold,' she protested.

Sir Roger pulled her around the side of the building and backed her against the wall. 'I can warm you up.' He grinned and kissed her. For a while all thoughts were obliterated, but as Sir Roger's hand once more began to stray towards her breasts a knot of anxiety formed in her stomach.

'We should go back inside. This isn't seemly.'

Sir Roger rolled his eyes. 'We are hardly alone.' True enough there were others who had taken the opportunities afforded to them by the shadowy corners and archways of the Common Hall. 'I have been away for months. You would not deny us this chance to get reacquainted?'

'No…only…when will you speak to my uncle?'

Joanna asked shyly. 'He spoke of other husbands, of men he knows would want me.'

Sir Roger's jaw tightened. 'And you would prefer one of these other men, is that what you are trying to tell me?'

Joanna reached hastily for his hands. 'No, I love only you, I swear!'

Sir Roger's mouth turned down petulantly. 'Good. I hate the thought of you belonging to someone else. You say you love me but how can I believe you when your kisses are so cold and chaste? You may as well be my aunt or sister! Give me some token of your affection so I can believe you,' he breathed.

Joanna smiled and began to unwind the scarf from her neck but Sir Roger caught her wrist. 'Not that sort of token,' he said. 'Save that for the lists.'

'Then what?' Joanna asked.

'I don't believe it was my conversation you craved when you came to my tent. Show me how much I mean to you. That you want to be my wife.'

He tugged her closer until his mouth covered hers, tongue forcing her lips apart. His hips ground against hers, one leg pushing between her thighs. She felt his hand slip from her hair and begin to travel across her body. His teeth grazed her lips and Joanna winced. She tried not to cry out as Sir Roger's fingers groped and dug into the soft flesh of her breast. Without warning he pinched her nipple hard.

Waves of unpleasant heat spread through her torso. She was dimly aware of what took place between a man and woman, but feeling these sensations bordering on pain the low cries that issued in the night from her aunt's bedchamber began to make sense.

Were women supposed to like this show of male affection? Perhaps in time she would learn to, but at that moment Joanna would have given up all prospects of marriage to make it stop. She closed her eyes, reminding herself that this was the price for getting what she craved. A life of excitement with the man who made her heart pound. Not a bleak existence in a damp Welsh village with old Thomas Gruffydd. No longer an unwanted inconvenience in Simon's household. Sir Roger would be satisfied soon and it would not happen again until after they were married.

The sound of someone whistling floated around the corner, a familiar tune that had been playing while she had talked with Hal. Sir Roger's hand dropped from Joanna's breast. He smiled down at her, his eyes still hungry. She returned his smile faintly, glad that she had pleased him.

The whistling stopped. For the second time that day Hal interrupted them but now Joanna found herself glad to see him. He sauntered across to where they stood, his eyes flickering knowingly from Sir Roger to Joanna.

'I had barely crossed the room to find you and you were gone, Roger. I thought you might be out here.'

Had he followed them deliberately? His face was grim. Joanna looked away shamefaced. Clearly his opinion of her virtue, or lack of, had been confirmed afresh.

'Joanna, go back inside. I'll find you later,' Sir Roger commanded. She nodded obediently and left, turning back briefly at the corner to glance at the two brothers. They mirrored each other, arms folded, legs apart and identical expressions of anger on their faces. Sir Roger's was easy to understand but why Hal should have seemed so furious was a mystery.

'Who is she?' Hal asked curiously.

Joanna was different from the women Roger usually favoured, preferring them slender with chestnut hair and flashing eyes, not small and shapely with the air of a startled cat when surprised.

Roger gave the satisfied grin that never failed to set Hal's teeth on edge. 'You were talking to her while I danced. Did you discover nothing yourself?'

'Only that she adores you and believes you feel the same,' Hal snapped. 'Do you?'

A guilty expression flitted across Roger's face. 'I'm fond of her I suppose. She amuses me and she's so devoted. So biddable. She's more innocent than I prefer but one can get tired of the same wine. White can provide a pleasant alternative to red occasionally.'

Hal wrinkled his nose. The description of Joanna struck him as apt. For all her indiscreet behaviour at the camp she had been modestly dressed. Her unhappiness when her virtue had been called into question had been real enough and her discomfort just now as she had submitted to Roger's clumsy caresses was genuine.

'You were doing your best to relieve her of any innocence she still possessed,' he said darkly. 'Is that fair? Or wise?'

Roger leered. 'If she's willing to play I'm not going to object.'

'Do you intend to marry her?' Hal asked.

'I did consider it for a while,' Roger said candidly. 'Though sadly I've discovered this vintage turns out not to be as rich as I first hoped it might be.'

'Stop jesting.' Hal glowered. 'Mistress Sollers is not the first woman you have deceived. If you do not intend to marry her make it clear and take no more liberties or I *will* inform Father of your behaviour. I don't have to tell you what that might do in his current state of health.'

He strode away and was swallowed up by the city.

Chapter Three

'Are you coming to the tournament today?'

They were the first words Roger had spoken to Hal since the previous night. Both had returned to the camp separately and Roger had stamped around the tent, reminding Hal of when they were both children.

'I wasn't intending to,' Hal answered, earning a petulant scowl from Roger who took the cup of warm milk Hal offered.

'I'm allowing you to share my tent so the least you could do is help me prepare. You know my armour better than my squire,' Roger grumbled. 'You'd have made a better squire too if you hadn't been so proud.'

Hal ignored the jibe. 'You know I have matters of my own to attend to.'

'Your work is all you think of. I'm on the lists

before midday,' Roger wheedled. 'You'll have plenty of time.'

Hal took a cloth-wrapped package from the chest at the end of his bed, laid it carefully on the table and unfolded it to reveal the sword he had crafted. The edge gleamed in the light as he drew it from the scabbard and weighed it in his hand.

Roger whistled in genuine appreciation. 'I don't know why you want to enter the guild. You're a good blacksmith already.'

Hal laid it carefully back on the cloth and ran his fingers over the wide, flat blade.

'Would you be content to stay aiming at wooden targets?'

Roger snorted. 'Of course not!'

'I don't want to spend my life shoeing horses and hammering plough blades. There are other skills and other metals.'

'Do you have plans for the weapon after you've presented it?' Roger asked hopefully. 'Something so fine deserves to be wielded by a knight.' He couldn't hide the note of longing in his voice and Hal's throat tightened in annoyance.

'I'm keeping it. Whatever you think, you are not entitled to lay claim to everything I possess,' he said archly.

Roger snapped his fingers to summon his page.

Hal drank his milk, feeling his stomach beginning to settle. He had not intended to drink so much the previous night, but after leaving the feast he had stalked around the city until he found a tavern where he could mull over what he had witnessed between Roger and Joanna. No doubt she would be at the joust. Anyone could see the foolish girl was blinded by the thrill of the tournament and her dreams of winning his brother's heart.

'When you spoke to Joanna last night did you mention your task today?' Roger asked.

Hal started as the name he was thinking was spoken aloud. 'Why would I tell her about that?'

Roger smirked. 'I thought you might have told her about your sword, that's all.'

'I doubt your lady would care about my sword. I think her interest lies entirely in the jousting,' Hal said.

Now Roger had introduced the subject Hal felt entitled to continue. Joanna was not the first woman Roger had caused to become infatuated and certainly would not be the last. If she was foolish enough to believe the sweet words that spun from Roger's lips it was no concern of Hal's, but her eyes brimming with sadness as Roger repeatedly ignored her presence had pricked Hal's heart. Moreover she intrigued him. He'd seen energy in her when she bickered with him that she hid from Roger, to whom she had submitted meekly.

Which was the real woman? He'd like to find out. A worm of guilt wriggled in his belly as he remembered trying to persuade his brother's woman to dance.

'Did you speak to her last night as I told you to?' he asked.

'No, she left early and I was caught up with other matters. I'll speak to her today,' Roger said with a careless wave of his hand. 'Now, for the final time, will you come help me this morning? If you're seen with me it will increase your standing in the eyes of the Guild members.'

Hal doubted how much influence a young knight of middling wealth from the North York Moors might have, but to say so would be churlish. Roger would not stop until he had the answer he wanted and it was better to be busy than wait here until he had to present his work. 'Very well. I'll spare an hour, no more. I cannot be late to the Guild Hall.'

'Good.' Roger swung his legs to the floor. 'I'm not entering the mêlée, but I could use a bout of swordplay to wake my senses. How about you pit your weapon against mine?'

Hal ran his fingers reverentially over the pommel and cross guard of the falchion. However much he craved it, Roger would not get this weapon.

'I'll spar with you, but not with this.' He slid it back into its sheath and folded the cloth around it. 'I'm not doing anything that might risk my chances of admittance to the Guild.'

Joanna could scarcely draw breath; her chest was tight with excitement. Last night Simon had secured admission from Sir Bartholomew's steward to one of the most prominent stands at the tournament ground. This morning a messenger had called him away, leaving Joanna seated alone amid guests of the castle.

She did not care that her dress was of linen, not silk, and the band drawing back her hair was embroidered with flax, not spun gold. She was closer than she had ever been to the knights and Sir Roger would not fail to notice her today.

Trumpets sounded and the knights processed in. They paraded around the field, each with his entourage of pages and squires. Joanna craned her neck to find Sir Roger and spotted two heads of black curls walking side by side. She gave a small cry of surprise, causing the woman next to her to glance round.

The procession reached Joanna's stand. She leaned forward once more, smiling and cheering along with the crowd. She waved at Sir Roger, but he did not see her. Beside him Hal turned and his eyes met Joanna's, lingering on her in a manner that sent an unexpected shudder rippling through her. Unsettled, she raised an eyebrow haughtily. He stared at her unsmiling, a small frown knotting his brow, then carried on walking. Dressed in a dark wool tunic, Hal was out of place among the procession of squires who wore their masters' colours proudly. From his bearing he could easily be a knight himself.

The knights took their places. Hal muttered something to his brother and both men stared in Joanna's direction. She raised a hand and Sir Roger inclined his head ever so slightly towards her. He turned away to talk to the knight who stood beside him. Joanna lowered her hand slowly, her smile feeling suddenly tighter and forced. Hal patted the horse, his gaze still on Joanna. She dropped her eyes, unnerved by his gaze.

The first three bouts passed in a blur, Joanna barely watching until it was Sir Roger's turn.

He mounted his horse and trotted to where Sir Bartholomew sat. This was the moment Joanna had been waiting for, when each knight would choose a lady to present him with a favour to wear as he rode. Sir Roger turned his horse in Joanna's direction and paused in front of her stand. She slipped the silk scarf from around her neck, her heart beating rapidly.

'Will you give me a favour to wear, my lady?'

Sir Roger's voice sounded loud across the tilt-yard. Joanna's heart stopped. He was not speaking to her. Slowly she felt the blood drain from her face.

Further along the stand a woman slipped a scarf of vibrant green over the tip of Sir Roger's lance. Through swimming eyes Joanna recognised the dark curls of the woman Sir Roger had danced with the previous night. The crowd cheered. Oblivious to what followed, Joanna slumped back on to the bench. She gazed at the wisp of pale-yellow silk that lay across her lap.

What had gone wrong? She had not been able to speak to Sir Roger since she had submitted to his touch in such an indiscreet manner the night before. He had seemed pleased with her then, so why now was he so cold?

She raised her eyes. Across the field Hal was

watching her still, his frown deepening. Joanna narrowed her eyes as she stared back. In response Hal's lips twisted into a sneer. Unable to bear the knowledge that he was watching her humiliation, Joanna dropped her gaze. She bundled the scarf tightly in her hand, digging her fingernails in her palms until a series of red half-moons marred the pale flesh. When she glanced up again Hal had gone.

The bout began. Joanna barely noticed as his opponent's lance splintered against Sir Roger's chest. As the crowd surged to its feet she slipped out of the stand and made her way to the gate at the end of the field that led to the arena where the knights waited. Head down she collided with someone. Opening her mouth to apologise, she discovered Hal blocking her path. He planted his feet firmly apart, the large knapsack over his shoulder swinging around.

'Let me past,' Joanna said, trying to dodge around him.

Hal put his hands on Joanna's arms. His grip was firm but not painful.

'Don't go in there,' he said gently.

'I need to speak to Sir Roger,' Joanna answered. Her eyes filled with tears and she blinked furiously.

'It isn't a good idea,' Hal insisted. There was a loud roar from the lists. Joanna turned in the direction of the tilt but could see nothing past Hal's broad frame.

'You can't stop me!' Joanna struggled against Hal and he loosened his grip. He stood back and raked his fingers through his hair.

'No, I can't.' He sighed, his tone heavy with exasperation. 'I have an appointment I must keep, but I advise you not to confront Roger today.'

He hitched his burden higher over his shoulder and stepped to one side. Joanna stood motionless, uncertain what to do. She nodded in defeat. Hal smiled in apparent satisfaction and walked away.

Another roar, this time accompanied by cries of astonishment, thundered in Joanna's ears. In an instant she changed her mind and rushed through the gateway into the field. Sir Roger was on foot and leading his horse away from the tilt. Joanna stared in disbelief. He had been unseated. Her anger forgotten, she rushed towards him.

'Are you hurt?' she gasped.

Sir Roger glared at her and she stepped back in alarm.

'Why are you here?' he snapped.

He sounded so cold he might have been a stranger in the street. Joanna swallowed nervously, wishing she had followed Hal's advice and not come. She raised her chin and spoke with as much dignity as she could, but her voice was no more than a whisper.

'You did not choose my favour.'

Sir Roger's cheeks turned crimson. He threw his arms out wide. 'Is that all you can think of at a time like this?'

'It would have been a sign of our intent to wed...'

Her voice tailed off as Sir Roger's face reddened further. 'Marriage? How can you talk of marriage at a time like this?'

A low buzzing filled Joanna's ears. 'But what we did last night? The way you touched me!'

Sir Roger gripped her shoulders tightly. Her throat constricted as if he was squeezing it. She tried not to picture him dancing with the dark-haired woman, nor Hal's observation that she was not the only woman trying to catch a knight.

'What does last night matter? I lost the bout and the winner's purse. I have no money to wed! Any money I have must fund my campaigns.'

'I'm sure you will win future contests,' Joanna said with a confidence she suddenly did not feel.

Sir Roger's lip curled and she lapsed into silence. He turned his back on her and took hold of his horse's reins. 'The king has planned a tournament for St George's Day in Windsor. I intend to be there. I shall be leaving York tomorrow.'

'But you will return to York for the Lammas Day Tournament as always? That's six months away. Perhaps then…'

'I have no means to marry now. Nor the intention to do so at this time.'

Sir Roger ran his hands through his hair in a gesture similar to Hal's.

'Farewell, Joanna,' he muttered through clenched teeth. He led his horse out of the courtyard, leaving Joanna standing alone. She covered her face with her hands, her fingers slick with tears. The crowd moved around her and she wiped her hand across her face. She could not stay here at the scene of her humiliation.

She pushed her way out, stumbling towards the city. Her feet led her on a path towards home but she could not go inside. Not yet. Not to admit to her uncle what had happened. She turned and walked through crooked streets of the city until her feet began to ache and her stomach cramped, reminding her she had not eaten all day.

For the first time she took notice of her surroundings. Unconsciously her feet had brought her back to Aldwark, opposite the Smiths' Guild Hall.

She gave a wry smile. She could wait for Simon in the gardens and inform him of her failure when he came out. Better he vent his disappointment there than in front of her aunt and cousins.

A fountain stood in the centre of the gardens. Wearily Joanna trailed her hand in the cool water, scooping up the heavy copper cup and drank. She sat on the step behind the basin and leaned back against the carved stone edge. She drew her knees up and, unwatched by anyone, started to weep in earnest.

Five guild officials sat at a long, oak table, chains around their necks and well-fed bellies bulging under tunics of fur and velvet, the visible signs of their prosperity. The calluses and scars on hands that now bore ornate gold rings were the only indications that they had once been in Hal's position: young and untrained, used to the heat of the furnace and the weight of a hammer. Admittance to the guild would set him on the path they had walked.

On the table before them lay Hal's sword. The Guild Master stood and placed his hands on the table either side of Hal's work. He affixed Hal with a steely gaze.

'An interesting choice of subject for your masterwork. You have pretentions to be an armourer? How many knights do you meet in your moorland village?'

A ripple of laughter ran around the room. Hal did his best to smile at the feeble jest. The Guild Master picked the weapon up, scrutinised it, then passed it on. Hal held his breath as each man examined it before it was returned to the centre of the table.

'Wait outside,' the Master commanded.

Hal walked to the outer chamber as the men turned to each other, muttering in low voices. He struggled to discern anything from their tone or expressions. Lulled by the heat of the fire on what had developed into another mild day his mind began to wander.

What had the roars from the tiltyard meant? Had Roger won or lost? He hoped Joanna had had the sense to heed his warning and save her confrontation. The shock on her face when Roger had chosen another woman's favour had caused Hal's heart to throb unexpectedly. Perhaps now she would understand how fickle Roger's affection was.

He realised his name was being called and snapped his attention back to the present. He re-entered the chamber and the Guild Master beckoned him forward, gazing down his crooked nose.

'You are young,' the Guild Master stated. 'Eight months out of being a journeyman, you said?'

Hal nodded slowly, locking eyes with the Guild Master.

'Your work lacks finesse,' the Guild Master announced stiffly. 'The blade is good, but the work on the quillon lacks technique.' There were murmurs of agreement from around the room.

'No subtlety in the ornamentation,' another man interjected. There was a familiarity about the man. Hal couldn't place the resemblance but something in the straw-coloured hair and pale eyes clawed at his memory.

'Your ambitions outstrip your skill at this time,' a third added.

A burning ache began to grow in the pit of Hal's stomach as he took in the meaning of their words. He had failed.

'Go back to your village, young man,' the second man said with a stiff smile. Once more the turn of the man's lips reminded Hal of someone, though now he did not care about remembering who it was.

The Guild Master stood. 'Practise your trade. Take a wife and increase your standing. Perhaps in a few years you will have acquired the necessary skills to see beyond the bare form of the metal.' He gestured at the weapon on the table.

Hal stepped forward and wrapped it in the cloth, casting his eyes over the twisted knots of the cross guard.

'Thank you, sirs,' he said as politely as his disappointment would allow. He walked out, head high. It was only when the door had closed quietly behind his back that he allowed his frustration full vent.

With a growl he turned and kicked the gate. It was childish but it relieved some of his disappointment. A greasy-haired man standing at the street corner with a tray of pies gave him a suspicious stare. Hal glared back and took a breath that rasped in his throat. He needed a drink. Water first to quench his thirst, then something more potent to numb the disappointment.

He strode to the fountain in the gardens and lifted the chained cup to his lips, drinking deeply. The lion's head grinned at him, its sightless iron eyes mocking. Irritated, Hal flung the cup back into the basin sending water slopping over the edge.

A cry of annoyance made him start. He had not noticed the figure sitting on the step at the other side of the fountain, but now a woman stood and rounded on him furiously.

'Watch what you're doing, you great oaf!'

Joanna stood before him. She seemed to register who she was speaking to for the first time.

'You!' She wiped her hands over her damp dress. Her eyes narrowed suspiciously. 'Did your brother send you to find me?'

'Do you take me for his lackey?' Hal said bitterly. 'I have better things to do than traipse around the city on errands for him!'

'Then why are you here?'

Joanna folded her arms across her chest with indignation.

'Don't annoy me, woman,' Hal growled. 'I have no idea what brought you to this part of the city, but I am here on my own business and I am most definitely not in the mood to listen to your accusations.'

Joanna's eyes glinted brightly and she gave a sob. Her eyes were red and swollen.

'You ignored my advice, I take it.' Hal sighed.

She bit her lip and nodded guiltily as if expecting recriminations while somehow still contriving to scowl at Hal from beneath long lashes. Being glared at by Joanna was like being scolded by a kitten.

'He said he cannot marry me. He chose another's favour.'

Remorse stabbed Hal's guts. He had been instrumental in bringing her to this state. He had told Roger to make his intentions clear but the girl had not deserved such public rejection. He mentally cursed his brother's unthinking cruelty. Assuming it *was* unthinking, of course.

His craving for a cup of wine increased but he could not leave the blasted woman here. Already they had attracted the attention of the pie seller who was eyeing Joanna with open interest. Recklessly he reached for her hand.

'What are you doing?' Joanna demanded, pulling against him.

'You're not the only one to have suffered a disappointment this afternoon,' Hal said firmly. 'I'm going to find a drink. I don't want to leave you somewhere this isolated alone so I'm taking you with me!'

Chapter Four

Her chin resting in her hands, Joanna stared moodily at the cup before her.

'Drink,' Hal instructed.

Joanna opened her mouth to refuse, but Hal's watchful expression made her think twice. She took a small sip. As the sharp, cheap wine hit her tongue she realised how thirsty she was and how dry her throat, no doubt the result of the weeping she had done. She took a deeper swig, then another until she had all but drained the cup. She slammed it on to the table and glared at Hal defiantly.

Hal raised his cup in salute to her and drained it in one. He leaned back against the wall, his shoulders brushing hers, and stared at the cup, rubbing his finger across the rim.

'Now can we leave?' Joanna asked.

Hal did not appear to hear her. Joanna stared

about the room. The customers were quiet, serious men dressed in rough work clothing, nothing like the company her uncle kept. It wasn't the sort of place she imagined a nobleman's son would choose to drink in.

Hal refilled their cups and turned his attention to the long, cloth-wrapped bundle that he had propped against the bench between them. He affixed it with such hatred that Joanna burned to know what it contained. She glanced sideways at her companion—this dark figure, so like Roger in appearance, yet so different from the carefree, easy-tongued young noble. Joanna shifted in her seat.

'If you're planning to keep me as hostage all evening, I'd rather know sooner than later,' she said archly.

The anger that had not left Hal's eyes since their unintentional meeting began to ebb and the crease between his brows smoothed. His lips flickered in what might have been amusement.

'Hostage? You do have a knack for overstatement.'

Joanna scowled. 'What else would you call it? I didn't ask to accompany you. You half-dragged me through the streets, despite my protests, barely speaking to me along the way. You barricade me

into the corner and now give me no indication
how long you intend to keep me here!'

Hal spread his hands wide and leaned back
against the wall. 'You are free to leave whenever
you like.'

Squashed into the corner by the fireplace, she
had no way of leaving without crawling under the
table or climbing across his lap. Her chest tightened at the idea of such closeness and she hurriedly took another drink. 'I'll stay...for now.'

Hal gave a brief, empty smile. 'Good. No one
should drink alone when they're sad.'

Joanna's eyes pricked at the reminder of how
distraught she had been when they had met. She
realised that her distress had vanished, replaced
by anger and curiosity at Hal's odd behaviour.
Now the memory of Sir Roger's callous words
reared up once more and a lump formed in her
throat. Her lip trembled and Hal's expression became sympathetic.

'We have established that I was not searching for you,' Hal said, 'but tell me why you were
skulking alone in a square?'

Joanna shrugged. It was none of his business.

'I was waiting for someone.'

Hal's eyes lit with interest. 'Who? Have you finished grieving for my brother so quickly?'

'Don't mock me! How can you suggest such a thing? Why do you seem to enjoy wounding me?' Joanna slammed her cup on to the table, causing the men at the next table to regard them curiously. 'I will never forget your brother. My heart is in pieces and my hopes are…my hopes…'

She broke off as the lump in her throat expanded to the size of a fist. Hal refilled their cups and held one out to her, a small gesture of apology. She took it and tossed the wine back.

'I have no hopes,' she muttered, self-pity enveloping her. 'I love him and it is for nothing.'

Hal picked up his cup and took a long, slow drink. 'I cautioned you not to approach him today but you didn't listen to me. If things are not going his way, his temper can be short. Surely you know this about him, though?' Hal's lip curled into a grimace. His face was so like Sir Roger's that it could be the knight himself mocking her.

'My brother only comes to York twice a year for the tournaments. In three years you can only have been in his company seven or eight weeks at most,' Hal said kindly. 'Has he ever asked for your hand?'

Joanna's stomach twisted. 'Never directly. He said he had to wait until he had enough money. He's suffered losses in other years, but now he says he can never marry me. What can have caused him to change his heart so quickly?' she asked.

She swallowed and buried her face in her hands, while the sadness flooded over her. She turned her face miserably to the corner until she had mastered her emotions. Hal said nothing, but when she finally raised her head he had moved her cup closer to her reach. She gave him a thin smile of gratitude and wiped her eyes on the end of the yellow scarf she had hoped Roger would take as her favour. She twisted it tightly between her fingers.

'How can you be so certain you love Roger?' Hal asked softly.

Joanna raised her eyes to meet Hal's defiantly. 'Anyone who knows him would love him. He's a great knight—or will be when his fortunes change. No one else has ever made me feel so desired.'

'Are you sure it isn't simply the idea of what he does that attracts you?' He sounded so scathing that the blood rose in Joanna's cheeks. Her head spun from the wine. She pointed an accusing finger at him.

'What he does is wonderful. Why should I be ashamed of loving him for that? You're bitter because he has what you'll never have,' she spat.

'And I've told *you* I have no wish for his position. I'm happy in mine,' Hal answered with a glare, his voice rising. Again, the men at the next table glanced over. 'Or I was!' he finished bitterly, lowering his voice. His eyes fell on the mysterious bundle once more and sorrow crossed his face.

'What is that?' Joanna asked quietly. 'You haven't told me what put you into such a dark mood. It's to do with that, isn't it?' she said.

Wordlessly Hal lifted the bundle and laid it on the table in front of him. He unfolded the cloth. A thick-bladed sword lay before Joanna.

'Is that Roger's?' she asked.

'It's mine.' Hal raised his chin and fixed Joanna with an intense stare. 'I made it. I'm a blacksmith,' he said with dignity.

Hal's presence in Bedern made sense now.

'You were at the guild,' Joanna said. She was about to admit her connection but Hal gave an angry sigh.

'For the little good it did me. I have finished my time as a journeyman and crafted this as my masterwork. I thought it was fine enough but I was wrong,' Hal said shortly. 'A pack of overfed, overgilded men who sit in judgement on over-stuffed chairs!'

He continued to rant and Joanna sat back to listen, hiding a smile at the description of her uncle and his fellow guildsmen. Hal's voice was heavy with disappointment and she did not want him to think he was the cause of her amusement. Instead she nudged his cup of wine towards him with her own and turned her attention to the sword.

Years of living and working with Simon Vernon told her at a glance why the guild had rejected it. The weapon was well proportioned, but the design was crude with too much clamouring for attention. With a scrap of parchment and ink she could have designed better herself. She merely nodded, suspecting Hal would not appreciate any further criticism.

Hal clearly misinterpreted her silence as a lack of opinion. He sniffed, giving her a condescending smile.

'Of course a woman wouldn't appreciate the work involved in crafting something of even this standard.'

'Of course,' Joanna agreed icily. She traced the tip of her finger across the heavy knotwork of the pommel and turned to face him with a cold smile. 'You should put this away or it may attract the attention of someone capable of wielding it.'

That blow hit home with alarming results. Hal's face hardened.

'I know how to use it,' he said. 'My father—and brother—intended me to be Roger's squire. I received all the training my brother did. I can fight as well as he can.'

He pushed the table back and stood. 'Now we have both succeeded in insulting the other I think our business here is done.'

'I agree,' Joanna said. 'Farewell, Master Danby.' She stood and brushed past him, affecting to make as little contact as possible, and stalked towards the door. She had barely taken ten steps into the street before footsteps pounded behind her and a hand seized her arm. She gasped in alarm.

'What do you think you are doing?' Hal asked.

'Going home!' Joanna answered, trying and failing to shake free of his grip.

'Not alone,' Hal said. He gestured at the darkening sky. 'It's growing late and a woman should not be roaming the streets alone.'

'These are my streets, I know them better than you and I don't need your protection,' Joanna said. She wrenched herself free and folded both arms tightly across her chest, staring moodily at Hal. 'Besides, I thought we agreed we had offended each other enough to merit parting company.'

'Offended or not, I insist,' Hal said calmly. 'You

are here at my whim and therefore you are my responsibility. I would not see you come to harm.'

'My hopes are dashed and my heart is broken. What further harm could befall me?' Joanna sniffed.

'Do you really want me to list the ways?' Hal asked darkly.

Joanna scuffed her foot and pretended to consider her answer. He was right; the city was no place to be walking alone, however much she wished to be rid of his company.

'Are you going to stop behaving like a foolish child or shall I throw you over my shoulder and take you anyway?'

'You wouldn't dare!'

The skin at the corner of Hal's eyes crinkled with amusement. Against her will Joanna smiled.

'Very well, as you give me no choice,' she said.

'You will have to direct me as I don't know where you live,' Hal reminded her.

As she slipped her arm through his Joanna suppressed an involuntary smile. Uncle Simon would have long since finished his business and she took great pleasure in anticipating the surprise in Hal's arrogant eyes when he discovered whose house he had arrived at.

* * *

'Where are you leading me?' Hal grumbled as Joanna turned down yet another snicket. 'We could have walked to Whitby by now.'

'You are free to leave me any time you wish,' Joanna replied curtly.

They were the first words she had spoken, the first acknowledgement she had given that he existed at all since reluctantly submitting to Hal's demand to accompany her. Occasionally what might have been a sob escaped but was quickly stifled. Hal could not pretend to be anything other than relieved that she was keeping her emotions in check.

Presumably she would give vent to her feelings once more when she was home, wherever that might be. Hal stared down the narrow street leading off into a warren of alleyways and grimaced.

'I swear we have passed this way three times already,' he said. 'These alleys are no place to be walking at night.'

Joanna stopped walking abruptly, causing Hal to bump into her. She finally met his eyes. 'You can defend us with your fine sword, can't you?' she said. The faintest trace of a smile curved about her lips, challenging rather than amused. 'Are you worried you'll get lost?'

'I don't like cities and this is the least welcoming I've been in for a long time,' he answered. *Though it could equally be the company influencing my mood*, he thought darkly.

'You'll recognise where we are soon enough,' Joanna replied. She motioned to carry on walking.

Her head barely came to Hal's shoulders. If she had not been holding herself stiffly at arm's length she would nestle in the crook of his arm quite satisfactorily. Hal glanced down at Joanna's bowed head. He preferred his women to be tall and willowy, but he decided Joanna's curves would be a pleasure to bundle up against in an evening that was rapidly becoming chilly. Perhaps he should have made good his threat to throw her over his shoulder after all.

Lost in thoughts he knew should be forbidden, Hal barely registered when Joanna stopped again. He found himself in the square where they had first met opposite the Guild Hall.

'So you *were* leading me in circles,' he said irritably. 'Why?'

'Because I had no wish to return home so soon,' Joanna said. 'I said you were in no danger of losing your way.' She dropped his arm and stalked past the hall, rounded a corner and stopped in front of an imposing house on the end of a row.

'You live here?'

She nodded.

'Yet you were sitting alone in the square?'

Another nod, this time accompanied by a loud bang as she lifted the ornate iron doorknocker and released it.

'I told you I was waiting for someone and I was.' Her eyes were wide and innocent, but the full lips were curved once more into a smile as the door flew open and light flooded the street to reveal the figure of a man.

'Where have you been so late?' demanded an irate voice that was sickeningly familiar to Hal. It was the man who had sat at the Guild Master's right hand.

'I believe you have met,' Joanna said sweetly. 'This is my uncle, Master Simon Vernon.'

Hal cursed to himself as he bowed, realising now what Joanna's half-secret smiles had meant. He turned to go but Master Vernon spoke.

'What are you doing with my niece? Is it your doing that she's so late back?'

'Master Danby kindly brought me home, Uncle,' Joanna said. 'For which I thank him and shall say farewell.'

'I know your face,' Master Vernon said. It sounded like half an accusation, half a threat.

Hal bowed again. 'I had the honour of presenting my work to you this afternoon.'

'Honour nothing!' Master Vernon snorted. 'You'd better come in and explain what has happened to keep her out so late.'

Joanna stiffened. Clearly this had not been part of her scheme. Now she was in the light Hal saw her eyes were once again red rimmed. For all her bravado she had been weeping as they walked. Hal stifled his sympathy, reminding himself that Joanna had led him intentionally to meet the man he had disparaged in such strong terms.

'Gladly, Master Vernon,' he said, and walked inside.

'You let me say all those things and did nothing to stop me,' he muttered to Joanna as Master Vernon walked into the back room calling for wine.

'Yes, though I don't intend to share what you told me. If you had not insisted on accompanying me you would have been none the wiser.' Joanna glanced to the door her uncle had gone through. 'I didn't intend you to come in, but if you think you can turn this meeting to your advantage, then do so. If not, drink your wine, go quickly and leave me in peace.'

Master Vernon returned, followed by a woman with a baby on her hip who settled herself by the fireplace. Joanna rushed to the woman, who must be her aunt, dropped to her knees and began to sob loudly while the woman patted her shoulder and made soothing sounds.

'What is this?' Master Vernon barked. He glared at Hal. 'Joanna, has this man played you ill?'

Joanna winced. 'No. Master Danby has done nothing wrong. Sir Roger told me he cannot marry me.' She stood and wiped a hand across her face.

'You swore he would ask,' Simon cried.

'Sir Roger will be back in August. He'll ask me then, I'm sure,' Joanna insisted. Hal frowned, hearing the desperation in her voice. What had Roger told her that she had pinned her hopes on him so deeply?

'Now what am I to do with you?' Simon thundered. 'I must find you a husband myself as you seem incapable, though I doubt I'll find anyone willing to take you off my hands if you go traipsing around the city with strangers like a common tavern wench!'

He rounded on Joanna. 'Is it not enough that you go chasing after one man but you have to go wantonly flinging yourself into the company of another?'

Joanna paled. Her eyes lit with the fire Hal had

been on the receiving end of, but surprisingly she bowed her head and folded her hands meekly.

'I asked Mistress Sollers to accompany me. She deserves no censure,' Hal said swiftly.

Master Vernon gave an angry snort. 'Go to bed, Joanna. We'll discuss this in the morning.'

Joanna curtsied to her uncle. She seemed younger and suddenly weary as she left the room with her aunt. Hal's heart lurched and he vowed to have a forceful talk with his brother as soon as he returned to the camp.

Master Vernon seemed to notice Hal for the first time. He walked close to Hal and pursed his lips. 'Master Danby, is it? You bear the same name as the wretch who has disappointed my silly niece. I assume it is not a coincidence that you brought her here?'

Hal took a deep breath. 'Sir Roger is my half-brother. My father is Robert, Baron of Danby and Westerdale, who holds land from William of Pickering.'

'A nobleman with a blacksmith for a son?'

'My mother was not of noble birth. I followed her father's path in life.' Hal's answers were clipped. Questions he'd been asked a hundred times before. Justifications he would have to make forever.

'Do you believe your brother intends to marry my niece?' Master Vernon demanded.

'No,' Hal replied honestly. 'I have tried to tell her as much, though as she will not believe the words from his lips she is unlikely to believe them from mine.'

Master Vernon crossed the room and poured two glasses of wine. He passed one to Hal and scowled. 'I am not an unfeeling man,' he declared, despite all evidence indicating otherwise to Hal. 'But I have fed and kept Joanna for a decade. I cannot afford to keep her forever. I have my own family to consider. She must find a husband soon.'

The reason for her desperation was becoming clearer now. Instead of insisting Roger did not marry Joanna, Hal should have persuaded him to commit to her. He'd caused this with his blunder.

'Bringing Joanna safely home was a kindness. I think you have a good heart,' Master Vernon said. 'Better than your brother's at least. Perhaps you are the sort of man the Guild needs—or could be in time.'

Hal smiled and drank his wine. Joanna had told him to turn events to his advantage and they seemed to be doing so of their own accord. He spoke rapidly of his ambitions, the forge at Ravenscrag, and his work for the abbey at Rievaulx and the villages on the moors. Master Vernon nodded approvingly.

'I told you this afternoon to go back to your home and make a life for yourself,' Master Vernon said. 'I mentioned marriage.'

Hal's smile froze. He had a sickening feeling he knew where Master Vernon was leading and the man's next words confirmed his fears.

'I have a proposal that could work to both our advantages, Master Danby. I want you to marry my niece.'

Chapter Five

How Hal found his way to the camp he couldn't say. His feet must have traced the path of their own accord because his brain played no part. He located Roger in the castle hall, drowning his sorrows in wine, and dragged him back to their tent.

'Tell me what happened between you and Joanna,' Hal demanded.

Roger threw himself on to his cot with his wine jug. 'I did as you asked. I told her I could not marry her. I dare say she will grieve for a while, but that can't be helped.'

'How forceful was your rejection?'

Roger stared at Hal through bleary, wine-reddened eyes. 'Completely,' he answered petulantly. 'I told her I cannot afford marriage and that I'm leaving York.'

Hal sat on his bed and rested his elbows on his knees. He closed his eyes wearily and wished he hadn't. Visions of Joanna's eyes, all the bluer for the red rims surrounding them, filled his mind.

'You have to change your mind,' he said.

Roger spat out an oath. 'Why would I do that?'

Hal fixed his brother with a stare. 'Because her uncle wants me to take your place.'

Roger stumbled unsteadily to his feet and pointed an accusing finger at his brother. 'This must be a jest. On your part or his?'

Hal scowled. His first instinct too had been to laugh at the suggestion until he had seen the earnest expression on Simon Vernon's face.

'Master Vernon was furious that Joanna had failed to win your hand. He all but offered me membership of the guild as a bribe for taking her,' Hal said, his bile rising at the memory.

The Guild might think more favourably of a man with the responsibility for a wife and family, Master Vernon had said, which Hal translated as *a man who rids me of my troublesome niece*! The man had shown little regard for Joanna's distress, thinking only of his own pocket. No wonder she had been reluctant to return home, knowing the reception that awaited her failure.

Roger gave a high-pitched guffaw. 'This is rich fun. My honourable brother finds himself ensnared. The lady's methods are more effective than I suspected!'

Joanna's face flashed before Hal's eyes once more, still clinging on to hopes of Roger, despite all signs to the contrary.

'She had nothing to do with it. She was not present at the time and I imagine the idea will be as unwelcome to her as it is to me.'

'Are you not tempted to accept the offer?' Roger asked slyly.

'No!' Hal exclaimed. 'When I enter the guild—and I will—I want to know it is because of my merit, not as a reward for ridding Simon Vernon of an inconvenience.'

Roger took another swig and let out a loud belch. 'Stop being so high-minded. You failed to get membership of the guild today. This would ease your admittance and Master Vernon would be a more useful connection to you than he ever would to me.'

Hal swung himself to his feet, ignoring the seductive voice that whispered in his ear of the sense of this. He crossed to Roger's cot and stared down at his brother. 'You are fond of Joanna, you said so yourself. Why not marry her?'

'Sadly, as you discovered, she is merely the niece of a guild member. He has a son now and she will inherit nothing. Her marriage portion will be small,' Roger sneered.

Hal set his jaw. 'I'll ask for the last time: will you reconsider your intentions towards her?'

Roger took a maddeningly slow drink from the jug. Hal's palm itched to slap it from his hand. Roger finally looked up.

'No. Sir Robin De Monsort has a daughter who comes of age in the next month. I intend to make sure I am her choice and am leaving with him in the morning.'

'Won't you care at all to see Joanna given to another man?'

'If she'd been richer I would have grieved more, but I care very little about it if I'm truly honest.'

Hal bunched his fists, his heart thudding with anger at the careless way his brother spoke. Roger swung himself unsteadily to his feet, wobbled and fell back on his cot.

'This morning you wanted me to bid farewell to Joanna forever. Now you want me to marry her after all. This has nothing to do with her feelings and everything to do with your wanting to escape from the situation. Just marry her and be done with it. She deserves a husband who at least has a passing interest in her.'

'And what makes you think I do?' Hal asked in surprise.

'The fact that you're even trying to persuade me,' Roger explained with the slow logic of the drunk. 'If you cared nothing for her you wouldn't worry who she married.'

Hal grimaced. He barely knew the girl, but his ire rose whenever he witnessed the dismissive way Joanna's uncle or Roger spoke of her or to her. Joanna's distress had touched him and he felt at least partly responsible for having caused the situation by insisting Roger make a decision. Blame lay at his feet, but surely not enough to require such a foolhardy step as penance?

'She's sweet-natured enough to keep you happy and has connections for you that no other woman does. If you won't have her Simon Vernon will find someone who will. I'm sure she'd prefer you to a fifty-year-old with stale breath,' Roger continued. He leered suggestively. 'You and I are enough alike. Maybe you'll please her in the night after all.'

Hal wrinkled his nose. 'You disgust me sometimes. If we weren't brothers I'd want nothing to do with you.'

'But we are and the choice is not yours.'

Roger laughed to himself, gave another great

belch, closed his eyes and began snoring. Hal ran his hands through his hair and gave an exasperated sigh. His eye fell on the wine jug still clasped in Roger's hand. He tugged it free and poured the remains into a cup before lying back on his cot, racked with indecision.

The morning brought rain, and with it a resolution. Hal packed his belongings and dressed in silence, slipping the thick wool tunic over his shirt as he stifled the yawns that resulted from a long night lying awake. Still angry, he avoided eye contact with Roger who was equally engrossed in dressing, ordering his young page back and forth with clothing of fine linen and silks. Once there was nothing left to do the brothers faced each other, their angry words lay between them, a barrier as real as stone and mortar.

Hal unbent first, clasping his hand on to Roger's shoulder. 'I wish you good fortune in the tournaments. Bring honour on our name.'

'Have you made your mind up about Joanna?' Roger asked gruffly, ignoring Hal's words.

Hal squared his shoulders, thinking he would rather stick his hand into his own furnace than reveal his intentions to Roger.

'You showed no interest last night. Why now? Unless you have reconsidered?'

'I haven't.' Roger said belligerently. 'In fact, I only asked out of courtesy. Whether you marry her or not is no concern of mine.' He clicked his fingers to the page, turned on his heel and sauntered out of the tent.

Hal hefted a bag across his shoulder, dragged his trunk to the waiting cart, then walked into the city.

Simon Vernon was not at home when he called. Sounds of family life drifted to Hal: children quarrelling, the clattering of cookware, a small dog yapping. Mistress Vernon peered at him through the partially closed door. Her gaze was suspicious rather than hostile and Hal wondered what Joanna had told her aunt of the previous night's events. He craned his neck to try to catch a glimpse of Joanna, but she was nowhere in sight.

Mistress Vernon informed Hal that her husband was most likely at his foundry. Hal retraced his steps to the Guild Hall along the alleys Joanna had taken him through the previous night. He suppressed a smile as he remembered her wide eyes full of innocence as she had led him in circles throughout the streets.

Even without instruction he could not have missed his destination. St Andrewgate was home to all York's metalworkers. The narrow street was lined on both sides with open-fronted workshops making and selling all manner of wares and the heat from the furnaces and heady stench of smoke meeting the drizzle greeted Hal like an old friend.

Master Vernon's foundry was located in an excellent position on the corner with two sides open to the street. Hal paused outside, aware of a clamminess creeping around his back. It was not too late; he could turn and walk away and no one would know. Except for him. He contemplated Simon Vernon's establishment, larger and grander by far than his own forge in Ravenscrag. One day he would be master of such a place and today, for all his reservations, he was setting his foot most decisively on that path.

Simon Vernon was standing with his back to Hal, barking orders at a pair of young apprentices. A figure was seated at a table in the corner. Hal stared in surprise as he recognised Joanna, head bent over a wax tablet with a stylus in her hand. No one had noticed his arrival so for a moment he stood drinking in the sight of her. She wore a dark-blue dress, high necked and tight sleeved beneath a sombre grey surcoat, belted tight beneath her breasts. Her hair was braided and held back from her face with a linen band. In such a setting she appeared as delicate and out of place as a wren in a nest of crows. The impression was such a contrast to the gaily dressed, flighty girl he had encountered at the camp that Hal was transfixed.

She was not beautiful, at least not in the way he preferred his women to be, but engrossed in her task Joanna's face was alight with enthusiasm, lending her cheeks a blush of rose. Her figure he already knew from having examined her the previous night. A slight stirring of excitement made him grin. Whatever other reservations he might have about marriage to Joanna, the physical aspects were not among them. He would enjoy getting to know his wife once they were wed.

Joanna muttered to herself, made a swift stroke with a quill and looked up. Too late to glance away her eyes trapped Hal's. She frowned, a small furrow appearing between her eyes before she broke into a wide smile. She jumped from her chair and crossed the room to him.

'Master Danby, what brings you here?' she asked warmly. 'Do you have a message for me?' Her voice was hopeful, leaving Hal in no doubt whose word she craved.

He ignored the faint stab of jealousy that pricked

his chest, deciding that whatever else occurred, Joanna would never discover Roger's indifference from him. 'I'm here to see your uncle.'

Simon Vernon finally noticed him. He strode to Hal, an eager expression on his face. 'You again. Should I assume you are here because of our conversation last night?'

Hal bowed. 'Good morning, Master Vernon. I am indeed here to discuss your proposal.' He glanced at Joanna who was still standing beside her uncle, her eyes bright with suspicion. Master Vernon followed his gaze.

'Joanna, go fetch ale for us. Make haste, girl!' he exclaimed, pushing her shoulder.

Hal's teeth gritted. If he had needed confirmation that he was making the right choice, the man's manner towards his niece was enough. Joanna left the building.

Simon Vernon watched her go, then turned to Hal. 'You're here to ask for her hand?'

Hal took a deep breath. 'I am.'

Now the words were out the weight of anxiety lifted from his shoulders.

'Last night I was certain you would refuse,' Simon said. 'What changed your mind? Was the promise of my good favour too much to resist?'

Hal smiled politely. 'Naturally.'

Simon Vernon held out a hand. 'Then the matter is settled. Now let's discuss terms.'

Joanna tapped her foot impatiently as the serving girl filled an earthenware jug with maddening slowness, all the while wondering what her uncle and Hal had been discussing. When she first saw him her heart had leapt, believing for one blissful moment that Sir Roger had changed his mind and sent his brother as messenger. Of course that had been foolish. From what she was learning of Hal he was too proud to consent to carry out such a task. This was not merely a visit for courtesy, however. From the way her uncle had dismissed her she knew there was more to Hal's appearance and she was determined to find out what it was.

She arrived back at the foundry with heels skidding in the mud. The two men were facing each other, arms folded and legs set wide, consciously or unconsciously mirroring each other's stance. They were both talking and smiling, but when Joanna entered Hal's face became serious.

'Bring the ale quickly, Joanna,' her uncle instructed. 'We have something to drink to.'

Obediently Joanna walked to the table at the back of the room and filled two cups. She picked them up and turned to find Hal standing close behind her.

'Let me help,' he said, taking the cups from her hand. He stared down at Joanna with an intensity that sent warm shivers running across her scalp.

'Come here, girl!' Simon called. As she joined them his jowly face split into a smile. 'I said last night I would find you a husband if you could not find your own. Master Danby here has asked for your hand and I have agreed.'

The room spun and grew hotter. Joanna looked at the furnace to check if it had flamed suddenly, but it burned as steadily as always.

'You must have misunderstood,' she said. 'Surely he means on behalf of Sir Roger.'

Simon snorted contemptuously. 'Of course he doesn't. You can forget any dreams of Sir Roger asking you. I know I have. The sooner you get him out of your head the happier you'll be.'

'I don't believe you.' Her voice echoed in her ears.

'Believe it, you silly chit,' Simon snapped. 'Master Danby has excellent prospects and will make a good husband. What possible objections could you have?'

'I don't know him!'

'You were happy enough to go flitting about

the city with him yesterday like a common wench with no regard for your name!' Simon barked.

'He's a bastard!' Joanna faltered. Hal's head whipped up as though she had struck him physically. His eyes bored into her, the pupils large and black, pinning her to the spot with their intensity. 'I'm sorry…' she began.

'I bear my father's name and I hold land on his estate,' Hal said curtly. 'My status does not shame me.'

'Master Danby is right. What does that matter?' Simon asked. 'He is a lord's son by birth and *his* children will be legitimate.'

Children. Joanna's stomach heaved at the thought of children and what creating them would entail. The thought of anyone touching her in the way Roger had made her want to scream.

Simon gripped Joanna by the arm and pulled her to the back of the room out of Hal's hearing. His face was stern.

'It is good fortune you happened upon someone who did not take advantage and make you completely unmarriageable, but enough is enough,' he growled. 'I have wasted three years while you waited for his brother and I'm not prepared to wait any longer. Master Danby has clearly seen the advantages such a match will bring. I suggest you do the same. This man or Thomas Gruffydd, but no more waiting.'

He dropped her arm and stormed out, leaving Joanna in no doubt that he intended to be obeyed. Hal was watching closely, his mouth a thin line.

'What advantages does he mean?' Joanna asked as soon as Simon was out of earshot. She closed her eyes as the answer struck her with sudden clarity.

'No, I understand. It's guild business, isn't it? How did you manage to coerce him?'

'The idea was not mine. Your uncle suggested it.' Hal frowned. 'Why do you assume I want the marriage any more than you do?'

A feeling of nausea told her he was speaking the truth. Hadn't Simon threatened to find her a husband only last night?

'So you're buying me?' Joanna said, her voice shaking. 'Do you gain admittance to the guild as a reward?'

'Actually, I don't!' Hal said. 'I'm not buying you. I gain nothing at this time other than a wife and the promise that I can petition for membership sooner than the customary year is up *if* I feel able. I'm not sure I get the best out of the deal.'

Hal stepped closer and put a hand gently on her shoulder. Joanna shrugged it off again violently.

'I don't love you,' she said coldly.

Hal raised an eyebrow. 'Nor I you. It would be rare if we did after such a short time knowing each other. I don't expect you to feel for me what you did my brother, but perhaps in time we will become fond of each other.'

Joanna crossed her arms, the mention of her adored knight sending waves of misery through her. 'If Sir Roger knew he would never let this happen. I need to speak to him.'

Hal's expression became blank.

'My brother has already left the city.'

Joanna's shoulders sagged and she stifled a sob.

'In truth, I have no real desire to marry you, knowing you are in love with him,' Hal said. 'However, as your uncle said, there are advantages for me. For both of us.'

'What is the advantage for me?' Joanna asked quietly.

'Perhaps nothing,' Hal admitted. 'If you would prefer to wait and see which alternative husband your uncle can find for you I will not stand in your way.'

Those words were all it took. He was right; Simon Vernon would find her a husband and, being anxious to be rid of her, would take less care than he did over choosing his belt. Thomas

Gruffydd's face swam before her eyes and she shivered.

Joanna walked to the front of the workshop where the breeze cooled her cheeks and she could think more freely. Hal did not follow, though she could feel his dark eyes on her. She examined him out of the corner of her eye: a tall figure, handsome when he stopped frowning, but so like Roger that the sight of him tore her to shreds inside. Simon thought him honourable. Perhaps he was right. Hal had come to her aid in the camp when the guards had made their lewd comments and last night he had insisted on accompanying her home. For some reason known only to himself he had set himself as her protector.

Uncle Simon came back inside. 'You've had enough time to think, so what is it to be? Make your choice, girl.'

Joanna swallowed, summoning the courage to speak. 'I do not wish to marry this man, but you leave me no choice.' Simon grunted his agreement. Joanna bunched her fists to stop her hands trembling and forced a smile she did not feel in the slightest.

'Master Danby, I will be your wife.'

Chapter Six

The wedding was arranged with indecent haste, being only fifteen days in preparation rather than the customary forty. Lent was fast approaching and, perhaps fearing Joanna would change her mind, Simon Vernon was insistent that the ceremony took place before rather than afterwards.

Hal had returned home to speak to his father the same afternoon as their betrothal had taken place and had not returned to the city. In vain Joanna hoped that his petition would be refused, but six days later a messenger hammered on the door of the house, bearing a letter for Simon agreeing to the proposed date and asking him to acquire lodgings for Hal and Joanna for the nights following the ceremony.

To Joanna the speed with which matters were put into place was the final seal on her hopes of escaping the betrothal.

'I agreed too rashly,' she muttered, pacing the floor of Simon Vernon's house as the day drew closer. 'I should have asked for more time to consider, or delayed somehow.'

Mary Vernon ceased her sewing and frowned. 'What good would waiting have done?'

'Sir Roger loves me,' Joanna said. 'He will never let the marriage take place. When he knows what I am being forced into he will come back for me, but the sooner the wedding, the less chance he will receive my letter in time.'

'You've written to him?' Mary frowned. 'If my husband finds out he'll be furious!'

'He won't find out. You won't tell him, will you?' Joanna pleaded. She stared into the fire where she had cast letter after letter before finally deciding on the words to explain her plight. She had sent the letter ahead to Windsor the day Hal had left York and nine days later there had still been no reply.

'Windsor is a long way,' Joanna said firmly. 'It will take time.'

No answer came, but three days before the wedding Simon Vernon returned home and tossed a bulky leather pouch to Joanna. With a thumping heart she opened it and tipped the unexpectedly heavy contents into her hand.

It was a brooch. Joanna's stomach plummeted as the meaning of the gift became clear and she could no longer deny what was happening. Hal must have made it and this was his marriage gift to her. The brooch was small, made of three strands of iron twisted around each other to form them into a ring. It was unadorned with gems or other ornament. It was neatly finished but a workmanlike piece. A marriage brooch suitable indeed for a match without passion. Joanna closed her hand over it, but Simon demanded to see what she had been sent.

He held it up to the candlelight. 'Your husband-to-be may be skilled with plough blades and horseshoes, but he'll need to improve his fine work if he wants to achieve the status of a master.' Simon laughed.

'Perhaps you should tell him how far away he is and he may decide to end this betrothal,' Joanna suggested.

Simon laughed. 'Don't be foolish, nothing is going to prevent this marriage.'

Joanna held a hand out. 'May I have my brooch back, please?' she asked coldly. He placed it in her hand and she excused herself and climbed wearily to her room. She took the brooch out again and noticed something else in the pouch. She opened it and in surprise found a letter from Hal.

Please accept this as a token of my fidelity to you. Although I am not the husband of your choice I hope in time we can be happy. Henry Danby.

The script was neat and precise. The author's hand was sure and bore signs of an education, but of course Hal was a nobleman's son.

Joanna smiled wryly to herself. In all the time she had known Roger he had never written to her. Now she began to suspect that he never would, or that if he did the message would come too late to save her.

On her wedding day Joanna woke with dry eyes, having spent all her tears the night before. She had hoped for rain or a black sky, something better suited to symbolising her mood, but the sun broke through wispy clouds. Mary eased herself into the room, panting gently. She handed Joanna a cup of warm milk, easing herself on to the end of the bed. Joanna stared at her aunt's swelling belly, which seemed to grow more each day. She had borne five children, four of whom had lived, and now a sixth was expected already.

Mary saw her looking, rubbing her hands over the bulge. 'It gets easier each time,' she said.

'You're wide in the hip, you won't have any problems when it's your turn.'

Joanna blushed. 'It isn't bearing the children that worries me,' she admitted in a whisper. Mary drew her into an embrace.

'That is bearable too. Not at first, but you learn to tolerate it. Some women even find pleasure in it.' Her lips narrowed disapprovingly. 'Or so I'm told!'

Joanna gripped the cup in her hands. A sob welled up in her throat and Mary patted her briskly.

'Come now, there's no use in fretting over what you can't change. Your new husband is handsome enough. I'm sure you'll find you're as happy as any woman can expect to be.'

Joanna bit her lip. She was devoted to Sir Roger with all her heart but even his touch had left her skin crawling. She remembered the last time they had kissed; Sir Roger's hands on her body, fingers nipping and twisting, digging into her flesh while his tongue forced its way between her lips. How could any woman endure, much less enjoy, such a thing? If it was like that with a man she loved, what would it be like with one she didn't?

Dressed in a pale-blue kirtle laced tightly beneath a darker-blue, sleeveless cotehardie, it was a source of amazement to Joanna that she managed to walk to the church without fainting. She stopped abruptly at the gate, every fibre of her body urging her to run, but Simon tightened his grip on her arm and pulled her through.

Hal was facing the church door, which gave Joanna plenty of time to observe him as she walked up the path. How ironic that this angle had been her first glimpse of him too. Whenever they had met Hal had always worn plain clothes, but today he was dressed in a dark-green jerkin with gold embroidery at the sleeves and collar over a black tunic. A wide belt pulled his waist in in a manner that accentuated the broadness of his shoulders and back and his close-fitting hose revealed well-formed legs. His hair had been drawn back into a neat cord at the nape of his neck, but dark curls were already beginning to break free, as unruly as ever. He turned as she approached and his eyes widened in obvious appreciation. Joanna smiled nervously at him and for a moment she allowed herself to believe things might turn out well. Hal's eyes slid to his brooch pinned over Joanna's heart. She raised her hand to it.

'Thank you.'

He broke into a wide smile full of pleasure. As reluctant as she was to become his wife, Joanna had to admit she was marrying a handsome man. If only it was his brother her happiness would be complete. She stifled a sob as Simon pushed her forward to stand beside Hal. The priest began intoning words that washed over Joanna's head and the ceremony began.

When she was later asked to describe her wedding, Joanna had no recollection. She did not weep and was proud of that. She spoke the required words in a clear voice, made and received promises. They must have exchanged rings—the plain narrow band that felt as heavy as a manacle on her finger was evidence of that. Throughout it all she kept her eyes downcast as a modest maiden should. No one would expect more, or censure her for her reticence.

There was stillness and the churchyard filled with an expectant hush. Finally Joanna raised her eyes to meet those of her husband.

'I believe a kiss is customary,' Hal said quietly.

'Oh! Of course.' Joanna obediently raised her face.

Hal hesitated before stepping towards her. He put his hands at either side of Joanna's face. They were warm and rough. The hands of a craftsman, not a noble. His fingers spread wide so that his thumbs caressed her cheeks and the little fingers brushed against the base of her skull. He leaned down, closing his eyes as he moved towards her. Much gentler than Joanna had expected he brushed his lips across hers.

With their lips still touching Hal opened his eyes. Joanna tilted her head back and parted her lips, waiting for the assault of his tongue but it never came. Hal's eyes narrowed and he frowned.

'Well, Mistress Danby,' he said gruffly. 'The deal is done.'

The wedding feast took place at the Guild Hall in Bedern. Seated at the centre of the high table Joanna and her husband were toasted and fêted, though in reality neither played much of a part in the proceedings. Her own connections were few, but it struck Joanna suddenly that her husband had brought no guests of his own. Even his best man had been one of Simon's older apprentices. There had been no one who might have tried to prevent the marriage from taking place.

Glad to be ridding himself of his niece, Simon had spared no expense so that all might know he was the host.

Once or twice Joanna caught her husband looking at her when she glanced his way but he quickly turned his attention elsewhere. What would they have spoken of anyway? Their kiss played through her mind. She was aware that somehow her response had been incorrect but did not know how.

Hal's plate was as untouched as hers and somehow seeing this was reassuring. He clearly felt as at odds with events as she did and this made her bolder.

'Do you regret what we have done?' she asked softly.

Hal put down his goblet and turned in his seat to face her. 'No, though I shall be glad when the day is ended and we can return to the inn. I dislike all this pageantry.'

A troupe of musicians struck up a lively tune. Mothers swept children out of the way as laughing couples filled the floor. Before long the sickly-sweet scent of lilies, crushed between the rushes on the floor, filled the air.

'We should dance,' Hal said, pushing his chair back and helping Joanna to her feet. He was quick on his feet and graceful. Under any other circumstance dancing with him would have been a delight, but as he led her through the steps Joanna's thoughts were on his last words. When the day ended they would return to Hal's lodgings with all that must happen between a husband and wife. The thought made her feel nauseous and she stumbled her footing through the next steps of the reel. Hal's arm came about her waist, leading her back into the rhythm.

'Are you ill?' he asked, concern clear in his voice.

'Just a little tired,' Joanna answered.

As she passed down the line one of Simon's associates overheard her words. He grasped her round the waist and lifted her high. 'The bride wishes to sleep,' he cried. 'We shall have the bedding ere long!'

Joanna's blood froze in her veins. That part of the wedding night had kept her awake night after night. She had steeled herself to bear whatever her husband bade her do, but to be disrobed in front of the guests would be unendurable. Cheers soared around the room, echoing his words. Joanna felt herself passed from guest to guest through the steps of the dance. Her protestations were ignored as hands gripped her skirts, pulling at the cloth as if they would begin undressing her right there. Laughing faces leered at her as for one terrible moment she became the centre of a circle of dancers before a pair of strong arms gripped her and she was clasped against someone's chest. She tried to pull free but a soothing voice hushed her, brushing her hair from her face.

'I'm sorry to disappoint you, gentlemen and ladies, but there will be no bedding,' Hal said.

Joanna gave a gasp of relief. He smiled down at her with eyes full of intent that caused a shiver to race along her spine.

'My wife is my own tonight,' he said quiet enough for only her to hear.

Joanna leaned against Hal weakly to catch her breath and felt his arms tighten reassuringly around her. Her heart thumped as he led her through the last steps of the dance and back to the table.

'Thank you,' she breathed.

'I have no desire to put either of us through that humiliation,' Hal muttered under his breath.

Curfew had passed long before the guests began to depart from the hall. Hal and Joanna were escorted through the streets by a crowd reluctant to see the end of the festivities. Joanna's throat tightened at the thought that, despite Hal's insistence, they would be accompanied into the inn and into the bedchamber itself. She need not have feared as Hal firmly bade the guests goodnight and shut the door behind him before leading Joanna up the narrow staircase to his room.

The chamber was large, clearly the best in the

inn. Lamps glowed in the corners of the room and on the table where a jug of wine also stood. A large, low settle stood in front of the fireplace that burned brightly. The bed stood against the furthest wall. Joanna tried to ignore it.

Hal removed his cloak and took Joanna's from her hand. He hung them on the peg behind the door, removed his outer tunic and untucked the shirt from his breeches. He sat on the edge of the bed and began to remove his boots.

Silently Joanna began to undress. She slipped her cotehardie off and let it fall to the floor. With her outer layer gone she became conscious of how closely her kirtle emphasised the curves of her figure. With trembling fingers she began to undo the laces at the side, but only succeeded in pulling the knot tighter until it was impossible to undo. She exhaled loudly in frustration.

'What's wrong?' Hal asked, looking up.

Joanna's cheeks began to flame as she admitted her predicament. Hal grinned, his brown eyes crinkling with amusement.

'Don't laugh at me!' Joanna cried, pulling angrily at the laces.

Hal crossed the room in easy strides and stood before her. Joanna's chest tightened. Shadows played across his face and torso where the light flickered. He exuded an air of unfettered masculinity that sent Joanna's stomach lurching with alarm. Despite the roughness of Roger's touch and kisses once they were in private, in public Roger had always appeared restrained, behaving with the decorum that etiquette had demanded. Now alone with Hal, Joanna was aware of just how different the brothers were. Facing him felt as though she had stepped from the saddle of a highly trained thoroughbred only to be confronted with an unmastered stallion.

'Put your arms out to the side,' Hal said.

His voice was so commanding that without thought Joanna obeyed. Hal's hands began to work at the laces. He was close enough that Joanna could feel the heat of his breath on her exposed neck causing shivers to play across her skin. Soon there would be no dress in between them and Hal's quick, dexterous fingers would be moving across her body. Her heart pounded in her breast with a violence that caused her head to spin. She reached out a hand to the table to steady herself.

Hal gave a small cry of triumph as he worked the lace free and Joanna felt the material of her bodice loosen. She took a deep breath of relief as the air filled her lungs. Hal stood back and held his hands with a flourish that reminded Joanna of a conjurer in the marketplace revealing birds from his sleeves.

With a nod of thanks Joanna turned away. She slipped out of her kirtle and dropped it to the floor. She unpinned her hair, running her fingers through it until it fell freely down her back. Clad only in her chemise, she turned back once more.

Hal had not moved. His eyes roved slowly over Joanna's body, eyeing her with unconcealed desire. He must have been watching her all the while. Unconsciously she tightened her grip on her chemise, drawing the ribbons of the neck closer together.

Hal's eyes followed the movement and his brows knotted into a frown.

'I'm not going to hurt you,' he said.

Joanna nodded. Hal reached a hand to her cheek and stroked it softly. He rested his hands on her shoulders and Joanna realised for the first time how much she was shaking. Hal took hold of both her hands, drawing them gently away from her chemise until they were by her side, still enclosed in his.

Joanna closed her eyes.

Let it be quick, she pleaded silently.

Perhaps not silently after all, as Hal abruptly released her hands. The floorboard creaked. Joanna opened her eyes to find he had moved away. He was leaning over the table with both hands resting on it and his broad back to Joanna. She crossed the room and stood behind him.

'I'm sorry,' she whispered. She lifted a hand to touch his back, but stopped short and lowered it again. She stood uncertainly behind him, waiting.

Hal stood straight and ran his hands through his hair, pulling the tangled curls loose from their cord. He poured a cup of wine and drained it before facing Joanna.

'You have nothing to apologise for.' He filled both cups and placed one in Joanna's hand. He saluted her with a bleak grimace. 'Happy wedding day, my dear wife!'

Sadness crossed his face. He looked weary and remorse flashed through Joanna. The first time would be the worst but that would only happen once. She sipped her wine for courage, then placed the cup on the table and stood before Hal. With her eyes fixed on the floor she unlaced the ribbon and pulled the neck of her chemise open. Cold air hit her shoulders as she began to ease it slowly down over her body until her breasts were almost exposed.

'What are you doing?' Hal asked harshly. He

seized Joanna's hands, his grip firmer than before, and prevented her lowering the chemise any further. Joanna lifted her eyes to meet his. His eyes were flashing with fury.

'I made promises to be a dutiful wife and within the day I have broken them,' Joanna said.

'Put your clothes back on,' Hal instructed. Joanna opened her mouth to protest but Hal drew her chemise back up. He crossed to the bed and began to pull on his boots.

'What are you doing?' Joanna asked in confusion.

'I'm going out,' Hal said. 'Your promises and "duty" will wait. I doubt either of us would get much pleasure out of anything we do tonight.'

He walked to the door, took down his cloak and spun it around his shoulders before opening the door. He paused, one hand on the frame. His dark eyes were unreadable.

'Go to bed and don't fear, Joanna. You *are* my wife and I will not wait forever, but I am not one to force myself on an unwilling woman. You can sleep safely tonight.'

He slammed the door behind him and was gone.

Chapter Seven

Hal woke up with an uncomfortable stiffness in his neck. He was slumped along the length of the settle with his cloak thrown over him in place of a blanket. He straightened his legs and groaned. He had not intended to spend his wedding night drinking alone in the corner of a gloomy tavern before stumbling back to the inn to fall asleep alone.

He opened his eyes slowly. He pushed himself to his feet, wincing at the crick in his neck—he was too tall to sleep on the bench—and stretched his arms wide. Joanna was still asleep in the bed. On soft feet he crept to her side and could not suppress the smile that came to his lips at what he saw. She lay on her side with one leg drawn up, the covers failing to hide the tantalising curves of her buttocks. One hand was tangled in the flaxen drift of hair that spread wide about her. Her face showed none of the anxiety that had twisted it the previous night when she had offered herself to him.

Hal went downstairs where the innkeeper's wife provided him with a large bowl of hot fried chunks of bread and milk.

'Your wife will be hungry this morning, sir,' she said with a knowing chuckle as she slipped a slab of honeycomb into the bowl.

Hal agreed pleasantly. He watched the comb begin to melt into the bread, wondering what the woman would say if she knew he had spent his night on the cold, wooden settle rather than in the warm arms of his pretty bride.

When he returned to the room Joanna was awake and sitting up plaiting her hair. She jumped as Hal entered the room. Her eyes widened and her hands moved instinctively to draw the counterpane higher. She had completed one side before he came in and the thick braid lay neatly bound behind her ear. The other side was loose, the pale hair falling over her shoulder in a manner that made Hal long to slip his fingers through the silken mass.

'You don't need to do that,' Hal said. 'I told you last night I don't force myself on unwilling women.' The fact his infrequent companions were never unwilling crossed his mind.

Joanna said nothing but returned to braiding her hair. Hal put the bowl on the table, drew up a stool and watched her fingers moving swiftly and surely. He took a chunk of bread and ate it hungrily. When Joanna had finished her braid, Hal hooked his foot round the second stool and pulled it closer to the table.

'Come join me,' he invited.

Joanna climbed from the bed and obediently padded across the room barefoot and wearing only her chemise. Hal's throat tightened as he stared at the contours he could see beneath the thin linen.

Joanna sat on the edge of the stool and selected the smallest piece of bread. She nibbled it slowly, keeping her eyes on Hal who munched his own with enthusiasm he didn't feel. He pushed the bowl closer to Joanna who took another, larger chunk this time, eating it with an expression of pleasure. A small trail of honey dribbled temptingly down her slender fingers. Hal pictured himself slowly licking it away and wondered what Joanna would do. Scream or faint, in all likelihood, or worse, quietly and obediently submit to him as she had begun to do the night before.

Visions of passionless nights and silent days stretching down the years ahead of them filled Hal's mind and an overwhelming feeling of frustration enveloped him. He pushed himself from his chair abruptly.

'What's wrong?' Joanna asked in alarm.

'Everything,' Hal admitted. 'This marriage was a mistake. I knew it before I even spoke to your uncle but I ignored my doubts. Last night you recoiled from me with such repulsion.'

Joanna jumped to her feet and faced him, hands on hips. 'It's far too late for regrets now!'

'If it was within my power to undo it I would,' he said.

'You would undo it? You!' Joanna cried. 'Unfortunately there is no way to do that.'

Her voice was high. She sounded on the verge of breaking down. Perhaps she was. Hal wouldn't blame her.

'You could sue for an annulment,' Hal suggested, his stomach curling at the thought. 'You have grounds. I refused to consummate the marriage after all.'

Joanna's face lit briefly. Would she do it? The humiliation of all that was implied would be hard to bear, but Hal would endure it if it meant the end of this farce.

'No,' Joanna said bitterly. 'What other prospects do I have? I cannot return to my uncle's house and no one else will have me.' Tears welled suddenly. 'For good or ill, I am your wife.'

Hal looked away, unwilling to see her large, blue eyes full of sorrow. She took a step closer to him and Hal looked up once more. She wiped the tears away with the sleeve of her chemise. 'I have made my vows to you and I will be a true and faithful wife.'

She reached for Hal's hands. Her fingers were cold and he squeezed them instinctively to warm them. Joanna's eyelids flickered. She chewed her lip then slipped her hands free and stepped so close to Hal that he could feel her full breasts pushing up against his chest through the thin chemise and his shirt. Hal pictured himself kissing them, teasing her nipples between his lips until Joanna cried out in pleasure. Excitement surged inside him.

He put his hands around Joanna's back. She slipped hers rigidly around his neck and raised her face, once more parting her lips in the manner she had in the churchyard. Her eyes were blank and the sight of them quashed all Hal's desire. Her arms shook and Hal's blood chilled in his veins.

A true and faithful wife in body perhaps, but

whose heart belonged to another man—what a prize that was! Roger's words echoed treacherously in his ears. *You and I are enough alike.* She didn't want Hal. That was clear enough. Would it be Roger she would think of when Hal finally bedded her? He'd swim the Ouse naked in front of the entire Guild of Smiths before he'd tolerate that.

He dropped his hands and stepped back. Joanna put a hand on his arm but he shrugged it off.

'Stop that!' he snapped, more harshly than he intended.

'Last night you said you would not wait forever,' Joanna said. Her voice was tight with anxiety.

'It was a stupid thing to say,' Hal answered. 'Call it the voice of the wine rather than mine.'

He walked to the window and flung the small shutter open, letting grey daylight into the room, and turned back to her.

'If I'd wanted you under any circumstance I could have taken you last night,' he said. 'It is my right as your husband but I chose not to. Where would the pleasure be for me in knowing you would hate every moment or be thinking of another?'

'I wouldn't be...' Joanna began but Hal hushed her.

'Yes, you would. Don't lie. I know your heart belongs to my brother,' Hal growled.

She had the dignity not to contradict him. There was no reason to expect her feelings to have ceased when she spoke her vows but jealousy flooded Hal's veins. Perhaps he should tell her of his brother's indifference to her marriage, but what purpose would that serve, other than to make her even more wretched? He wasn't that cruel, but if he waited for her love to die of its own accord he would be old and grey.

Roger was not the only man capable of capturing a woman's attention, though. Hal crossed the room in two strides and before she could protest he pulled Joanna to him.

'I'm a proud man, Joanna,' he breathed, staring at her intently. 'I don't want to see you quaking with terror whenever I speak to you and I certainly don't want you forcing yourself to seduce me. I will not come to your bed until you ask me. I'm going to kiss you, though. I deserve that at least.'

She gasped in surprise and he nearly released her, but instead slipped one hand behind her neck, tilting her face to his. The other he put around her waist and held her gaze, silent and unblinking, his expression commanding her not to look away. Still watching, he bent towards her and covered her mouth with his. Joanna's eyes widened as she pushed her lips hard against him, opening her mouth wide. It struck Hal that for all his enthusiasm, Roger had no subtlety if that was what she had come to expect. Hal drew away. He lifted a finger and placed it over her lips.

'Wait,' he ordered. 'Close your eyes.'

He captured her bottom lip between his and tugged gently. Joanna gave a soft moan of surprise but he ignored her and held still, waiting for her top lip to close over his before he began to move his mouth slowly and firmly over hers. She tasted of honey and was as soft as rose petals. Hal increased the pressure of his kiss before running his tongue lightly over Joanna's lips and parting them gently to allow him entry to her mouth. His tongue flickered briefly against hers and he felt the breath catch in Joanna's chest. Her hands clutched his arms and Hal realised for the first time that his heart was pounding strongly. At some point he had closed his own eyes.

Enough! Before he was caught in a current from which he could not pull free.

He withdrew his tongue and took one final taste of her lips before he pulled away and examined his wife. Joanna's eyes were closed, her lips still parted. Her cheeks were suffused with a scarlet flush that brought a smile of victory to Hal's lips.

He withdrew his hands and Joanna opened her eyes like one waking from a dream. The colour in her cheeks deepened and her eyes widened.

'I have business to attend to this morning,' Hal said pleasantly, as though he had done nothing more than kiss her hand. 'I'll leave you to dress in peace.'

He left the room quickly and walked downstairs, grinning. He would wager she had not been thinking of Roger during *that* kiss and from the look on Joanna's face, Hal had a feeling that he would not have long to wait before he was in her bed.

Hal was as true as his word. Each night Joanna left the noisy public room of the inn and returned to their bedchamber first where she lay awake, listening for Hal's step outside the door. He would come in—never too long afterwards—extinguish the candles and undress silently, then pause, waiting for her word. She never gave it. Hal would make his way to the settle and stretch out wrapped in his cloak and blankets until morning.

He appeared to bear Joanna no ill will for this. Why should he, when she knew he felt as little affection for her as she did for him? Less even because the tremors that had run through her at his kiss had unnerved her in a way she had not expected.

His only sign of dissatisfaction was the way he turned his neck back and forth to rid himself of cricks each morning. Every time he did, a pang of guilt stabbed Joanna. More than once it was on her lips to invite him to share the bed with her, but she swallowed back the offer, knowing that when he did come to her bed he would not be content with sleep.

On the third evening after their marriage they dined with Simon and Mary. Hal was in good humour, laughing with Simon, gracious to Mary and smiling as tenderly at Joanna as any true husband would. She doubted an outsider would suspect how little fondness he felt for her.

After the meal Hal and Simon traded stories while Joanna and Mary sat together, keeping the children from intruding as best they could. Small Betty wriggled from Joanna's grasp and ran across the room in pursuit of one of the kittens. Hal reached out an arm and effortlessly scooped her up. He jiggled the child on his knee until Betty screeched with excitement and demanded more. Joanna walked over and held her arms out.

'You'll make her sick,' she scolded.

'Nonsense! She's having fun,' Hal answered. He bounced the child a couple more times to make his point before passing her back to Joanna with a grin.

'How do you like your husband?' Mary whispered as Joanna returned to her seat.

Mary would never ask anything in an obvious manner but from the raise of her eyebrow her meaning was clear.

Three days after his kiss Joanna's lips remembered his touch and taste. It had been nothing like Roger's kisses which were fierce, rough even, his passion for her too great to be easily controlled. Hal's touch had been slow and measured, but Joanna had lost all sense of where she was or who was kissing her until he stopped so abruptly and walked from the room without a second glance at her. It had clearly meant nothing to him so how had it caused her limbs to weaken and her breath to stop in such an alarming fashion?

She should not have felt anything. Had not wanted to. She cringed whenever she thought how her body had betrayed her. Worse, her mind had betrayed her because now when she tried to bring Roger's face to mind his features were jumbled together with Hal's until she could not pick them apart.

Hal was gazing towards them. He could not have heard Mary's words but Joanna smiled faintly. How could she explain that she was denying her husband that which was rightfully his and that he was content to allow it? The moment would come soon when she could no longer refuse, and she was unsure whether the thought of her body responding with such abandon scared her more than it excited her.

When Hal offered his arm as they walked home that night Joanna took it happily, still amused by the image of him surrounded by children and company. He had appeared surprisingly comfortable with Betty and she pictured him with children of his own. Her heart gave an unexpected throb as she realised they would be her children also. She should have borne children for Sir Roger. It should have been him sitting by the fire, not Hal. The unfairness of it drove a fist into her belly.

'We'll need to leave early tomorrow,' Hal said.

Joanna had always known they must leave the city, but now the day was here it felt as though her heart was being cut from her body.

'Surely there's no need to leave straight away?'

'I've completed my business here,' Hal said,

'and I have other commitments to attend to at home. Aren't you curious to see your new home?'

Joanna stared at her feet. 'I suppose so,' she mumbled.

Hal gave her arm a comforting pat and said nothing more until he bade her goodnight with a light kiss on the back of her hand, his eyes dark and thoughtful.

Hal was already up when Joanna woke the next morning. He was naked apart from his braies. Through half-closed eyes Joanna watched him wash in the ewer of water. Even on their wedding night he had been clothed and what Joanna saw aroused her curiosity. His back was broad and his arms firm, each muscle clearly defined by the light that filtered through the shutters. Why this surprised Joanna she couldn't say. He was a blacksmith after all and a man did not spend all day in such a job without some effect but Hal could have been cast from the very iron he worked with.

She gave an involuntary shiver at the thought of Hal's hands on her and he turned around. Not wishing to be caught spying, Joanna gave an exaggerated yawn and rubbed her eyes before sitting up. Hal grinned and she smiled back innocently, prepared to deny completely that she had been watching, yet convinced Hal was aware of the fact.

Hal had acquired a cart for the journey, which he had already loaded with sacks and boxes before Joanna's own chest was carried down by the innkeeper's boys. She held her leather bag close to her body and climbed on to the seat beside him. Hal clicked his tongue, gave a snap of the reins and the horse moved forward.

Soon the city walls were behind them. Joanna turned back for one final view, then pulled her hood forward to hide the sorrow that crossed her face. Hal said nothing, but after a while he spoke.

'Unless you married a man from York you would have left eventually.'

'I know that!' Joanna snapped. She fell silent. He had meant to be kind and to point out that she had dreamed of leaving with Sir Roger seemed unnecessarily harsh. Perhaps Hal realised what she was thinking anyway because he reached behind him, pulled out a wineskin and wordlessly passed it to Joanna, who drank deeply. She rested her hands on her knees and watched the countryside roll slowly by, listening to Hal whistling the tune that had been playing at the feast.

* * *

Night had fallen by the time they reached the inn at Malton. Joanna climbed down wearily. Her back was aching from the hours sitting on the hard cart bench and she began to walk in a wide circle around the deserted market square.

'Keep close by me,' Hal cautioned.

'I've lived all my life in a city. I don't think I'll have anything to fear here,' she countered.

Hal scowled. 'You'll still find cutpurses and men who will not think twice about relieving you of your goods—or your virtue.' He held an arm out, but as Joanna reached for it Hal drew her to his side and held her tightly. The gesture was unexpected and, caught off balance, Joanna flung her arms about his waist. Hal looked down at her and opened his mouth to speak but then closed it again. Silently Joanna held on to her husband, body flooding with warmth as he led her down the narrow alleyway between the stables and the inn.

As the only inn in the town it was much busier than the one in York where travellers had a choice. Exhaustion hit Joanna like a fist and she slumped on to a stool, knowing that if she had to stand any longer she was in danger of never rising again. Hal dropped his bags and immediately called for wine and food. Joanna closed her eyes and allowed the bustle to carry on around her as Hal secured their lodgings and directed their baggage to be taken upstairs.

Soon two bowls of stew stood on the table before Joanna.

'Eat,' Hal urged, nudging the bowl towards her.

She took the smallest taste. The stew was good—rich and thick, tasting of beef and cinnamon—and Joanna found she had an appetite after all. She emptied the bowl and leaned back against Hal. He put an arm around her shoulder. Despite the noise her eyes began to close as she nestled against him, glad to be held so comfortingly.

'We don't have so far to travel tomorrow,' Hal said gently. 'Go to bed. I'll be up shortly.'

Joanna picked up her bag and climbed the stairs. Hal had succeeded in obtaining one of the private rooms on the second floor. It was small and dark, but at least they would not have to bed down in the common dormitory with a dozen other travellers. The bed was narrow and unlike the inn in York there was no settle for Hal to sleep on. Joanna's scalp prickled. She could hardly expect him to sleep on the floor but if she was asleep—or at least gave the impression of being—he would surely not wake her. She undressed quickly and climbed into bed, pulling the covers up tightly.

* * *

When the door opened not long afterwards Joanna buried her face in her arm. She listened as Hal moved stealthily around the room, muttering under his breath. From the sounds of rummaging and chests opening he seemed to be searching for something. Joanna shifted slightly and risked a peek.

Her blood turned cold. The figure in the room was tall, but wiry instead of broad. By the light of the moon Joanna saw tufts of pale hair sticking out about his head. The intruder began to empty the contents of Joanna's bag on to the floor. He cackled in triumph as he discovered the scrip containing Joanna's money, sending her scraps of parchment fluttering to the ground.

'That's mine!' Joanna exclaimed before she could debate the wisdom of drawing attention to herself.

The intruder jumped in alarm and looked towards the bed. He snarled as his eyes met Joanna's, but she was already leaping from the bed, running towards the open door and screaming 'thief'.

She felt her hair seized from behind, a sharp pain that stopped her in her tracks, and she was wrenched roughly to the ground. The intruder kicked the door shut and turned back to Joanna, his eyes wide and greedy as he regarded his unexpected spoils.

Chapter Eight

Hal rolled his shoulders back, the knots brought on by a day's driving making their presence known. The cart had been slow and awkward and made him long to be on horseback. No wonder Joanna had been so pale and ill if she felt anything like as tired and stiff as he was. No one paid him any attention as he sat by the hearth and warmed his back and he decided he liked the feeling.

Here he was unknown; just another traveller weary from the road instead of the lord's bastard son or the shining knight's brother. He cradled his wine cup, thinking back to his years as a journeyman, travelling the country with his master, never stopping for more than a month or two in any place. How strange that idea would be for Joanna who had never left York until today.

As the thought of his wife crossed his mind Hal drained his cup and placed it on the table.

She would doubtless be asleep by now, or feigning such. The prospect of another night alone while she lay silently at the other side of the room filled Hal with melancholy. He wondered what she thought of as she lay alone. The answer came to him that in all likelihood it was Roger who filled her dreams. He did not believe it had been Simon Vernon's house or company that she had been crying for as they left the city this morning.

He reached for the wine flask but it was empty. He was tempted to call the serving girl over and ask for more. She was pretty, dark-eyed and laughing—more to his taste than Joanna, who regarded him with such sadness or hesitancy whenever he spoke to her. Without too much coaxing she would probably provide other enjoyments along with the wine. His wife did not want him so why should he not take comfort elsewhere? Joanna could spend her nights foolishly grieving for a man who did not want her and he could find pleasure in more willing arms.

And do what? Produce more bastards with no place in the world as his father had and countless other men did? He would never make *that* mistake. Guilt at the thought of breaking his vows so lightly made him wince. He was already using Joanna ill by marrying her to gain favour with Simon without heaping that indignity on her head too.

He put his cup on the table and made his way upstairs. As he reached the landing and turned the corner a scream cut through the noise rising from the rooms below, cut off abruptly by a door slamming. It only took a moment to realise that the voice was familiar, but that moment seemed to last for years before Hal broke into a run towards his room.

The door was wedged. Not locked, but something behind it was preventing him from entering. Hal pushed harder and the object shifted. The room was in darkness but enough light from the lamps on the landing allowed him to see what had blocked his way. Joanna lay on the floor, twisted beneath a shabbily dressed man who knelt astride her, one hand across her mouth. Her shift was raised to her knees and one leg was splayed out to the side, but she was not submitting easily. Her left arm lashed out at the man's face while the fingers of her right hand scrabbled on the floor towards her heavy-soled boot that was almost within her reach.

Hal roared in anger and lunged towards the man, grabbing him by the collar. He wrenched him off Joanna and spun him around. The man snarled and fought to free himself, delivering an unexpected punch to the side of Hal's jaw that made lights burst behind his eyes. As Hal's grip loosened the intruder elbowed him in the chest and sprang for the door. Hal bunched his fist and drove it into the man's back, then turned him around and delivered a series of blows until his fists hurt, aiming to block out the idea of Joanna enduring the ordeal he had narrowly prevented as much as to subdue his opponent. The man succeeded in landing a few punches, but Hal barely felt the impact.

When the man went limp in Hal's arms Hal threw him to the ground and drew his dagger from its sheath at his waist. Snarling, he gripped the man by the hair and bared his throat. It was only Joanna's cry of alarm that stayed his hand.

She was standing at the foot of the bed. In her hand was Hal's sword, the tip dragging on the ground from the weight she could barely lift. Despite the situation Hal barked a laugh.

'What were you going to do with that?' he asked.

'In case he overpowered you,' Joanna said, her voice faltering.

'That was never going to happen,' he said fiercely. 'I know how to fight.'

'I wanted to help you.'

Hal studied Joanna properly. Her face was ashen save one red mark across her cheek, but her eyes blazed with a defiance he had never seen. He reached once more for the man's throat and again Joanna cried out.

'Don't!'

'Why not?' Hal asked irritably. 'He'll hang in the morning anyway. After what he tried to do to you he doesn't deserve a clean death!' Images of Joanna's bloodied, broken body lying on the floor, her eyes lightless and unseeing, raced through Hal's mind. His throat tightened. If he'd stayed downstairs and ordered more wine as he'd considered...

'His blood won't be on your hands, though,' Joanna whispered, her voice barely audible. 'Don't become a killer, please.'

She lifted her eyes to meet Hal's, wide and imploring. He nodded, knowing he could not deny her this, and sheathed his dagger. He dragged the man to his feet by the neck of his tunic, twisted one arm behind the man's back until he yelped in pain and marched him downstairs, loudly demanding the landlord's presence.

Hal's was not the first room the man had ventured into, but the only one that had been occupied. Amidst the angry shouts of the other guests the man was roughly stripped to his braies, and pouches of money, jewellery and other valuables were discovered and claimed by their owners. The last Hal saw of the man was as he was dragged by the furious mob from the building to the town square to spend the night in the pillory with the gallows in clear view.

Hal felt no sorrow at the man's fate. He eased himself into a chair by the table and retrieved his money pouch and the scrip embroidered with the initials 'JS' that must belong to his wife. His eyes fell on another item that lay discarded and he picked it up, rubbing his fingers over the twisted metal of Joanna's marriage brooch. He slipped it into his own pouch, wondering if she would notice, or care about, its absence.

Joanna! Hal's scalp prickled and he spat an oath at his own thoughtlessness. He took the stairs two at a time.

She was sitting on the edge of the bed, her thick travelling cloak wrapped tightly around her and Hal's on top of that. Her bare feet were pressed tightly together on the floor and her hair fell across her face. She jumped to her feet as Hal stepped on a loose floorboard. Her shoulders sagged in relief as she recognised him.

'The townspeople have him now,' Hal stated. 'It's out of my hands.'

'Thank you,' Joanna said.

'Are you all right?' Hal asked. Ridiculous question! He could see how tightly her hands gripped the edges of his cloak. She bowed her head, trembling.

In two strides Hal was beside her. He opened his arms wide, expecting her to refuse, but wordlessly Joanna fell into his embrace. Her hands clutched tightly about his waist, fingernails pressing into his spine. The terror left her in gulping sobs that came faster and stronger. With each one her breasts rose and fell, forcing Hal to be acutely aware of their fullness as they pushed against his chest.

Hal tightened his arms about her slender torso, moving his hands in slow comforting circles until the anxiety that filled them both had diminished. She shifted slightly as she rested her cheek against his shoulder. She was just tall enough that her cheek rested in the curve of his neck. Unexpected waves of desire rippled through Hal and his breath caught in his throat. Joanna continued to sob, seemingly unaware of the effect she had just caused in him. He rested his chin on the top of her head, waiting while her distress burned itself out.

Finally Joanna's sobs ended, though her body still shook with occasional tremors. Reluctantly Hal eased his hold and smiled down at her. She needed something to calm her. If it came to that, so did he!

'Wait here,' he commanded. He raced back downstairs and called for hot, spiced wine. The heady, cinnamon-scented steam filled his nostrils as he carried it back upstairs.

Joanna was sitting where he had left her. 'I thought you'd gone,' she said, her voice dull.

'I said to wait,' Hal rebuked her gently. 'That meant I would come back.'

He drew her to the bed and sat beside her and pushed the wine into her hand. They passed the jug back and forth in companionable silence until it was empty. Hal's jaw was beginning to throb from the blow. Other aches would make themselves known soon. He rubbed his face absentmindedly. He was not expecting Joanna's fingers to cover his and he gave a start. She started to withdraw her hand, but Hal captured it and held it in place.

'Your hand is cold,' he joked. 'It helps ease the soreness.'

She gave a faint smile. He noticed her cheeks were no longer ashen.

'I should never have left you alone,' he told her. 'I warned you myself, but took no heed of my own advice.'

Hal ran a thumb across the bruise on her cheek, another burst of anger knocking the breath from him. The devil would hang in the morning and Hal swore to himself he would be there to witness the man's end as his feet kicked against nothing and his face turned crimson.

Joanna was watching him carefully. 'Don't leave me tonight,' she said quietly.

Her eyes were dark smudges against her pale skin. Hal thought back to the sight of her brandishing a sword she could barely lift. Even after what she had suffered she was prepared to risk herself defending him. She had looked wild and fierce, more alluring than ever before. He fought down his rising desire. Perhaps he had misunderstood.

'If I sleep in your bed you'll sleep in my arms,' Hal said. His pulse quickened. 'Do you understand what I mean?' If she said no now he did not know how he would bear the disappointment, but Joanna raised her eyes to his.

'I don't want to be alone after what happened,' she whispered.

Hal crossed the room and extinguished the lamp, pinching the wick between fingers that were unaccountably shaking. He removed his outer clothing until he stood in his braies and shirt.

Joanna turned the covers back on the bed and smoothed her long shift down. By a shaft of moonlight Hal caught a glimpse of one calf. It caused more excitement than such a sight really warranted and he hid a smile at his own foolishness. He climbed into the bed and pulled the thin covers closely around them both. Their hips brushed together as she arched her back slightly to settle her balance. Even before his back touched the mattress he was harder than he could remember being for months and his anticipation began to mount. Beside him Joanna lay rigid, her rapid breathing the only sound in the room. He rolled on to his side, raising himself on to his elbow and reached a hand to Joanna's shoulder to pull her towards him.

Her breath caught in her throat. It was only a small sound but, coupled with the way her body felt like lead as she came reluctantly to his arms, a sense of dishonour filled Hal. Joanna had suffered terrors tonight he could only imagine and had accepted the surrender of her virginity as the price for comfort and safety. To claim her now would make Hal no better than the brute he had saved her from. Only a contemptible man would exact such a payment as the price for safety.

Though every part of his body cried out to continue Hal relaxed his hand. 'Go to sleep, Joanna,' he whispered close to her ear. She turned her head—so close that her lips were within reach.

'But you said…' She faltered.

'Never mind what I said,' Hal replied gently. As he took his hand from her shoulder he felt the tension flood from her body. After a pause she rolled on to her side facing away from him. Hal closed his eyes, smiling in the darkness. He had gained an unexpected victory tonight. There would be no more uncomfortable nights alone. He was certain of that. Still grinning, he allowed the sound of Joanna's breathing to lull him to sleep.

The sky was barely light when Joanna woke. The counterpane felt curiously heavy until she realised that the weights pinning her down were Hal's leg and arm. At some point in the night they had moved closer together and he had wrapped himself around her from behind. His other arm was spread out across the pillow above.

He was deep in sleep. She could not move without waking him and he seemed at peace. The room was chilly and Hal's body was warm. She remembered the feeling of Hal holding her tightly as she cried. The safety she had felt in his arms had been unlike anything she had experienced and after the trials of the previous day Joanna was in no rush to relinquish the memory. She shifted carefully on to her back, nestling into the space between his chest and arm, and waited for the sun to rise. Hal shifted slightly and muttered something unintelligible. His fingers spread out across Joanna's shoulder as he shifted closer to her. Chills raced down the length of her arm.

She craned her head to look at Hal. His jaw was swollen and she wondered if it was as painful as her own cheek felt. She ran her hand over his bruise as she had done the night before. His beard growth was scratchy under her fingers. As she touched him Hal's free arm closed around her, his fingers tangling into her hair. She was firmly trapped in his embrace now, her arm crushed between their bodies with her fingers still resting against his cheek.

He opened his eyes and his lips curled into a smile. He had been awake for longer than Joanna had realised. He turned and kissed her open palm, then drew her closer to him and gently kissed her lips. Joanna's heart pounded in surprise yet she did not pull away. Wordlessly they rolled to face each other.

The time had passed when she might have slipped from his arms while he slept and delayed the inevitable yet again. Last night she had steeled herself to submit but Hal had reprieved her. There would be no escape now. Memories tumbled through her mind: Sir Roger's hands tight upon her breast, the intruder's fingers digging painfully into her thighs. She whimpered in apprehension. Hal paused mid-kiss and looked into her eyes. He put his hands either side of her face and caressed her with more tenderness than she would have expected.

'It will be nothing like last night, I promise you,' he breathed.

Joanna nodded. Hal began to kiss her again. She put her arm about his waist and he sighed deeply, his tongue running across her lips. She barely realised she was kissing him back until his lips left hers and began travelling slowly to her neck, planting feather-light kisses on her skin. She sighed in pleasure at these sensations, gentler yet more stimulating than any touch of Roger's had been.

Hal's hands dipped below the sheets as he removed his braies. The same hands began to inch Joanna's shift higher. Cold air hit her feet, her calves and finally her thighs as his fingers teased their way upwards until they reached the place her legs met. His fingers brushed against her, spreading wide and stroking the soft mound of hair. A moan of alarm erupted from her as a violent throb shot through her lower half.

The sound seemed to excite Hal because he growled and eased himself astride her, covering her body with his. His legs eased hers apart as his weight pinned her down. A strange calmness descended upon Joanna and she closed her eyes. It would be over soon, she told herself. Hal stroked his hand between her legs once more, firmer this time and sending ripples of heat coursing through Joanna's body.

Hal shifted his weight, there was a slight pressure, a little pain, and he was inside her. He took hold of Joanna's hands and guided them about his waist. He was gentle at first with a slow rhythm and Joanna was aware of every stroke as he moved within her. She felt him grow harder, his thrusts becoming faster and deeper. His hands roamed across her hair and face, his breath hot and rapid on her neck. A sensation of pressure began to build in Joanna and breathing took more effort. She was starting to fear it would never come to an end when Hal's arms slid behind her back and he clutched her tight, lifting her towards him. He gave one long groan and a final deep thrust then sagged down, burying his face in Joanna's hair.

When Joanna opened her eyes he was smiling at her with a warmth she had never seen before. Her cheeks flamed as he kissed her gently. He rolled on to his back, wriggled one arm underneath Joanna and held her close in the crook of his arm, shutting his eyes. Joanna wrapped her arms around her body and stared at him curiously. He was clearly content with what they had done. For her part it had been neither as painful nor as unpleasant as she had feared it would be. It had not even been as uncomfortable as the embraces Sir Roger had cajoled her into. Mary Vernon had been right; it could be tolerated.

Her stomach tightened with guilt as Sir Roger's face flashed into her mind. Her longing for him tore a hole in her heart whenever she thought of him, but she had promised to be a faithful wife to Hal and today she had put the seal on that promise. If she had ever entertained the thought she could be freed from her marriage that was behind her now. For Sir Roger to come to mind when she had just committed such an intimate act felt tantamount to a betrayal. She squeezed her eyes tight in an attempt to banish him and gave a heavy sigh of regret.

'What are you thinking about?' Hal asked sleepily.

'Nothing,' Joanna replied, much too quickly. She could hear the guilt clearly in her voice.

The muscles in Hal's arm tightened. Joanna glanced away.

'Liar!' Hal withdrew his arm and sat up, his eyes hard with jealousy. 'You don't need to tell me. I can guess well enough,' he said bitterly.

He climbed from the bed and pulled his braies and tunic on.

Joanna pushed herself on to her elbows. 'It wasn't what you think!'

Hal folded his arms and scowled, his mouth twisting downwards. 'Was it all night you thought of him, or only this morning?'

'Just now!' Joanna answered without thinking. 'No! I don't mean… Not while we… Only afterwards…'

All her words were coming out wrong. She hit her pillow in frustration.

'We need to leave soon. We've stayed too long already,' Hal said curtly. He picked Joanna's dress from the floor and tossed it on to the bed. He busied himself repacking their belongings while Joanna dressed silently.

As Hal opened the door he stopped, dipped into his money pouch and folded Joanna's hand around something cold and hard.

'Your brooch, Mistress Danby,' he said.

Joanna pinned the brooch on her dress, wishing she could turn the time back, or had the words to explain to Hal. Maybe then his eyes would not be so full of hurt that made her heart ache in response.

Chapter Nine

Joanna said nothing as they left the inn. She sat silently as Hal led the horse and cart towards the town gate, but the sight of the gallows and their occupant drew a sharp breath from her. Hal turned to offer her a word of comfort, but the memory of her deceit rankled and he bit his tongue, turning a grim eye on the limp body that twisted slowly from the end of a rope.

Last night he'd vowed to be there to see the man's end but this morning finding Joanna warm and peaceful in his arms had proved too much of a temptation. It should have struck him as suspicious that Joanna was so amenable when the night before her reluctance had been a wall between them, but it had been far too long since Hal had woken with a woman in his bed. The touch of her fingers on his flesh as she believed him still asleep had inflamed him beyond resisting and he'd broken his intention without even thinking about it.

Now he reflected that he'd have been better off ignoring the urges that whispered so enticingly and gone down to the square with the rest of the townspeople. He'd never enjoyed witnessing suffering, however, and the sense of satisfaction at seeing the man meet his deserved end would have been hollow before long. As hollow as the pleasure he had taken from his time in Joanna's arms, he thought bitterly.

They passed through the gate and Hal climbed beside her on the seat. She stiffened as their shoulders touched, drawing her arms closer to her sides.

'Sit behind if my touch is so alarming to you,' he muttered, not bothering to keep the resentment from his voice.

Joanna turned her blue eyes on him reproachfully, but she settled her arms by her side again until they were touching Hal's. Scowling, he urged the horse faster as they reached the open road and they made their way along the familiar route towards Pickering.

Crops gave way to sheep, green pasture to yellow moss and the scraggy, twisted bushes where purple heather would bloom. Hal's mood began to lift as the track began to climb into the hills.

However far he had travelled he never returned home without joy at the sight of the moors as they rolled away into the distance. His hair whipped about his face and he brushed it out of his eyes.

Joanna spoke, dragging him from his reverie. Her voice was quiet, the sound carried away by the wind and drowned out by the rattle of the wheels. Hal had to strain to catch her words. He raised an eyebrow questioningly.

'I never thanked you properly for what you did last night,' Joanna repeated, a faint blush tainting her cheeks.

'No thanks needed,' Hal replied stiffly. 'Anyone would have done what I did.'

He regarded Joanna surreptitiously from the corner of his eye. She had wrapped her cloak tightly around her body and sat hugging herself. Her hair was braided back from her face, trapped under the linen filet that all married women wore. It gave her pale face an air of solemnity, further accentuated by her lips tightly pressed into a thin line. If she had been a more welcoming companion he'd have tugged the band free to allow the wind to tease the pale locks loose.

He could scarcely credit the fact that not half an hour ago he had been kissing her, his fingers tangling in the mass of hair, his hands upon the body that was now shrouded in the thick wool cloak.

'But if you hadn't arrived...' Joanna continued.

She placed a hand hesitantly on Hal's wrist and looked into his eyes. Her fingers were cold on his skin. Hal's pulse quickened as his body recalled her earlier touch, reminding him treacherously that it still wanted her.

Their coupling had been silent and brief. He had expected nothing more of his first time with Joanna. His release when it came had been muted and the act had lacked the true pleasure that an hour or two spent with a more enthusiastic, good-humoured bedfellow gave him. He had not expected the laughing, fumbling urgent joining of two people who had craved each other's bodies for so long, but afterwards she had given that traitorous sigh and Hal had realised that all the time she had been picturing Roger in his place. It was a revelation more sobering than a bucket of seawater across his body, and one that sickened him to his stomach when he thought of it.

'You thanked me well enough this morning,' Hal snapped.

Her eyebrows shot up in shock. 'Do you think that is why I lay with you?' she gasped.

'Wasn't it?' Hal asked. He tightened the grip on

the reins as the cart began to climb the hill. 'You could have thanked me any number of ways, Joanna. You didn't have to repay the debt with your body!'

'Is that what you think?' Joanna's voice trembled.

'You've shied away from my touch ever since our wedding so you'll have to forgive my suspicion at your timing,' Hal said grimly. 'Would you have invited me into your bed last night if that hadn't happened?'

'No. But that wasn't why I did it,' Joanna protested. She lowered her voice. 'I knew I would have to eventually. After what you did for me last night I was feeling fond of you.'

Hal snorted.

'Fond!' he remarked archly. The resentment that had been gnawing at his heart bubbled to the surface. He'd sensed again the undercurrent of passion in her he had touched when he first kissed her and it pained him to know it had been thoughts of Roger that ignited it.

'And of course you were able to bear my touch by conjuring the man you wanted to be with,' he sneered.

The slap came out of nowhere. There was surprising strength behind it and Hal's cheek stung.

Joanna's hand was still raised and she was shaking visibly. Her face was contorted with anger as she spat out a word Hal was surprised she even knew. She leapt to her feet, causing the cart to rock alarmingly. For one moment Hal though she was about to hurl herself from it. Her cloak billowed in the wind, rising up behind her. He grabbed hold of her wrist firmly with one hand while with the other he pulled sharply on the reins until the horse stopped.

'Are you trying to kill yourself?' he raged. 'If you had fallen you could have broken your neck or been crushed by the wheels!'

Joanna struggled under his grasp. Hal loosened his grip and she wrenched herself free and jumped down from the cart. She stumbled as she landed on the rough stones but caught her balance and stalked away.

By now they were far from any settlement. Distant bleating of sheep and the lonely cries of crows were the only sounds of life. Hal watched Joanna's retreating figure. She found a clump of moss and sat down with her back to Hal, curling herself into a tight knot and wrapping her arms around her knees. When he was sure she did not intend to go any further Hal put his elbows on his knees and rested his head in his hands with a sigh, waiting for her to return once her anger had burned away.

When he looked round again she was gone. He leapt to his feet and searched in every direction. She was heading across the moors. Hal leapt from the cart and raced after her.

'What do you think you're doing?' he yelled. She turned back to him.

'I'm walking,' she said angrily.

'Were you planning to run away back to York?' Hal asked.

'I'm not running away. I like to walk when I'm angry.'

Joanna's face was tearstained but her expression was defiant. Hal recognised the same set of her jaw as when she had faced her attacker last night: a mixture of apprehension and determination not to let her opponent see it. That she could ever view him in the same light made Hal's heart split in two. He lowered his voice, trying to speak calmly.

'You don't know where you are, or what the land is like here.'

She shrugged. He crossed the ground towards her, the peat spongy beneath his tread.

'Look,' he said, gesturing around him. 'The twisted boughs are heather, but the brown and yellow are moss. Tread on the wrong patch and you'll find yourself sinking into a bog up to your knees. If you're fortunate.' He eyed her darkly. 'Further than that if you aren't.'

He took a few steps to the side, where the moss was thick and yellow and put his hand down, pressing until brown water oozed between his fingers. Joanna's gaze followed his hand, her eyes wide.

'I didn't know,' she said.

Hal held his hand out in a gesture of peace, thought twice and wiped it on his tunic, then held it out again. Joanna regarded it suspiciously but took it.

'You wouldn't know. How could you?' he said. 'But you'll learn once you've lived here for a time.'

It was the wrong thing to say because Joanna gave another muffled sigh. Hal had been mistaken to think the anger she had felt had subsided. Once more he found himself wishing he had never agreed to marry her. No guild membership was worth living with this for.

'You don't want me—' he sighed '—I understand that but here we are. If it comes to it I hoped for a wife who cared for me. Not one who bears my touch under sufferance and longs for another man every time she's in my arms.'

Joanna pulled her hand free from Hal's. She rounded on him and put her hands on her hips.

'If I was thinking of Sir Roger—and I wasn't, as I have already tried to explain—then what does that matter to you?' she shouted. 'You don't love me! You say you wanted a wife who cares for you, but it wasn't *me* you wanted to marry. It was Simon Vernon's niece.'

The wind had whipped Joanna's cloak from round her body. It billowed out behind her to reveal the dress she wore beneath. Her breath came hard and with each inhalation her breasts rose, pushing up against the tight bodice. They were standing close and an overwhelming urge to kiss her washed over Hal.

He wondered how different her lips would feel if he was the man she wanted to be with. She had the capacity for passion, he had seen hints enough of that. When he had bedded her this morning he had sensed the need within her, but she had fought against it.

'It was never my intention to hurt you,' he said gently. 'I believed marrying was of benefit to both of us.'

'What was the benefit to me?' Joanna asked, laughing incredulously.

Hal folded his arms. 'I hope that despite everything I'm more agreeable than the old widowed Welshman I believe was your alternative,' he said drily.

Maybe he wasn't. Would her feelings die quicker if she had not married someone so similar to Roger? Hal honestly did not know. He stepped closer, but Joanna's hands shot up between them.

'That's an easy justification to salve your conscience,' she cried. 'You took me from my home, from everything and everyone I know because it suited your purposes to make my uncle happy and further your interests.'

She was raging now, her ferocity unexpected and alarming. The words were nothing new to Hal, but before she had shown a quiet resignation: sad at times, but accepting, and he had genuinely believed she would become accustomed to him before long. Now her emotions were spilling out uncontrollably as she gave vent to the feelings she kept inside, and for the first time he grasped the enormity of her pain.

'When you bedded me were you thinking of me or only the admission to the guild it was buying you?' she finished.

'It was you!' Hal insisted, though in truth he could not remember what had gone through his mind at the time. He had been filled only with the need to quench his desire for his wife. Afterwards he had lain beside her in a contented, fog-headed mood, daydreaming of the joys he would introduce her to next time.

'Do you intend to spend the rest of your life pining for my brother?' Hal asked sullenly. He found himself curiously reluctant to speak Roger's name to her.

Joanna waved her arms in exasperation. 'Do you expect my heart to change promptly just to suit you? That isn't the way love works!'

'And does dwelling on that make you happy or sad?' Hal shot back.

Joanna wrapped her arms around herself and turned to stare across the moorland. Hal wondered if she was even seeing it. Witnessing her sorrow now felt like an intrusion.

'I'll wait by the cart,' he murmured. 'Take care to walk back exactly the way you came.'

Joanna rubbed her burning eyes. Hal's words had knocked the fight out of her, as quickly as it had risen up, leaving her exhausted. Her palm stung and she swallowed a knot of self-reproach at the memory of hitting Hal. It was deplorable to have done it, but Hal's insinuation had been unacceptable. The idea that he thought her capable of such infidelity had been too much of a slur to tolerate, especially when she was innocent of the fault he accused her of.

What right did Hal have to command her thoughts? He had known her feelings for Roger when he married her.

She walked back to the cart, making sure to follow the route Hal had taken. Part of her doubted his caution was genuine, but now was not the time to provoke another argument.

Hal kept his attention focused on the horse as she drew near, stroking the velvety nose and muttering in the animal's ear. Joanna spoke his name. He looked up and gave a thin smile, making no mention of the bitter words that had passed between them. She eyed him suspiciously.

'Roger may have given me up, but that doesn't mean he didn't love me. He felt he had no choice and couldn't give me what he wanted me to have. That shows he loved me more, not less.'

Hal eyed her for a long time before speaking slowly. 'That can be the case,' he agreed. 'What matters now is what you will do with the knowledge. Are you determined to spend the rest of your life being miserable or will you at least try to be happy with me?'

Tears began to prickle her eyes again and she

bit her lip. 'I only had one chance of happiness and it's gone forever.'

Hal ran a hand through his hair and sighed in exasperation. 'That's your affair, but if that's the case you're more foolish than I thought!'

'I promised to be your wife and I will. I'll keep your house and aid you in your work. I'll…I'll lie with you and bear your children—'

'Children!' Hal interjected. 'I think we're getting far ahead of ourselves there! Don't worry, there are ways to prevent that sort of occurrence.'

'Oh.' Joanna blushed. Perhaps Hal had no intention of repeating the morning's incident. Her spirits lifted slightly.

'But please, carry on' Hal prompted.

Joanna folded her arms and lifted her head defiantly. 'I'll do all you ask of me and in return you don't expect me to pretend I love you and you don't condemn me for not doing. You can have my body, but my thoughts and my heart are not yours to lay claim to.'

A shadow crossed Hal's face and his mouth turned down. 'Thank you for your frankness, Mistress Danby,' he said coolly. 'The terms are acceptable to me.'

Joanna shot him an angry glare. She spun on her heel and pulled herself into the cart. She stared down at him, her face impassive. 'Hadn't we better be going if we want to reach your home before nightfall?'

Hal climbed beside her. 'We aren't going straight home. Didn't I tell you? We're going to my father's house.' He cracked the reins and gave her a twisted smile. 'He's waiting to meet my wife!'

Despite the harsh words Joanna had flung at him, Hal had seemed determined to forget they had even quarrelled. He talked of pleasantries, of his house and forge and the people she would meet in Ravenscrag. He was an amusing storyteller and the journey passed quickly, but he told her nothing about what she should expect in Wharram Danby. Perhaps he thought she had already been told everything there was to know, but in reality Roger had barely spoken of his home.

It should have been Sir Roger who brought her here, not Hal, Joanna thought with a stab of regret. He should have been beside her as they drove down the main road of Wharram Danby, alongside the millpond and past the longhouses and cottages. Villagers were returning from the fields and paused as they passed. Some called warmly to Hal and he greeted them by name, earning smiles and waves. He was clearly popular among his father's tenants. Many of them stared openly at Joanna. She resisted the urge to bury her face deeper in her hood and forced her lips into a smile.

The stone walls of Wharram Manor glowed pink in the sunset. Joanna was captivated by the long, low house at first sight but it should have been Roger's arm she linked hers through as they walked through the large oak doors as wife of the future owner. She pushed the feeling of regret deep into her heart, chiding herself for her disloyalty to Hal once more.

Her stomach growled from a mixture of hunger and nervousness as they entered the Great Hall.

Hal grinned. 'We'll eat soon enough,' he said. 'My father keeps a good table.'

She flashed a look of fury at him. Eating was the last thing on her mind.

A tall, thickset woman waited alone in the middle of the Great Hall. Hal knelt and took hold of her hand, pressing it briefly against his lips.

'Lady Danby, I am at your service,' he said.

A ripple of shock ran through Joanna. This was Roger's mother. She dropped into a deep curtsy, her legs shaking.

Lady Danby looked down her nose at the couple before her. Her hazel eyes regarded Joanna as if she had thrown a fistful of rats on to the table, but when they turned to Hal they flashed with very real disdain. Joanna tried to imagine Lady Danby greeting her more warmly as Roger's wife, but could not summon the vision of her smiling at anyone.

'Is that Hal?' a deep voice called from the end of the room.

Hal's face broke into a smile of joy. A tall figure stood in front of the fire, facing into the flames. He turned as he heard their footsteps. The man's right eye was fused shut, criss-crossed with deep scars and the pupil of the left was milky. Joanna's mouth dropped open and her fingers tightened on Hal's arm. He glanced down at her and raised an eyebrow.

'Did you not expect this?' he whispered in surprise. 'Has my brother not told you of our father's condition?'

Joanna shook her head, embarrassed at being caught unawares. It seemed there was much Roger had not told her and she felt an unfamiliar rush of resentment towards him. If he had not told her something as important as this, what else had he failed to share with her and had he ever truly intended to share anything at all?

Chapter Ten

Hal left Joanna's side and strode to the fireplace. He drew his father into a warm embrace. The older man patted his son on the back with his left hand. His right arm hung limply at his side, his hand concealed by a glove. Joanna burned with curiosity to know how this affliction had come about.

Beside Joanna Lady Danby stood straight, her shoulders back and her eyes narrowed. Once again Joanna got the sense that she had no liking for Hal. It was understandable of course. What woman would be happy seeing her husband's illegitimate offspring received with such affection?

'Did you bring your wife inside or have you left her with the cart?' Hal's father asked. 'Let me see her.'

Hal beckoned Joanna forward. She studied the man as she walked slowly towards him. There was no mistaking that this man was Roger and Hal's father. Despite his disfigurement and the additional years he bore, he was as handsome as his sons. He was as broad and tall as both of them and shared their dark curls, which on him were beginning to be tinged with grey. The similarity between the men was so strong that Joanna could not for the life of her decide which part of their mothers each son had inherited.

'My wife, Joanna,' Hal said. 'My father, Lord Danby.'

Lord Danby reached a hand forward and felt towards Joanna. She held her hand out and he grasped it tightly.

'Welcome to my house,' he said, his voice booming.

'Thank you, my lord,' she replied, sinking into a curtsy.

'No, no. Get up!' he instructed. 'I want to look at you properly and see what my son has won himself.'

Was he feeble minded? With only one milky eye how did he intend to do that? Joanna stood upright once more.

'Stand over by the large window,' Lord Danby instructed. 'Take me there.' He felt his hand along Joanna's arm and looped his through hers. Joanna guided Lord Danby to the centre of the room and paused in front of the arched window. Lord Danby let go of her arm.

'Stand in the light if you please.'

Joanna straightened her back, smoothed her hair and walked to where Lord Danby indicated. The sun was low, but streamed through the oiled linen that covered the window. It warmed Joanna's back and cast her shadow on the rush floor, throwing it out of shape.

'You're thinking I can't see you, aren't you, girl?' Lord Danby laughed good-naturedly. 'You're right in some ways. Faces I can't do well, but gestures I can see and I can make out forms well enough. In the dark we're all equally sightless and a shapely figure is all that counts at the end of the day, isn't it, Hal!'

Joanna glanced at Hal uncertainly. He stood beside his father, arms folded, watching her closely.

'Not all,' he said gravely.

His eyes flashed as they met Joanna's. A flurry of excitement took her by surprise as she recognised his desire. She remembered his declaration of wanting a wife who cared for him and sorrow gripped her that she was not that woman. She fixed her eyes on the floor.

'Father, if you've finished inspecting my wife

we'd be thankful for something to eat and drink. Joanna is unused to travelling so far and much less used to being examined like a horse in the marketplace.'

Hal walked to her side and held his arm out. 'You must ignore my father's peculiarities,' he told her, loudly enough for Lord Danby to hear but with humour in his voice. 'He thinks that his condition gives him licence to behave as he chooses.'

Lord Danby laughed. 'Hal is right. I expect everyone to indulge me. I crave your pardon, my dear.'

He was like his sons in so many ways, yet when his face broke into a smile, Joanna saw he was completely unlike them. He had given them the shape of their jaws and lips, however his smile exhibited none of Roger's shameless grin that suggested he was planning to undress her where she stood, nor the caution that played about Hal's lips when he seemed uncertain of her response. His eyes bore lines in the corners at the same spot where Hal's creased with humour.

Joanna found herself liking him a great deal.

'No pardon needed,' she said, placing her hand in his.

He lifted it to his lips, then clapped his hand on Hal's shoulder. 'Well chosen, lad,' he murmured.

Hal's eyes met Joanna's once more, his approval clear. They creased at the corners and a warm glow spread inside her. If it had been a test, she had passed. She found suddenly that Hal's esteem mattered a great deal more than she had expected it to.

Lady Danby clapped her hands sharply and a waiting servant sprang to attention. Lady Danby's face was taut as she issued orders for food and drink, then she swept to the fireplace, seated herself on a high-backed chair and turned her attention to the tapestry she was working on.

Lord Danby seemingly did not notice his wife's temperament. He began to talk to Hal in a loud voice about matters relating to the running of the manor and lands which were still recovering from the blow caused by the Great Pestilence. Arm in arm the two men left the hall. Joanna wavered, torn between joining Lady Danby and admitting her acquaintance with Roger and following her husband. In the end Lady Danby's face was so stern and unwelcoming that Joanna picked up her skirts and hurried after the men.

Hal looked surprised but not displeased to see her. He held his free arm out and the three companions walked across the moor where great grey-coated sheep stared at them with baleful expressions, bleating rudely. Over the next hour Joanna learned more than she ever wanted to discover about the afflictions that plagued the wild-eyed beasts—along with facts about their mating that made her cheeks burn with mortification and looking at her husband excruciating.

Dinner was mutton stew, rich with red wine and rosemary, onions and parsnips. More wine accompanied it and Joanna ate eagerly, unable to remember a better meal. The fire was well stoked and a dozen candles burned on the table in holders of twisted iron that Lord Danby told her with amusement were Hal's early attempts at the craft.

'You'll have to produce something more inspiring if you want to enter the guild,' Lord Danby said.

Joanna shot a glance at her husband who, surprisingly, grinned. 'They're crude, I know. I've improved since and I have no fears I will gain my admittance before the year is up.'

For one horrible moment Joanna feared he was about to reveal the conditions of their marriage. She was not sure she could bear that humiliation.

Lord Danby clapped his son on the shoulder. 'I hope so, lad. You've got a wife to support now. You'll need more than the income that crafting farm tools brings. You'll see he doesn't slack, won't you, Joanna?'

Joanna inclined her head rather than answer. Her finger traced a pattern across the table where a trace of wine had spilled, the arms of her candelabra more symmetrical than Hal's design. She realised Lady Danby was watching and wiped her hand through it with a demure smile.

Lady Danby's temper had improved. She guided her husband's hand to his knife or cup when he fumbled for it, waving away the pageboy who stood ready to provide assistance. Clearly Lord Danby was not entirely resigned to his lack of ability because he gave small sighs of frustration, though Joanna noticed he squeezed her fingers affectionately when they touched and allowed her to aid him.

Hal caught Joanna staring and leaned closer to her to speak in an undertone. 'My father was injured four years ago.'

'My hearing was unaffected however,' Lord Danby said loudly. 'If Joanna wants to hear the tale I'll tell her myself.'

Hal sat back in his chair and smiled at Joanna. He cocked one leg over the other, resting his ankle on his opposite knee and rolled his cup between his hands. She had never seen him at such ease and she returned his smile warmly.

'I was tilting,' Lord Danby told her. 'I have another son as Hal may have told you…'

Joanna opened her mouth to say she knew this already but Hal caught her eye and she closed it.

'Roger wanted to train, but Hal had begun his time as a journeyman and gone west. Roger's lance was not tipped and it struck me full in the face. It splintered into my eye. I fell and the horse crushed my arm. It was the last time I tilted. I wouldn't let them take the arm though!' he said proudly.

'It was not our son's fault!' Lady Danby's voice was mild yet reproachful.

'I have never blamed Roger, as well you know,' Lord Danby said, patting her arm. 'I merely say he might have taken more care knowing it was a practice, not a tournament, but it is always his way to be rash. He forgot he was competing against an old man instead of his equal.'

'He was young!' Lady Danby insisted. 'And as for equal…'

Hal leaned forward abruptly. 'More wine, my lady?' He reached across and filled Lady Danby's cup. She eyed him with resentment.

'If you had accepted your role as his squire it would have been you Roger rode against.'

A chill crept over Joanna at the idea of Hal blinded and maimed. Instinctively she reached for his hand and felt his fingers close around hers.

'If I had accepted my role I would still have bested Roger in every bout,' Hal muttered, sitting back in his seat.

'Enough!' Lord Danby spoke quietly but his voice carried more authority than if he had shouted. 'These are old grievances and we have a guest.'

He turned his sightless eyes towards Joanna. 'Tell me about yourself. Who is your family? I'm a little surprised at the speed this has taken, though it is not unwelcome.' He turned to his wife with a wicked grin. 'At least one of my sons shows signs of giving me a grandchild!'

'Though not an heir,' Lady Danby replied, glancing at Hal who looked at his hands.

Joanna's stomach twisted. Surely that had been Roger's intention too.

'My name was Joanna Sollers,' she said to fill the awkward silence that ensued.

She searched for a glimmer of recognition in the faces of Roger's parents, some sign that Roger had spoken of her. There was none. A lump formed in her throat.

'My uncle is Simon Vernon,' she continued. 'Of the Guild of Associated Smiths in York.'

'Ah, that explains it,' Sir Roger said. 'Hal so rarely tears himself from his work that how else would you have met other than through the guild?'

The familiar prickle of tears stung Joanna's eyelids. Roger had told his parents nothing of her, just as he had told her nothing of them. His life was split into two parts that never met. Maybe they were never intended to.

Hal filled her cup and placed it within her reach. She took it and raised it to her lips that were suddenly twitching. She looked his way to thank him and stopped short as she saw the pity that filled his eyes as he looked at her.

'An unexpectedly advantageous match for one in your position, Henry!' Lady Danby said with a cold smile, glancing from Joanna to Hal. 'How fortunate you were to win the heart of such a well-connected woman.'

Joanna gaped at the rudeness.

'Indeed so,' Hal answered, his lip curling into a smile.

'Mistress Danby, you've gone pale,' Lady Danby

said, throwing an accusing look at Hal as though it was his fault. 'Are you ill?'

'I am very weary,' Joanna said. She realised it was true. She felt unaccountably heavy and her eyes wanted to close of their own accord.

'We've travelled from Malton where we stopped last night,' Hal explained, squeezing her hand gently.

Lady Danby lifted her chin. 'Now you have succeeded in finding a wife I would expect you to have had more regard for her safety even if you disregard her comfort. You should have carried on to Pickering or the abbey at Rievaulx.'

'Hal is perfectly able to protect me,' Joanna cried. 'He saved my life last night.' She put her hand to her mouth in surprise at her forwardness. Where had that burst from? She blushed as all eyes turned on her and haltingly recounted the previous night's events.

Lady Danby's expression suggested she only saw this as further evidence of Hal's thoughtless behaviour, but Lord Danby smiled in approval. He congratulated Hal on his skill and dismissed them with a wave of his good arm.

They climbed the stairs to the bedchamber in silence but once there Hal caught Joanna by the arm. He waited until she lifted her eyes to look into his face.

'There was no need to defend me to Lady Danby,' he said sternly. His face softened and he dropped a kiss unexpectedly on to her forehead. 'I thank you all the same.'

'She dislikes you so much,' Joanna said indignantly.

Hal shrugged dismissively. 'Would you expect otherwise? The first accord she and I ever reached was that I should leave her household as soon as I was able.'

'But to be so openly rude!'

'I've learned to tolerate it and my father indulges her as he has always indulged everyone he loves.'

He stripped to his undershirt and braies and climbed into the bed. He bent one knee up, threw an arm out across the pillow and regarded Joanna with serious eyes. She hesitated, but remembered the unexpected contentment of waking in Hal's arms. Perhaps in his father's house he would not expect to bed her. She unwound her hair and stripped to her shift, conscious of Hal's eyes following her movements, and blew out the candle. She lay alongside him, resting the back of her neck against his outstretched arm and drew the blanket over them both.

The wind whistled around the end gable of the building. The sound was eerie after the noise of the inn and the familiar cries that echoed late into the York night. In the stillness she shivered. Hal rolled on to his side, wrapping his arm firmly around Joanna.

'Are you cold?' he asked.

The closeness was comforting after a day that had been so exhausting from travelling and she nestled her head into the crook of his arm.

'Not now,' she answered softly. She lay in the darkness, waiting for Hal's hands to begin working their way across her body as they had done that morning, but he made no move. Perhaps he was as tired as she was and only intended to sleep. She wondered whether he expected her to begin by touching him and how she would go about such a thing.

Her worry was ended by Hal speaking.

'My father's wife was not of his choosing. He loved my mother, but she was the daughter of a blacksmith in Pickering. He could never wed her, but he needed an heir so married Anne Sedbergh, the daughter of a knight from Guisborough.'

Joanna's heart stopped beating at the way in which Hal so easily dismissed the idea of a lord and a blacksmith's daughter. Before this evening she would have declared that of course such a match was possible, but now she wondered if Roger had ever intended to marry her. The thought was like a knife to her heart.

Hal continued his tale. 'My father swore he would not end his association with my mother. He continued visiting her in secret after his marriage, but before long there was evidence he could not deny.'

'What do you mean?' Joanna asked.

Hal raised himself on to his elbows. 'Me. It's hard to pretend there is no mistress when presented with a swelling belly. Much less when the curly-topped infant so clearly bears the signs of being a Danby.'

Joanna looked at her husband now her eyes had become more accustomed to the dark. His face was shrouded in shadow obscuring his features, but she could picture all too clearly the dark eyes and black curls of all three Danby men. Lord Danby would have been unable to deny fathering the man in whose arms she lay.

'That must have been hard for Lady Danby,' Joanna ventured.

Hal nodded in the blackness. 'She threatened to return to her father, taking her dowry with her.

Unfortunately she was already with child herself when my impending existence was revealed.'

He sighed and his fingers curled around Joanna's shoulder.

'She can hardly blame you for your conception,' Joanna protested.

'No, but hearts are not always rational. I don't bear Lady Danby any ill will for her resentment towards me or my father. To live with someone and know every day that they wish to be with someone else cannot be easy. When I was brought into her household that must have been humiliating.'

They lay in silence. Joanna's stomach curdled with shame. She wondered if Hal thought of their circumstances when he had said that. He had showed no bitterness, but she renewed her resolve to bury her feelings for Roger deeper so that Hal would never know how her longing scorched her heart. She pictured Anne Danby, married to a man who did not love her, bearing his child and rearing his bastard. Anne, like Joanna herself, had known from the outset that their marriage was nothing more than a business contract. She appeared fond of her husband now, but how long had it taken for them to reach that state?

'Why were you brought here to live? Where is your mother?' Joanna asked.

Hal's jaw tightened. 'It's commonplace that men keep mistresses, especially those who have a marriage thrust on them, but do you think my father is the sort of man to flaunt another woman under his wife's roof? Or that Lady Danby would tolerate such a thing?'

'Of course not!' Joanna exclaimed.

'Until I was six we lived in Pickering with my grandfather,' he said in a whisper. 'My mother assumed I would follow my grandfather in his trade, but whenever my father visited he told me tales of knights and tournaments. I begged him to bring me to live here so I could learn to be a knight.'

He stopped speaking and gave a cough, as though it embarrassed him to be caught showing such emotion.

'My mother died when I was seven. All I really remember is her laughter.' Hal's voice was tight with grief. Impulsively Joanna reached for his hand. He grunted in surprise, but laced her fingers in between his.

Joanna turned on her side and touched Hal's cheek. His beard grazed against her palm and Joanna's heart thumped disconcertingly.

'Her heart was broken because you left?' Joanna asked.

Hal gave a bitter laugh. 'Do you think such a thing can really happen? She died giving birth to the child who would have been my sister.'

'I'm sorry,' she whispered.

Abruptly Hal rolled on to his back but kept Joanna's hand enclosed within his, drawing it across on to his chest as he moved his arm. Through the light linen of his shirt she could feel the steady, powerful thump of his heart.

'My family died in the Great Pestilence,' Joanna offered quietly. 'My mother first, a day later my sister, my two brothers within an hour of each other, finally my father. I don't know why I survived.'

A deep pit of sadness opened in her belly. She had never told anyone of this, not even Roger, but in the dark, in Hal's arms, she spoke freely.

'Simon took me in, but he never wanted me.' Her voice cracked. 'No one did.'

No one until Roger had walked into her life. She'd eagerly clutched at every glance, caress or kind word as proof of his devotion. Now seeds of doubt began to grow into vines that wound around her heart, squeezing the life out of it. Her eyes filled with tears.

They weren't just for her pain but for Hal's, for the trials of the day, their earlier quarrel, for her heart aching for Roger with an intensity that would never leave her in peace. It was too large to be stifled. She tugged her hand free and rolled away from Hal as hot tears burned her cheeks. She drew her knees up to her chest and made herself small, crying silently as she had done so many nights before.

This night was different, however, because now Hal's arms came protectively around her. Her body moulded itself to his as he held her tightly and silently until her tears were done and sleep claimed her.

When she awoke in the morning he was gone.

Chapter Eleven

Hal danced and spun, parried and thrust until his muscles cried out in protestation and his lungs burned. Over and over his sword locked with that of his opponent as strike and counterstrike increased in speed and intensity. Lost in the fight, Hal forgot all sense of time and place. His heart thumped beneath his padded leather surcoat. Shadows shortened as the sun rose higher.

A swift lunge forward and the short blades slid together until the cross guards were touching. The points tilted skywards, trapped close between the swordsmen's bodies. Through gaps in visors their eyes met, both pairs screwed tight with determination and effort. His opponent was burly, carrying more weight than Hal, but Hal had the advantage of height. The two men edged round, feet digging into the sandy earth in an effort to gain the upper hand and still remain within the boundary of the square. Neither would give ground until, with an inward grin, Hal feinted to the left, then smoothly stepped backwards, sweeping his weapon away to the side.

His adversary lurched forward, losing his balance and landing on his knees. A quick feint to the side, a final twist and Hal was behind him, the point of his sword at the fallen man's neck where helmet and surcoat met.

'I submit!' the man cried between heavy breaths, throwing his sword to the ground. The wooden blade bounced across the yard.

Hal lowered his sword arm and placed his own weapon alongside. He held the other out to help his opponent upright.

Ralf Ashby, Lord Danby's bailiff of twelve years, lifted his visor, removed his glove and unstrapped the helmet. He scratched the grey thatch of close-cropped hair and gave a weary grimace. Hal removed his own helmet and loosened the neck of his surcoat. He disliked the garment, but even a wooden sword could leave a painful bruise.

'Thank you, my friend. I'm glad you chanced by,' Hal said, clasping Ralf's arm tightly. 'A half-hour striking at the dummy was becoming tedious and it's good to fight a flesh opponent. I know your time is precious, but it's been a while since I sparred with anyone.'

'Too long by my reckoning. I nearly took you that time,' Ralf remarked.

'Never!' Hal scoffed gently at his friend. 'You've not beaten me once in the past five years.'

'I'm twenty years your senior, if you can't win against me you may as well melt down your weapon and join the brothers at Rievaulx. You were slower than last time.' Ralf grinned wickedly. 'Perhaps your new wife is keeping you up too long at night?'

Hal drew his lips back into an approximation of a smile. The bout had lifted his mood and the mention of Joanna threatened to plunge him into gloom again. True enough he had got precious little rest last night, though Ralf would no doubt be surprised as to the true reason why.

He tallied up the nights since his marriage. Four he'd spent sleeping alone on a wooden settle and the two he'd shared his wife's bed she'd spent weeping or lying in trepidation of his touch. Last night, wrapping his arms tightly about her, he had been unable to ignore the sensation of Joanna's body close to his. Her back curving against his chest, her buttocks brushing inadvertently against his crotch, the tangle of her legs between his had sent flames of lust pulsing through him that refused to be quenched, leaving Hal burning with frustration. He had been awake for hours, thinking about her words long after she had fallen asleep.

No one had wanted her.

Joanna's voice had cracked with loneliness and Hal's heart had cracked with it. He wondered if she had included Roger in her statement. Was she starting to realise that his professed affection had been a falsehood or was her regret that the man she believed *did* want her lacked the means to claim her?

More than that, did she include Hal himself in her assessment? After all, he'd made no secret of the fact that for him their marriage had been a convenient and advantageous match. He'd never given her reason to suspect there was anything more to his feelings than that, but last night it had taken all his strength to resist the temptation to wake her and demonstrate how much he craved her. It was fortunate Ralf had called on Lord Danby this morning and given him the opportunity for release of another kind.

'Hal!'

The sound of his name dragged him from his

reverie. He looked up to discover Ralf was watching him, a knowing smirk on his face.

'Hal, were you listening at all?' Ralf asked. 'Are you going to tilt as well or is it another kind of lance you're thinking of aiming?'

Hal rolled his shoulders back, feeling the ache from the unfamiliar positions he had forced his limbs into. He ignored the bailiff's insinuation.

'Not today. I plan to be home before dusk. I have work waiting for me.'

'And a new wife to spend time with, surely?' Ralf laughed.

'Of course,' Hal replied. He clapped Ralf on the shoulder. 'Come, I need a drink and I'll wager you do also.'

A bath, too, he decided, as side by side they crossed the yard. Two days travelling and his exercise this morning had left Hal craving a plunge into the nearby beck. Even in late summer it rushed in ice-cold foam over the rocks. In spring it would be bitterly cold; enough to cool the hottest ardour. He unbuckled the surcoat as he glanced across to where Lord Danby stood by the barn leaning on his stick.

His father was not alone. Joanna was standing by his side. Their heads were bent together and Joanna was whispering in his father's ear. Lord

Danby had been alone when they had begun the bout so how much had Joanna witnessed? The thought of her watching while he was unaware of her presence sent a tremor of excitement through Hal.

As he and Ralf approached she took a step to the side, folding her hands demurely in front of her. She was wearing fresh clothing; a deep-green kirtle he had not seen before laced tight beneath her breasts. Her cheeks were pink and her hair, smoothly parted in the centre and coiled in thick plaits high above her ears, was damp. She had clearly taken the opportunity to bathe, too, though he presumed in the house rather than the fast-flowing beck that he intended to hurl himself into.

Hal's heart gave a violent thump as the image crossed his mind of Joanna swimming naked, the current twisting her hair in fierce tangles and icy water caressing her skin. He could not prevent the grin that formed on his lips.

'Good morning, Mistress Danby.'

Joanna's eyes widened as they travelled the length of Hal's body. He became acutely aware of his own appearance and how unkempt he was. Even though the bout had been friendly Ralf never gave quarter and Hal had fought hard. When he eased the surcoat off his damp linen tunic clung to his chest and back. His face bore a week's growth of beard and as he pulled the linen cap off, shaking his hair free, it stuck in thick tendrils to his scalp and cheeks. Sweat trickled down his neck and he lifted an arm to wipe it away on his sleeve.

Joanna looked away, biting her lip. The gesture reminded him of Lady Danby who never bothered to hide her distaste and his heart sunk.

'Who won?' Lord Danby asked impatiently.

'Your son, of course,' Ralf answered. 'I believe he has been practising despite his assurances he has not. Something has given him vigour he did not previously possess.'

Lord Danby gave a satisfied snort as though he had never doubted the outcome.

Hal looked down to find Joanna's long-lashed eyes on him again. Her expression was intense and her lips slightly parted. Her cheeks flushed pink as their eyes locked.

A fist drove into Hal's chest and he realised he had been mistaken at first. It was not distaste that had made her look away, but a hunger she either did not recognise in herself or did not know what to do with. A hunger for him. His blood rose once again. His fingers itched to touch her and awaken the desire he had sensed brimming below the surface when he had lain with her before. Tonight they would sleep in his bed and nothing would prevent him quenching the thirst he felt.

'Why are we out here when there is wine and food inside?' he asked. 'Joanna we need to leave soon and should eat before we do.'

Joanna put her hand on Lord Danby's arm to lead him back towards the house. Hal smiled at the sight.

Lord Danby patted her hand. 'Thank you, but I must ask Master Ashby to escort you back. I would like words with my son.'

Joanna glanced towards Hal. He gestured her to go ahead, watching as she took Ralf's arm and returned to the house.

'I like her,' Lord Danby said. 'I don't know what kind of woman Roger will eventually present as a bride, but I'm glad to see one of my sons is capable of finding a sensible woman.'

Hal gritted his teeth at the irony of his father's words. He said nothing, his eye still on Joanna's shapely figure.

'Your marriage wasn't for love, I don't need eyes to see that. You aren't at ease with each other,' Lord Danby continued. 'Is she with child?' His face darkened. 'Is it yours?'

'No!' Hal bunched his fists. 'There's no child. Joanna was a virgin.'

His mind flew back to Joanna's promise to bear his children. Yesterday morning he had been reckless. He would have to take more care in future. He intended to produce no unwanted accidents himself.

'The man she hoped to marry did not want her.'

Your son, he wanted to rage. The urge to reveal the truth to his father was overpowering.

'So you took his place? Would this man be someone known to me?' Lord Danby asked shrewdly.

Hal stared at his father in surprise. Because of his condition Lord Danby seldom travelled further than Pickering, yet no information seemed to pass him by.

'What makes you say that?' he asked warily.

'You went to York with Roger and returned with a wife. I know my sons. We both know you see Roger's transgressions as something you need to handle. You aren't obliged to make amends for all his mistakes.'

Hal's mouth twitched. A feeling of nausea began to fill his belly. He folded the surcoat over his arm, his throat tightening. 'I didn't marry Joanna for Roger's benefit. It suited us both to marry,' Hal said.

'I hoped you would marry a woman you cared for.' Lord Danby sighed.

'Why?' Hal asked.

Lord Danby closed his cloudy eye and stared unseeing towards the moors. His voice became wistful. 'Because you share my nature…and you've always known your mind. Bastardy can be a curse, but it gives you the freedom I never had.'

'Freedom, yes. Advantages, no,' Hal snapped. He regarded his father. A man who had kept a mistress far too long after taking a wife, who held romantic notions like a character in a troubadour's tale. Hal owed his existence to this man's weakness, but their natures were nothing alike.

'My status closes as many doors as it opens. Joanna needed a husband and her family connections will open doors for me no other wife could. How could the notion of love compete with such an opportunity?'

'In that case I'm sure your marriage will be happy,' Lord Danby said. 'Or at least no more unhappy than any.'

Lord Danby reached for his arm and in silence father and son returned to the house.

Midmorning came before they bade their farewells to Lord Danby and Lady Danby. Wrapped in their travelling cloaks, Hal and Joanna stood side by side as Lord Danby's stable boy led Valiant,

Hal's tan courser, to the front of the house. Joanna's mouth became a circle as the animal tossed its head and stamped impatiently.

'Where's the cart?' she asked in alarm.

Hal took the reins and held his hand for Valiant to catch his scent. The horse snickered in recognition and he ran his hand along the animal's smooth flank.

'We're leaving the cart here,' he explained as he led the animal closer to Joanna. 'One of my father's servants will drive it over. I stabled Valiant here before I came to York. The hill to Ravenscrag is steep and the cart would be too slow for my liking today. I want to get home quickly.'

Joanna took a step backwards. 'I don't know how to ride,' she protested.

'You don't have to know how to ride,' he told her in what he hoped was a reassuring manner. 'You just have to know how to hold on.'

'To the horse?' She sounded doubtful.

Hal took her hand. Did he imagine the catch in her throat or the way her skin seemed to flutter at his touch?

'Not to the horse. To me.'

He swung himself on to Valiant, then pushed the stirrup back. 'Put your foot in and get ready to swing your leg across,' he instructed. He twisted round in the saddle and slipped his hands beneath Joanna's arms. She was light and he lifted her with ease behind him as she obeyed his instruction.

'Now put your arms around me.'

Her hands slid beneath his arms and tightened around his waist. She pressed herself against his back. Hal allowed himself a moment to enjoy the sensation before he looped his foot back into the stirrup and spurred the horse into a trot. Joanna gave a muffled cry of alarm and her grip tightened, squeezing the breath from him. Casting a look behind him, he saw Joanna's bowed head hidden beneath the hood of her cloak.

Hal almost turned back for the cart, but he'd spent too long away from his forge. He was impatient to get back to the heat of the flames and smell of the charcoal. His muscles were complaining from the bout with Ralf and his skin still stung from the icy water of the beck. Now he craved the aches that came from a day hammering and lifting the iron. There would be work waiting—jobs that he could not leave, but that would take time from his new masterwork. Whatever he might tell his father, he knew marriage to Joanna was no guarantee of admission to the guild. He wondered if he should have negotiated harder with Simon Vernon for greater concessions.

They reached open ground and Valiant began to gallop. The moor was flat here and they could make good speed. Hal felt Joanna's grip shift and glanced over his shoulder. She was gazing around and a wide smile had transformed her face.

'Are you all right?' he shouted over the wind.

Joanna nodded, her eyes burning with excitement. Her hood fell back, caught by a gust of wind, and she laughed out loud, causing Hal to do the same.

Valiant was tired by the time they began to climb Horcum Bank along the ridge that would take them to Ravenscrag. Foam flecked his muzzle and his shoulders glistened with sweat. Hal slowed the horse to a trot.

Joanna's arms loosened and she wriggled her fingers. They brushed against Hal's torso, leaving a trail of warmth on his skin that was impossible from the coldness of her hands. He stifled a sigh, wondering if she suspected the effect such a small gesture was having on him.

When they reached the top of the ridge Hal pulled Valiant to a standstill. He dismounted, then put his hands around Joanna's waist and helped her slide down. As her feet touched the ground she put her hands on his shoulders to steady herself and looked into his eyes.

Time ceased to exist for Hal. The wind that buffeted them stilled. The gulls that cried in the distance were silent. Hal spread his hands about Joanna's waist—so slender his trembling fingers nearly touched each other. He remembered to breathe again.

'You did well,' he murmured.

'It's like nothing I've ever done before!' She glowed with joy—a beauty he had not recognised before. A *frisson* of excitement ran through him.

'Will you teach me to ride properly?' Joanna asked.

She had not removed her hands from his shoulders. He was tall and she had to lift her arms high, arching her back to reach him.

'With pleasure!'

Hal realised his lips were parted, ready to kiss her. He felt himself growing hard. A moment more and he would abandon all respectability and take her here and now on the heather. That would be foolish, though. She would hardly countenance such a thing and he would risk losing any ground he had made so far. He stared up at the sun. It was nearly midday.

'We've made good time. Let's rest for a while.'

Joanna sat on a clump of grass and drew her knees up. Hal sat beside her and took hold of her hand. She did not pull away, nor did she acknowledge his touch, but carried on staring at the land that stretched before them. Hal said nothing. Each time he returned home the wild beauty of the moors took his breath away. After the flatness of the Vale of York it must be extraordinary to Joanna. He pointed to where the rolling moors met the sky.

'Look, you can see the sea if you stare hard enough. I'll take you one day.'

She smiled and waved a hand across the expanse of moorland. 'Who owns this land?'

Hal gazed around. 'William, Earl of Pickering, owns the greatest share, Rievaulx Abbey a third. My father's portion is small by comparison, long and thin. Ravenscrag is the furthest village on the edge of his estate.'

'It's a long way from Wharram Danby,' Joanna mused.

'I've been further.' Hal shrugged. He lay back and stretched out his legs, crooking his arms behind his head, admiring the graceful tilt of Joanna's head and neck silhouetted against the sun.

'My father sent me to Guisborough to serve my

apprenticeship when he realised I had no intention of following the path he set out for me. My master decided to travel for three years and I went with him round the country.'

'Why didn't you do what was expected?' Joanna asked curiously. She turned to face him, leaning on one elbow. 'You ride well and I've seen you fight.'

'You saw a brawl in a tavern and a friendly bout with a man twenty years my senior. Hardly a spectacle to excite the crowd!'

Watching him had excited her though, hadn't it? The thought of that thrilled him further. He rolled over to face her, close enough he could feel her breath on his cheek. His earlier impulse whispered enticingly in his ear. There was no one around to witness what they might do. Before he could reach his hand to touch her Joanna spoke, her eyes blazing.

'But you could have become a knight. You didn't have to be a blacksmith.'

The sky seemed to darken. Hal sat up so Joanna could not see his face.

He waved his arm across the expanse before them. 'Roger is the legitimate son. He will inherit these lands and what little wealth goes along with them. The stain of bastardy might be washed away with enough gold, but I learned after I moved to Wharram that my father did not have the wealth to champion two sons. For all the tales he told me of the glorious tournaments I was never intended to be a knight. He brought me there to train as my brother's squire. I won't serve any man.'

'Squires can become knights in time,' Joanna said obstinately.

Bile rose in Hal's throat. Fool, to think it had been he who had woken the fire in her. It had been imagining him in the role of the knight she could never have.

Hal snapped his head round to look at Joanna. She drew a sharp breath. The desire in her eyes had vanished. Hal grimaced and pushed himself to his feet. He held out a hand to help Joanna from the ground. Once again she put her hand on his arm to steady herself, but this time Hal remained unmoved. He helped her mount Valiant in silence and when her arms came around his body he ignored the brush of her hand against his waist.

With a yell and a crack of the reins he was off.

Chapter Twelve

Hal's body remained as hard as iron for the rest of the journey and his manner as unbending. Joanna clung on with her arms about his waist as she had done before, but this time there was no joy in the ride.

She knew Hal had been offended by her words, but they had been intended as a compliment and she could not suppress the hot indignation that boiled in her belly. However much he denied wanting it, Hal would have made as good a knight as his brother and the unfairness of his situation struck her.

His face had been alive with happiness when he had walked across the yard towards her so he clearly enjoyed swordplay. She had only witnessed the end of his bout but he had fought with gracefulness and strength.

A tremor passed through Joanna as she remembered the contours his sweat-drenched tunic had revealed as it clung to his broad chest. She must have sighed aloud, or perhaps Hal felt her shiver, because he twisted his head to the side. The muscles in his neck were taut and his lips pressed firmly in a line. Was he still angry with her?

Roger always made his displeasure known much more forcefully, but Hal's expression gave nothing away. She bit her lip anxiously, wondering when she would face the repercussions.

On their first ride she had moved in unison with Hal, their bodies rising and falling to the rhythm of the horse as the miles flew under their feet. It had been one of the most exhilarating experiences of her life. With her chest pressed close to his back and her hands clasped around his waist Joanna had been unable to ignore the way Hal's muscles moved with such vitality under her palms. The rider was as powerful as the horse he mastered with such ease, both possessing a strength and wildness that she had never experienced before.

If Hal was still angry with her, to hold on so tightly and press her body against his would be inappropriate. He would not welcome the intimacy. She eased her grip and shifted backwards a little so they were no longer touching.

'Don't let go,' Hal commanded gruffly. 'Take care you don't fall off.'

'I won't fall,' Joanna replied. She concentrated on keeping upright, gripping Valiant's flanks tightly with her thighs. The wind tugged at her skirt and the ground was uneven, but she was determined that however much she slid and bounced she would neither fall nor need to cling tighter to Hal.

Those were the only words Hal spoke to her as they climbed the steep ridge. Stone buildings, barns or shepherd's huts began to appear at regular intervals amid the folding hills and as the rough ground became an equally rough track, Hal dug his heels into the horse's flanks. They broke into a gallop. Despite her intention Joanna's arms tightened around Hal once more of their own accord, but she could not recapture the rhythm, nor the pleasure. She barely noticed when the buildings became more frequent and closer together. Valiant slowed to a rolling walk and by the time they reached Ravenscrag her stomach was churning with every lurch.

They rode to the centre of the village, coming to a halt outside a long, low building with another smaller structure set closer to the river where the road continued over a bridge. Hal jumped from the horse. It took Joanna a moment to realise this must be his house. It was larger than she had expected when she had pictured it.

'Wait here. I'll stable Valiant,' Hal instructed as he took Joanna by the arm and helped her dismount.

She slid from the horse and landed on wobbly legs. As her feet hit the rough ground her stomach churned once more and her legs shook violently. She dropped to her hands and knees in the dirt, retching loudly. Her stomach was mercifully empty otherwise she knew she would have emptied it into the road.

Hal had taken hold of Valiant's bridle and begun to lead the horse away, but at the sound he turned back.

'What's the matter?'

'You did that on purpose,' Joanna groaned weakly.

He dropped the reins and walked to her side. 'Did what?' he asked in surprise.

Joanna gave a shiver and her stomach heaved once more. 'Rode so fast. Made it so rough.'

'Why would I do that?' Hal asked incredulously.

'To punish me,' she whispered.

'Do you really think I'm so malicious?' Hal exclaimed. His brow knotted as he stood over her, hands on hips.

Joanna wiped her hand across her mouth, tasting bile at the back of her throat. She sat back on her heels and stared at the ground in misery. 'It wasn't so bumpy the first time and I know I angered you.'

Hal folded his arms. When he spoke his voice was low and cold.

'I may be many things but I'm not petty. Angry or not I wouldn't set out to deliberately cause you harm. You simply aren't used to riding. I told you to hold on tightly, but you didn't so it's little wonder you feel sick. Stay sitting and recover until I come back.'

'I feel perfectly well again now, thank you!' Joanna climbed to her feet. She bit her lip as she felt the colour drain from her face. Hal's belligerent expression vanished instantly. He put his hand on her arm to steady her. Joanna took a step and as she did her thighs protested and her legs began to wobble. Before they gave way completely Hal bent and lifted her into his arms.

'What are you doing?' she cried.

'Carrying you,' Hal answered. He began to walk towards the house.

'Put me down. I can walk,' Joanna protested.

'I'd prefer not to take that chance,' Hal answered. 'It's fortunate my neighbours were not around to witness my wife sprawling in the dirt, but I'd rather not have them see you collapsing as you enter my home.'

'What about the horse?'

Hal stopped walking. He frowned down at Joanna, his expression odd. 'Are you determined to rebuff all my attempts at taking care of you? The horse is not feeling faint. The horse can wait.'

Joanna made no more protests as he carried her inside the house. His arms were comfortingly firm around her and his words echoed in her ears. She wrinkled her forehead in confusion. She had offended him, yet he swore he had not intended to do her harm. She had accused him of deliberate cruelty, but now he held her close and had shown concern for her. He could have left her sitting outside but he had thought to help her. She raised her eyes to look at her husband, wondering who exactly she had married. Hal had been looking down at her, but as she caught his eye he glanced away quickly.

'I'm sorry for what I said,' Joanna said. 'It was uncalled for. I don't think you're cruel.'

He looked down at her once more and a smile briefly flickered across his lips though he did not answer. Joanna slipped her arms around his neck and he pushed the door open and entered the house. He walked to a low-backed chair beside the hearth at the far end of the room. His hand lingered on the small of her back as he stood her on her feet and her skin fluttered where she felt the warmth of his fingers. Reluctantly she took her arms from around his neck and sat down.

Hal left the room and she heard him rummaging in what must be a pantry because he returned carrying two earthenware cups and a bottle. He pulled a stool beside her chair, broke the seal on the bottle and poured two measures. He lifted his cup and knocked it gently against the rim of hers.

'Welcome to my home,' he said, smiling.

He waited for her to respond and when she said nothing he lifted the cup to his lips and tilted it back, draining it in one. Joanna sniffed the cup warily. The scent was rich and made her eyes water. She sipped it cautiously and coughed as the liquid set her lips and throat on fire.

'What is it?'

Hal laughed. 'It's mead. It's better to drink it in one go. You'll get used to it that way.'

He poured himself another measure. Joanna took another, larger sip. The liquor did not burn so much this time. Under the heat she could taste sweetness and a hint of honey mingled with the tang. She licked her lips.

Hal watched her approvingly. 'See. You can't do everything by stealth. It's like riding a horse. You didn't hold on the way I told you so your legs ached. Some things you just have to give your all to. If you're timid and cautious around an animal you'll get hurt. Do you still want to learn to ride?'

'I do,' Joanna said firmly, fixing him with a bold stare. 'Will you teach me?'

'I'll teach you anything you ask,' Hal murmured, lowering his voice in a manner that sent chills racing down Joanna's spine. She took another drink and shivered as the warmth in her belly contrasted with the chill of the air and she wondered what else he intended to teach her.

Hal jumped to his feet. 'What kind of husband am I to make you sit in the cold and dark!' he exclaimed.

He began heaping logs and kindling on to the hearth from the pile that stood beside it. A jar on the hearthstone contained twisted strips of linen. Joanna looked at them curiously. The precious fragments of linen and discarded vellum she used for her drawings were in her bag and that was on the cart. She wished she had brought it with her.

She knelt by Hal's side and began to thread the strips through the kindling.

'Do you have a flint?' she asked.

'There's no need,' he said. He left the house and came back shortly after carrying an iron bucket holding glowing charcoal that he tipped into the hearth, setting the kindling alight with ease.

'I never let the furnace go out,' he remarked.

'Even when you're away for so long?' Joanna asked.

'I'm rarely away for more than a day at a time and a day doesn't go by when I'm not at work.' He jabbed viciously at the coals with the poker to wake the glow. 'I don't have the indulgence of spending my time at leisure. If I don't work I don't eat.'

He lit a pair of tallow candles and set them into holders. Light filled the room and Joanna looked properly around her new home for the first time.

'It isn't as grand as Wharram Manor, I'm afraid, but it suits me well enough,' Hal said apologetically as he followed her gaze.

Apart from the seats they were currently sitting on there was a large table with a bench running down each side. The usual assortment of cookware hung from hooks above the hearth and knives, bowls and cups stood on a heavy oak dresser in front of the window. A brightly coloured rug added a touch of warmth to the room, but otherwise there were few signs that the house was lived in.

Two doors led off, one into the pantry from where Hal had brought the mead. The other must lead to…

Joanna's hands tightened around her cup as she thought of the room that lay beyond and the bed it would contain. She stood and held her hand out for Hal's cup to prevent him seeing her thoughts so clearly.

'Let me clean these,' she said.

Hal took hold of her wrist. 'There's no need at the moment.'

'But it's my duty,' she answered. She thought wistfully of Lord Danby's house. Of the servants who stood ready for any task, of the life Lady Danby led and that any future possessor of that name would lead.

Stop it, she ordered herself. 'I'm used to working hard to earn my keep. I spent my days helping in my aunt's house, or assisting Simon in the foundry. I can do the same here.'

Hal's fingers tightened, then loosened once more. 'I may not have the horde of servants that my father does, but a woman from the village comes to serve me each day. A widow; you'll meet her tomorrow morning. I think you'll like her. I did not marry you to be my servant. You're my wife.'

He sat back on his stool and stretched his legs towards the fire that was now burning fiercely. He pulled the cord from his hair and shook his head until his black curls fell around his neck.

'What would you like me to do with my days?' Joanna asked. Her neck grew hot as she thought of the role she would play in Hal's nights.

'You're mistress of this house now.' Hal smiled. 'Run it as you see fit, but don't think you have to act as a servant.'

Mistress. The word enveloped Joanna like a blanket. The house did not feel like her home. That was to be expected, but in time perhaps it would. For now it was enough to know she had a roof over her head. She might not have Roger's love, but she had security. There would be no Simon Vernon hinting her presence was unwelcome. No threats of banishment or marriage to a stranger.

'Thank you.' Impulsively she took his hand. He stiffened, perhaps expecting trickery. 'I'm sorry I offended you earlier. Truly it wasn't my intention.'

He nodded in acknowledgement.

'Do you mind knowing you'll never inherit?' she asked.

Hal gestured around the room. 'You have to remember I grew up a fatherless boy in a house smaller than this. I never expected anything more. When I was taken from Pickering to Wharram it gave me a life I would never have known. I was given an education. I had a family and opportunities I never dreamed of.'

Firelight caught his face and Joanna saw his eyes were as black and hard as iron.

'When a man produces a bastard he's responsible for it the same as for any child. My father gave me the best life he could. I can't say I'd make the same decisions in his place, but I won't condemn him for his.'

'Even though you're a blacksmith, not a lord?'

'Smithing is in my blood as much as anything else. Why should I deny that side of my past? Even my father had to accept that. I'm a blacksmith,' Hal agreed, 'but a better one than I might have been. I'll be better still before long—richer, better connected, more skilled—and I'll have you to thank in part for that.'

He lifted Joanna's hand to his lips and kissed it, his good humour seemingly restored in an instant. Her chest tightened as his lips brushed her skin and her stomach turned over slowly. Hal raised his eyes to hers and they brimmed with challenge, then unexpectedly his mouth fell open.

'Valiant! I left him outside!'

He dropped her hand abruptly. 'He won't have roamed far, but I should see to him.' He rushed to the door. 'Explore the rest of the house and I'll be back soon.'

Joanna returned the bottle to the pantry. It was cooler than the kitchen and the heat that had raced across her flesh at Hal's touch began to fade. The pantry was well stocked, but disorganised. Cobwebs hung down and dust had collected in the corners. The widow Hal had mentioned must have failing eyesight.

Joanna returned to the kitchen and ran her fingers along the mantelpiece. They came away dirty. She wiped them on her skirts and began to compile a list of tasks for the days ahead. She opened the door to the room she had not been in yet. It was not the bedroom as she had expected, but a chamber that contained a large wooden chest, a low stool and a table overflowing with piles of papers and boxes. This must be Hal's private room. She glanced around, searching for any insight into Hal's interest, but stopped short of moving the papers.

The house was not rectangular as Joanna had supposed but shaped like an 'L' and a door in the side wall led to the bedroom. A pile of sheep-skins, below which Joanna could glimpse a red-and-green counterpane, covered the bed. Seeing it brought the reality of her situation crashing down on Joanna in a way nothing else in the house had. She would spend her nights here in Hal's arms. She remembered the feeling of Hal's hands on her body and, more recently, her own hands roaming across the muscles she had discovered when she held him so tightly as they rode. Even lovemaking was no longer an unknown terror. The prospect of what Hal would expect of her did not seem so daunting as it once had. She had faced that and had survived.

Hal found her there, still standing in the door-way, still staring at the bed, her fingers gripping the doorframe.

'Are you still feeling faint?' he asked, his face full of concern.

Joanna shook her head. 'I'm fine,' she lied. 'Just a little tired from the journey still.'

He stared at her quizzically. 'You can go into this room too. It's yours as much as any of the house.'

When she said nothing in reply Hal grinned. His

eyes roved across her body. Could he be thinking of the same thing she had been? 'Come with me,' he instructed gently. He took her by the hand and drew her into the room, closing the door behind him. His smile vanished as Joanna bit her lip nervously.

'You're reluctant still,' he said.

Joanna shook her head. 'It isn't because it's you,' she said hurriedly, thinking of their quarrel the previous day. 'What we did yesterday…'

She turned away and wrapped her arms about her body. Hal came behind her. He turned her round, and gently but firmly tilted her face until she was looking into his eyes.

'Yesterday morning was new to you,' he said. 'It will be easier now. It can be so much more than that, I promise.'

'What do you mean?' Joanna asked warily. She remembered the sensation of his mouth hot and eager on her flesh, his kiss driving all thoughts from her mind.

'You know what I mean,' Hal said, his voice deep and low. His eyes bored into Joanna, pinning her to the spot. He drew her closer until he filled her vision and she could feel the kiss of his breath on her face. 'There may not be love in a marriage, but there can be pleasure, for both of us. For you. I can show you.'

He traced his thumb from her cheek down to her jaw, then continued downwards slowly, sensuously. His fingers traced the contour of her neck until they came to rest in the hollow of her collarbone. His touch was as light as the breeze lifting her hair, waking every nerve in Joanna's flesh. She drew a sharp breath. Hal had told her that caution would hold her back. Would being bedded be more pleasurable if she was less reticent? The feeling of Hal moving inside her had left her raw, and the disconcerting pressure building within had threatened to suffocate her, but afterwards she ached for something she could not articulate. The urge to satisfy her curiosity flickered within her and she nodded slowly. She closed her eyes, her lips parting.

Hal's lips touched hers, sweet with the taste of the mead. He was kissing her and she was kissing him back feverishly.

From a long way off a door slammed and a voice called out, 'Master Danby, are you there?'

The voice was female. Hal froze, his lips still on Joanna's. She opened her eyes. He gave her a look of apology, then strode to the door and flung it open.

'I'm here, Meg,' he called.

Joanna followed him into the outer room in time to see a woman not much older than she was sidle in from the kitchen. The woman dropped into a curtsy that she held for a touch too long, giving Joanna full view of a pair of freckled breasts that were straining against the low neckline of her dress. Joanna's eyes narrowed as it struck her that she was not the intended audience. The woman stood, revealing a face as freckled as her bosom. Wisps of curly ginger hair escaped from her tight cap. She was not beautiful, but her green eyes glinted and her wide smile gave her face a vitality that bore its own beauty.

'Joanna, this is Meg Parry. I told you about her earlier,' Hal said.

This was the widow Hal had spoken of?

'Yes, you did,' Joanna said hesitantly.

'Mistress Parry, let me introduce my wife, Joanna Danby.'

The woman dipped another curtsy, much briefer than before, and if the surprised twist of her mouth passed Hal by it had not gone unnoticed by Joanna.

'I was not expecting to see you until tomorrow, Meg.' Hal's voice was warm.

'I saw your horse outside and thought you might

need some bread,' Meg replied. She smiled coyly at Hal.

Two things struck Joanna immediately. The first was that Meg Parry had a fancy for Hal and the second was that Joanna found she did not like that at all.

Chapter Thirteen

Meg soon recovered from her surprise at finding her master had wed and began chattering aimlessly, promising to return the following day to show Joanna around the village. Hal listened with one eye on Joanna. She seemed less than enthusiastic about the prospect. Her smile only flickered briefly across her lips and never reached her eyes. He was surprised. Surely the prospect of a companion her own age would have appealed?

Hal inwardly cursed Meg's timing, though she could not know she had unwittingly interrupted his seduction of Joanna. That last kiss had been the closest Joanna had come to showing genuine pleasure in the experience. He was still very much aware of the nervousness that coursed through her whenever he touched her, but it seemed to be melting with each encounter. A minute or two more alone he would have had her in bed.

He grinned to himself as heat filled his veins, losing the thread of what Meg was telling him about the continuing feud with her neighbours regarding their goose. He smiled and let his thoughts drift again, watching Joanna tilt her head on one side in sympathy, revealing her smooth, shapely throat that begged to be kissed.

Their first coupling had been rushed and awkward. Now Hal was filled with a determination that Joanna would not regret the next time. Her love might come or not, but her desire was growing. When she turned those cool blue eyes on him other parts of his body began commanding his attention louder than his heart.

If Meg left soon it was not too late to carry on from where he and Joanna had left off. He took Meg by the arm, led her to the door to bid her farewell and ushered her out with promises to sort the matter of the errant goose. When he turned back Joanna had followed him into the kitchen and was standing by the table. Her lips were pressed together and she was cutting the loaf of bread with vicious thrusts.

Hal folded his arms and studied her carefully. When he had found her standing in the bedroom doorway her expression had been unreadable, but her body had been rigid and her knuckles white, as though she was relying on the wooden frame to hold her upright. Her face had the same drawn appearance now. She had said that she was not faint, but perhaps she had not been entirely truthful. The journey must have tired her more than he had first realised. Lady Danby had accused him of neglect yesterday and today that judgement would be valid.

'Leave that and come sit with me,' he said.

He'd sit by the fire to warm her through, take her on his lap and kiss her slowly. Lips first, then her neck, perhaps the soft hollow behind her ear where her hair was escaping from its cap, next her collarbone and further down beyond that. He could imagine the taste of salt on her skin. Excitement began to build within him at the thought.

Joanna's lips tightened further. 'We should eat while the bread is fresh,' she replied. 'After all, Mistress Parry has gone to the trouble of bringing it for you.'

'There's no hurry,' Hal said. 'You look weary.'

Joanna looked at him, her chin jutting out obstinately. 'Do you have anything to accompany the bread?' she asked, ignoring his words and holding out a plate.

Very well, if she was determined to eat now they might as well. There was little to be gained from trying to satisfy a woman in one way if her body was demanding other nourishment.

His fingers touched Joanna's wrist as he took the plate from her hand and he saw her fingers tighten on the rim. She was aware of his touch, however much she resisted admitting it. He thought back to their arrival and Joanna's obstinate insistence she could manage unaided, despite the evidence otherwise. He doubted she would have refused Roger's offers so coldly.

Don't think of that, he warned himself. Only self-pity lay in trying to delve inside her mind. He'd married her knowing her heart was not his so it was too late to start wondering if it ever could be.

He walked into the pantry and grabbed a chunk of yellowing cheese and butter and a ham bone that was not too sparse. He presented his offerings with the solemnity of a steward at a feast. Joanna giggled, a sound that sent Hal's spirits soaring.

'The first meal we have prepared together,' he commented. 'Not much, but for tonight it will suffice.'

'I suppose Mistress Parry usually cooks for you?' Joanna asked in an offhand manner. She broke a morsel of cheese and nibbled it gracefully.

'Sometimes, though I can feed myself when I

choose to,' Hal answered. He bit into the bread and chewed. Still chewing, he returned to the pantry and brought a stoppered bottle of wine to the table. He spat a piece of grit into his palm.

'Meg has a good heart and she tries hard, but her skills do not lie in the kitchen.' He grinned.

There was a clatter as Joanna put two cups down on the table rather fiercely. Hal was pleased to note her cheeks had turned pink. Clearly all she had been lacking was food.

'I suppose there must be other reasons you employ Mistress Parry,' she said, pouring the wine. She took a cup and sat by the fire. Hal joined her.

'There are always a number of reasons we do anything,' Hal agreed.

Joanna's wide eyes regarded him expectantly. He lapsed into silence before recounting the tale of two years ago when he'd returned from Durham in a blizzard only to be set upon by a couple of brigands waiting by the roadside. One he'd slain, the other he had roped and dragged back to Ravenscrag, only to discover the man was an occupant of the village. Hal's testimony had put the villain's neck in the noose.

The man had been Meg's husband and the sight of the young woman standing alone and dry eyed before the gallows had pricked Hal's conscience.

He had found his home overrun with rats and in need of care and offered her employment rather than see her destitute.

'Employing Meg worked to both our advantages,' he said.

'Yes. Advantages on either side seem to be your strong point,' Joanna said curtly.

She was white faced once more and gripped her cup tightly between her hands.

'And why not?' Hal asked, taken aback by the venom in her voice. Perhaps she was comparing Meg's position to her own. They weren't so different really, Hal considered. He'd always had the compulsion to help unfortunates when he could, but why this should have raised Joanna's ire was beyond him.

'You can hardly criticise me for trying to aid someone when I've done the same for you.'

'Yes, another waif no one wanted. But you never decided to marry Mistress Parry,' Joanna remarked, her voice higher than usual.

'Why would I want to do that?' Hal asked. He would concede that marrying Joanna had been a step further than he usually took, but the advantages had been greater for both of them.

Joanna's face reddened once more.

'Why indeed. I suppose you had no need to.'

She picked up the poker and gave the fire a half-hearted prod. It hit Hal like a bolt of lightning that Joanna suspected him of relations with Meg. He could scarcely believe she could be jealous, but there was no other explanation he could think of.

Anger rippled through him. Why should she care what he did when her own heart belonged to someone else? He took the poker from Joanna's hand and stabbed it into the flames violently until sparks flew on to the hearthstone.

'If there's something you want to say to me please say it,' he said tersely.

If she was about to admit her suspicions Hal never knew because there was a loud hammering at the door. The second interruption at a crucial moment caused Hal to grind his teeth in exasperation.

'We'll discuss this another time,' he snapped as he strode to the door and flung it open.

A man swathed in a heavy cloak in the colours of Lord Danby's livery stood there. Moisture clung to the nap of the material. It had started to drizzle.

'I've brought your cart,' the visitor said.

Hal grimaced. The timing could have been better, but at least their belongings had arrived safely.

He reached for his cloak that was hanging on the peg by the door and threw it over his shoulders.

'Let's get it unloaded before the rain starts in earnest,' he said.

Between the two of them Hal and Lord Danby's servant carried the chest bearing Joanna's possessions into the bedchamber and deposited it against the wall. Joanna lingered in the doorway, watching anxiously. She followed them back outside to where the cart stood and seized on her leather bag that was stuffed between the seat and a crate of apples Lord Danby had presented Hal with. Relief spread across her face.

Hal watched as she threw the strap across her body and clutched the bag beneath her arm, hugging it tightly. He wondered what it contained that made her so anxious to reclaim it. Her scrip containing money was belted securely at her waist and she wore her marriage brooch over one breast—not that Hal imagined she viewed that as worth protecting.

Joanna's eyes were on Hal when he looked up. As their eyes met she clutched the bag tighter to her breast and glanced away guiltily. Whatever the bag contained he was not intended to know. Jealousy that Hal had so recently scorned Joanna for flooded him. Was it full of trinkets and letters from Roger? That seemed unlikely to Hal. His brother was a reluctant writer and from Hal's experience his idea of a memento was a coin if his partner had pleased him and a bruise or teeth-shaped scar if she had not. The unpleasant question crossed his mind whether Roger had ever struck Joanna and his fists clenched. Perhaps that would explain her earlier reticence to accept his aid.

'Where do you want everything else?' the servant asked.

Hal shook himself from his reverie and directed the man. When all their belongings and the food supplies were inside the house Hal climbed on to the cart and drove it the short distance to the forge by the river. The rest of the baggage was equipment and supplies for Hal's work. He dismounted and ran his hands over the boxes in anticipation. Some of this was from Simon Vernon: a marriage gift to Hal—or perhaps further thanks for relieving him of Joanna—of various metals and stones to help him in his work. More than he could have afforded himself. Excitement rippled through him. Tomorrow afternoon he would start planning his new masterwork.

Joanna walked over to the cart, still holding her bag.

'What are you doing?' Hal asked.

'I'm here to help,' she answered.

'I don't expect you to lug bars of iron. The forge is no place for a woman. Go back to the house. If you want to help I'm sure our friend here would welcome a drink of something warming.'

Joanna narrowed her eyes. She spun on her heel and stalked back to the house.

When Hal and the servant retuned to the house the scent of wine mingling with cloves and cinnamon filled the kitchen. An iron pot stood warming by the hearth with two cups beside it. There was no sign of Joanna.

By the time Hal left the servant curling up on a straw pallet in front of the fire and made his way to bed Joanna was asleep. She was facing the wall, knees tucked to her chest and the bolster pulled tightly up to her shoulders. As he climbed into bed her breathing paused. Hal tensed. He tugged some of the covers over himself. Joanna did not move, but her breathing took on the regular rhythm again. She was not asleep, just feigning.

Frustration coursed through Hal. Was she waiting for him to touch her? Was she anticipating the idea or dreading it?

Let her lie there and wonder. He was tired enough that all thoughts of lovemaking had gone out of his head anyway.

The raucous screech of a cockerel woke Hal the next morning. He climbed from the bed, sluiced himself down in the ewer of cold water and pulled on a fresh pair of hose and tunic.

He cracked open the shutter, letting light flood into the room. Joanna sat up and stretched her arms upwards. Her breasts jutted forward beneath the fabric of her shift. Hal watched them keenly, not bothering to hide his interest.

'I have to leave today, but I'll be back before nightfall,' he told her.

'Today? But we've only just arrived!' Joanna rubbed her eyes and drew her knees up.

'That can't be helped,' Hal said. 'I have a commitment I must keep that takes me away from time to time. Meg will be along shortly and my father's servant will want feeding before he returns to Wharram Danby. Have a pleasant day.'

'Wait!' Joanna climbed from the bed and crossed to the doorway, intercepting Hal. 'Where are you going?'

Hal sucked his teeth. Joanna would have to find out about his obligations at some point, but after her suspicions regarding Meg Parry, today was not the time. When she was settled more and had come to accept her life here he would begin to tell her the aspects of his life he had not yet revealed.

'You told me the other day that your thoughts were your own.' He took her face between his hands and smiled into her eyes.

'So are mine.'

Lord Danby's servant departed shortly after Hal left on his mysterious errand. Joanna was mildly curious where Hal had gone, but this mattered less than the fact he was absent.

Perhaps he would be away frequently and she would have the house to herself, in which case marriage might be bearable after all. When she considered the alternative husband she could have been forced to endure, this was a better result than she could have anticipated.

A quick walk from room to room confirmed Joanna's belief that whatever reason Hal had for employing Meg, tidying was not one of them. She resolved not to begin work on cleaning the house and instead spent the morning arranging her few belongings on a low table that stood empty in the corner of the room. With a finger she traced a spiral in the dust, then another and a third.

She pulled out her rolls of linen from her bag and found a spare corner among the other drawings and redrew the pattern, adding further twists and whorls.

When the door slammed late in the morning she started guiltily and slipped the paper back in her bag.

Meg, as she entreated Joanna to call her, had put a jug of milk on the table and was straightening the plates on the sideboard. She bobbed a curtsy to Joanna and wiped her hands down her skirt. She looked expectantly towards the door Joanna had come through.

'Master Danby left early on an errand,' Joanna said. There was no reason Meg needed to know, but Hal had implied the commitment was long standing and she might know where Hal had gone. If she did she was not about to share the information with his wife.

Meg shrugged. 'Aye, Master Danby is always coming or going. No one knows when to expect him,' she said, seemingly unconcerned. 'Shall we go into the village now?'

Joanna reached for her cloak and the two women walked to the centre of the village. It did not take long, no more than two hundred paces, Joanna estimated, until they were standing on common green. Joanna's heart sank as she surveyed her new home. Wharram Danby had struck her as small, but in comparison to Ravenscrag it seemed as large as York.

A half-hour was sufficient for Joanna to meet the widow selling ale from her door, the miller, the workers in the fields, the small boy guarding geese on the green and sundry other men and women. Without exception they greeted her with politeness, but their wide eyes and incredulous expressions made it abundantly clear that it was not just Meg who had found her appearance unexpected.

Anger bubbled up inside her. Hal had not told anyone of his intention to marry and now he had slipped away on a business he would not even share with her and left Joanna alone to face her neighbours. She forced a smile to her face and introduced herself, all the while imagining Hal suffering torments untold for his desertion.

When Meg suggested they return to Hal's home Joanna agreed readily, but as they neared the smithy her eyes drifted to the road that led across the river and to the hills beyond.

'I want to go that way,' she said and began walking before Meg had time to answer.

The road climbed steeply upwards, but as it reached the brow of the hill it levelled and split, one path leading to the sea, the other across the moorland. A light gust of wind blew around Joanna's neck like the breath of a lover. The image was startling and she blinked, wondering how on earth such a comparison had crept into her mind. Hal crept into her mind, his arms slipping around her from behind and his lips teasing her neck. A shiver ran down her spine. She blinked to rid herself of the image, reminding herself that she was too cross with him to even think of such a thing!

She stared at what lay before her, no buildings in any direction for miles but heather and hills that rose and fell.

'It's beautiful,' she exclaimed.

Meg shrugged as though there was nothing astonishing about what they saw. A lone figure was riding towards the village along the inland road. As he drew closer Joanna's heart began to thump as she recognised the posture of the horseman she had ridden with the day before.

It was Hal.

Meg waved her arms aloft and called his name. They walked to meet Hal, who climbed from the horse and bowed to the women.

'Good day, mistresses. I was not expecting a welcoming deputation.'

Joanna took a deep breath, intending to scold him for leaving her, but as she looked again at her husband her sarcastic retort died on her lips. His hair was tangled from the wind. He wore no cloak and the neck of his tunic was loosely laced, a dark shadow hinting at the soft hairs that covered his chest. A shiver of exhilaration took her by surprise.

All she could find to say was, 'I wanted to see beyond the village.'

'Joanna, you want to learn to ride, why not start now?' Hal said.

Before she could protest his arms were about her waist and he had lifted her on to the horse. She gasped and clutched her fingers into Valiant's mane as the animal stood patiently waiting for her direction. Hal put a hand in the small of Joanna's back to hold her steady, gathered the reins and began to lead the horse steadily towards Ravenscrag, giving instructions she tried to follow.

Meg walked silently alongside Hal. Joanna slid a glance down at her. Was this woman her husband's bedfellow? Joanna's instinct in the light of day was that she was not. From Hal's heated reaction to her hints the previous night he had suspected her thoughts. Whatever circumstance had led to Meg's employment, Joanna felt that bedding her was not part of it.

Perhaps it was only Meg who harboured feelings for Hal and they were not returned. It would not be surprising—he was extremely handsome, more so when he gave one of the rare smiles when he was genuinely amused that etched lines of laughter on to his face.

He was smiling now, only it was not Meg he was bestowing it on, but Joanna. She smiled back and Hal's dark eyes filled with intense hunger that set Joanna's stomach spinning over. She felt a blush begin between her breasts, creep across her chest and rise to her throat and was glad of the warm cloak she wore that hid it from view.

She considered the situation they found themselves in. Meg might want Hal, but if the hunger in his eyes was any indication, Hal wanted Joanna.

And Joanna wanted Roger.

Didn't she?

With Hal holding her on Valiant with such care for her safety, his dark curls lifting in the wind and his hand firm against her back, she could not truthfully say at that moment that she did.

Chapter Fourteen

Hal rose before daybreak, slipped from beneath the covers and began moving silently around the bedchamber in the grey half-light, pulling on his braies and breeches. Joanna watched him from the bed, woken by the unwelcome gust of cold air that curled around her replacing the warmth of Hal's arms where she had once again found herself in the night.

'Are you going away again today?' she asked sleepily.

'No. Today I can get back to work. I'll be spending the day in the forge.' Hal sounded relieved and Joanna wondered if the destination of his secret journey had been entirely voluntary. She hid a smile of glee that at least he would be gone to the forge and she would have the house to herself again.

Hal walked to the window and dipped his

hands in the ewer of water on the chest. Joanna watched him through half-closed eyes as he ran them across his face and through his hair. She wriggled sleepily down into the cosy hollow Hal's body had left. He had been warm beside her and she almost wished he had stayed there.

'Will you begin work on your masterwork today?' she asked.

'If I have the time. I have too many orders I need to fulfil that have had to wait,' Hal said.

'What are you intending to make?' Joanna asked curiously.

Hal frowned as he glanced quickly over his shoulder at her. 'That remains to be seen.'

The muscles in his broad back rolled as he lifted his arms high to pull a rough woollen tunic over his breeches and shadows caressed the curve of his neck. He shook his hair out of his eyes and faced Joanna. She tore her gaze from her husband's body just a beat too slowly and a knowing grin played around Hal's lips. An expression of such desire crossed his face that shivers raced the length of Joanna's spine.

She tried unsuccessfully to slow the beating of her heart that raced to double speed. From the glint in Hal's eyes now she suspected that all it would take to make him return to the bed was a single word. She dared not give it, but she recognised the way her stomach leapt to her throat, then plummeted back to her core.

Embarrassed he had caught her so openly staring at him, Joanna threw the covers back and climbed from the bed. The room was chilly—this part of Yorkshire felt colder than the Vale of York itself, and a violent shiver shot through her as her feet touched the bare stone floor. She exhaled loudly.

Hal picked his surcoat from the chest.

'Here, I don't want you catching a chill,' he said and wrapped it around Joanna's shoulders with a flourish. His fingers lingered on the neck of her shift and Joanna wondered if he could feel the pulse in her neck hammering beneath her skin.

The scent of more than the wool itself caught her attention—a heady mix of wood smoke and beneath that a trace of saltiness and musk that was uniquely Hal—and she pulled the surcoat closer around her. Hal was watching her keenly.

'Thank you,' she murmured, swallowing. She took a step back from him and opened the shutter to let the morning into the room. The oiled linen covering the window frame rattled in the wind and shadows of clouds raced over the cloth.

'Is it always this cold here?'

'The wind's blowing from the sea today,' Hal said, coming to stand beside her. 'You'll get used to the weather soon, though it isn't unheard of to have snow into April.'

Joanna winced. By late March York would be warm enough to walk around with only a light cloak. A pang of homesickness struck her. It must have shown on her face because Hal's lips twisted.

He moved away from her again to sit on the edge of the bed where he pulled on his boots. 'What will you do with your day?' he asked.

Joanna stared around the room. Cobwebs caught in the dawn light. 'Begin putting your house in order,' she said teasingly.

'Our house,' Hal remarked.

'Of course,' Joanna agreed. She wrapped the thick surcoat around her body, holding it close with her arms defensively about her chest. 'Our house.' The words felt strange on her tongue.

'I'll bid you good day for now in that case,' Hal said. He crossed back to her and took her face between his hands and Joanna's heart began to thump with anticipation. Instead of kissing her he gently brushed her forehead with his lips.

He dropped his hands and the door was banging shut behind him before Joanna had time to register that the emotion assailing her was disappointment. She began to brush and twist her hair into a plait, the scent of Hal's surcoat lingering on her skin long after he had left.

It wasn't until her limbs were burning with effort that Joanna stopped cleaning. She paused on her way back from the river, bucket in hand, and looked upwards, noting with surprise that the sun was over halfway across the sky. She had eaten nothing all day and the hollow feeling in her stomach was becoming harder to ignore.

She left the bucket by the door, rinsed her hands and beat the dust from her skirts, then returned to the kitchen and surveyed the results of the morning's work: freshly scrubbed walls and a cobweb-free ceiling. The house would soon be clean and ordered to her satisfaction.

She looked outside, but the forge door was closed. There had been no sign of Hal since he had walked out of their bedchamber that morning. He would surely be in before long as he, too, had eaten nothing. Joanna cut bread and cheese and sat at the table, drumming her fingers and waiting for his return. When Hal still did not appear Joanna wrapped the food in a cloth, poured a mug of ale and carried it down to the forge. The door was closed. The only signs that the building was occupied were the sound of rhythmic hammering and singing that accompanied it.

Joanna blushed as she recognised the song describing a flirtation with the miller's daughter and how the singer intended to barter for his bread. She glanced down at the slice in her hand and felt her cheeks flush as she remembered what they had done the night before. This time there had been no pain as Hal had slipped inside her. He had held her tenderly, his kisses slow, his hands gentle as they caressed her, guiding her hands around his body. She smiled to herself and knocked timidly. There was no response so she bunched her fist and hammered louder.

The door swung open and Hal peered out, blinking in the sunlight. He wore an air of concentration, but his face creased into surprise replaced by pleasure as he recognised Joanna.

Hal came outside, wiping the sweat and grime from his face with his bare arm, leaving streaks of black across his tanned face. Joanna held the cloth-wrapped food and mug towards him.

'You brought me food?' he asked incredulously.

'Here. It's nothing of consequence.' Feeling foolish, Joanna shoved her offering into his hand. She turned to go, but Hal caught her by the hand.

'Don't go!' he said. 'Thank you, it was a kind

thought. I don't normally eat until I finish for the day, but I'll gladly accept this.'

He unwound the vast leather apron from around his waist and sat leaning against the wall.

'Sit with me,' he said, patting the grass beside him.

Joanna lowered herself beside him, conscious of the way her flesh tingled as their legs brushed. Hal divided the bread into two and passed her half. They ate in companionable silence. The wind had dropped and the sun provided enough warmth that Joanna did not miss her cloak as she leaned against Hal.

'Has your work gone well?' she asked.

Hal gave a half-smile. 'Fair. Watt had let the fire die so I couldn't cast anything new. Fortunately I had some finishing to pass the time.'

'Is Watt your apprentice?' Joanna asked. Another new name and person. She wondered how many more she would meet.

'He's Meg's son. He tends the forge for me when I'm absent,' Hal said. He stood and held out a hand to pull Joanna to her feet. He led her inside the smithy. A red-headed child of five or six sat on a stool, alternately pumping on a bellows and wiping his nose on a trailing sleeve. As her eyes became accustomed to the darkness Joanna realised that the disorder of Hal's house did not extend to his workplace. Tools were precisely laid out, fuel stored tidily and work in progress methodically stacked or hanging from large hooks set into the walls. The heat from the furnace hit her and she inhaled deeply, allowing the smoky warmth to fill her lungs.

Hal was watching her as she stared around, his arms folded and his head on one side. Amusement lined his face.

'You seem more at home here than in the house,' he said.

Joanna ran her finger along the edge of the anvil where Hal's hammer lay beside a neat stack of doornails he had been crafting.

'When my aunt did not need my help I used to spend most of my time in the smithy on St Andrewgate,' she explained. A sudden impulse struck her. 'Perhaps I could help you in your work?'

Hal laughed, his eyes crinkling at the edges with genuine amusement, but his voice was kind.

'I'm sure Watt would gladly let you take his place, but I cannot afford an apprentice at the moment, nor am I permitted one until I become a master. I doubt you have the strength to hammer a plough blade anyway.'

Joanna felt her cheeks go as red as Watt's. For

Simon she had designed ornamentation for everything from swords to sconces and etched the fine patterns into belt buckles and gauntlets, but of course Hal would not know that. She smiled frostily, thinking of the sheaf of papers covered in her designs that even now lay in her clothes chest.

'I know my numbers and letters and I have a good hand,' she declared indignantly.

'My own hand is good. I'm not uneducated,' Hal said coolly.

Joanna's jaw tightened. 'If you want my assistance I'll give it gladly. The choice to accept it or not is yours. For now I shall return to the house. Goodbye.'

She lifted her chin and tugged the mug from Hal's hand. She ducked under the low doorframe and stalked back to the house where she flung herself on to a stool and sat with her chin in her hands, staring moodily into the fire.

Despite marrying her for her connections to the guild Hal clearly did not want her involved in his work. She could have told him of her drawings and convinced him to let her join him, but the condescending manner in which he had dismissed her offer set her blood boiling.

Very well, her designs would remain her secret for now. A wife should not keep secrets, but neither should a husband. Hal had still not told her where he had gone before and each day she was discovering more about his life that he had neglected to tell her.

Mary Vernon's whole purpose was to warm Simon's bed, bear his children and keep his house. Sir Roger would doubtless have expected the same. Why should Joanna expect more from Hal? She let out a sigh of exasperation. It was her own doing, of course. She had told Hal that her thoughts were hers alone and could hardly hold it against him if he decided to pay her with the same coin!

The days blurred seamlessly into one another, each much the same as the one before. Only the heather blossoming into deep purple flowers gave any indication that time was passing. Ravenscrag was a small village and alone would not have provided work enough for a blacksmith, but customers came from far afield with commissions.

Hal started work early and finished late, the same each day. He emerged to speak with the customers who called or briefly escape the heat of the furnace. Other than that Joanna rarely saw him. Wryly she remembered how she had once hoped he would be frequently away. Only the absence or otherwise of the songs accompanying the hammering gave Joanna any indication of whether he was content or dissatisfied with his labours.

By day she threw herself into the task of putting Hal's house in order and before long it was settled to Joanna's satisfaction. If Hal noticed the change in his house he made no mention of it, but he was so absorbed in his work Joanna doubted he noticed what day it was.

Some nights he did nothing more than throw himself on to the bed, others he strode around the room barely noticing her presence. He did not speak of his work, but lying in his arms Joanna did her best to ease his frustration. She knew he lay awake long after she slept, her head on his chest listening to the steady drumming of his heart.

Hal did not claim his rights every night, but when he did Joanna no longer dreaded what was to come. He was gentle, never causing the pain that Roger had. Joanna slowly became familiar with his reactions. How Hal's breath caught in his throat when she kissed the hollow of his neck and how her fingernails grazing his lower back would drive him deeper inside her. Sometimes she felt the hint of sensations that alarmed her with their intensity, but nothing that ever left her as exhausted and content as the act seemed to leave Hal.

After his rejection of her help Joanna vowed she would never again cross the threshold into Hal's domain, though she frequently found reasons to pass by in case he emerged. It was a warm evening when she was at the bank of the river, filling a bucket on bended knees, when Hal appeared from the forge.

He strode down to the bank a little further along from where Joanna was, pulling off the tunic that clung to his chest and back in patches. She stopped in curiosity to watch what Hal was doing. He did not appear to notice her as he tugged off his hose and boots and threw himself headfirst into the cold water, disappearing beneath the surface. He emerged moments later, arching his back and stretching his arms wide before he began to scrub the sweat and grime from his body and hair.

Joanna watched open-mouthed, her task forgotten. She noticed too late that she had let go of the handle and the bucket had begun to drift downstream. She cried out in annoyance, lunging after it, but stopped short as it floated out of reach towards Hal.

At the sound of her voice Hal's head snapped round. His eyes widened.

'Is the sight of me so alarming it makes you cry in shock?' he asked archly. 'I should warn the goatherd to keep his flock away in case I curdle the milk.'

Joanna pointed dumbly towards the bucket. He could not really believe he was so hideous as to alarm the livestock, but she had no words to answer his jest that would not cause her to die of embarrassment.

Hal retrieved the bucket. He splashed through the river and handed it to her. Joanna could barely mumble her thanks. She gathered her skirts and blundered up the bank and back to the house with cheeks flaming. When she reached the refuge of the kitchen she leant back against the table and closed her eyes, running her hands through her damp hair.

For all that they spent their nights in the same bed Joanna had seldom seen her husband other than by candlelight or in shadows. In broad daylight the water trickling down his muscles, droplets glistening in the downy thatch that covered his chest, and the hose clinging to his lower half, sent her thoughts spiralling down untravelled paths. She wished she had a river of her own to hurl herself into. Maybe that would quench the fires that the sight of Hal's body had caused to ignite within her.

When Hal returned to the house Joanna was stirring a pot on the hearth and did not raise her head as he entered the kitchen. He stomped into the bedroom, removed his wet hose and braies and pulled on fresh clothes. He took the ones he had discarded into the kitchen and hung them to dry on the hook above the fire.

Joanna said nothing, but walked into the pantry and returned with a cup of ale. Hal took it gratefully and downed it. A knot of tension speared the back of his neck. In need of something stronger, he went to the pantry and found a bottle of wine. The pantry was tidier than he remembered. He emerged and looked around with interest.

Joanna had transformed his house into somewhere welcoming and he hadn't even noticed. He wondered if he should compliment her on the changes. He had told her she was not a servant, but nevertheless that was how she seemed to spend her days. He wondered what else she did, but to ask would be to intrude into her thoughts. Better to wait until a time when she might choose to share the information.

He brought a second cup and gave one to Joanna. She accepted it quietly, staring at him with wide, wary eyes that tore into Hal's heart. She blinked rapidly as his fingers touched hers.

Hal suppressed a sigh of irritation. From her reaction when she came across him by the river Hal felt as if she had expected him to throw her to the ground and violate her against her will. Joanna had lived with him for long enough that she should have lost some of her fear by now. He did not expect passion, but hoped for more than indifference. She received his attentions without shrinking from his touch as she had the first time, but afterwards they seldom spoke. He never asked what or who she was thinking of and she never volunteered the information.

He pulled a chair closer to the fire and watched as she cooked, his mouth watering at the rich odour of stew that wafted from the pot. His stomach growled. Since the first day when Joanna had brought him her offering of bread Hal had hoped she would return to the forge. He found himself timing his tasks so they could be put down if she arrived, but she never came. He was not about to insist she bore his company more than she wanted, but the disappointment gnawed at him.

The stew was excellent and he ate ravenously. He held his bowl out for more and Joanna showed the first sign of pleasure he had seen that day. He was pleased to see she devoured her own share equally heartily.

He stared into the glowing coals of the hearth. The hearthstone was covered in marks. After an afternoon spent attempting to create the pommel and cross guard of a sword it looked to Hal's imagination as though someone had done the same here. He wiped them away, irritated at himself for seeing things where they clearly weren't.

He closed his eyes and tilted his head back, digging his fingers into the sore muscles of his shoulders. He was unprepared to feel Joanna slip her fingers between his. He sat rigid and the already tight muscles hardened.

'I'm sorry!'

Joanna whipped her hands away as though he had stabbed her, but Hal captured them and brought them back.

'Don't stop, you surprised me, that's all,' he said. Her fingers were still for what felt like eternity, then she began moving them slowly in circles across his shoulders.

A smile crossed Hal's lips. Her fingers were slender and cool, yet surprisingly strong. He settled back, enjoying the unfamiliar sensations as Joanna worked on easing the aches from his body. He imagined her hands moving downwards across his back, slipping sinuously round his chest to become a more intimate exploration of his body.

When she touched him in this way he could almost convince himself she was fond of him. He did not expect her affection, much less her love, but he found himself increasingly caring that she did not.

Chapter Fifteen

Joanna stood upright and put her hands in the small of her back, pushing her spine forward. She was glad of the rushing water that played around her legs as she stood knee-deep and barefoot in the river and let out a sigh. Beside her Meg did the same. The two women exchanged a look of weary understanding. Washing was backbreaking work.

For the past five days the temperature had risen steadily and the opportunity for washing sheets was too good to pass up. All along the riverbank women and girls from the village were engaged in the same task. Some sang or chatted, others were silent with exertion, and some obviously hoped to catch the eye of one of the men who stopped by the bank to watch.

The women dragged clothes and sheets from the river, twisted and wrung them before spreading them out to dry over the bushes. Small boys, including Watt who had been temporarily released from his bellows duty, raced back and forth scaring away the large gulls that watched proceedings with interest.

Task accomplished, the women sat on the grass to pull on their stockings and boots, in no rush to move. Joanna had tucked her skirts and shift into her girdle at the waist, doubling the layers, and the thick woollen kirtle was becoming uncomfortably warm. The wind that blew from the moors and had chilled her to the bone since her arrival now came as a welcome breeze, cooling her neck as it lifted the damp hair that escaped from beneath her cap. She noticed Meg had replaced her wool under-tunic with a second one of linen, lower at the neck and with loose sleeves. Joanna watched with envy, fanning herself with the back of her hand.

'I need to make another shift,' she said. 'Something lighter.'

'Ask Master Danby to take you to the market in Pickering. You haven't left the village since you arrived.'

Joanna glanced towards the smithy where even in the heat the door remained closed to provide constant dimness. She thought of Hal, returning to the house later each day, barely concealed frustration simmering in his eyes.

'I doubt he will agree. He's barely left the forge for days now.'

'It's the feast of St George next week,' Meg said. 'There's always a market. He'll go to that.'

A jolt like lightning shot through Joanna. Sir Roger's face rose in her mind for the first time in days and she reeled, starting forward abruptly.

Meg put a hand on her arm. 'Are you ill?' she asked in concern. 'You've gone pale.'

Joanna wiped her brow. She counted up the weeks since her marriage, wondering how they had gone without her spending every day grieving for the life she had lost.

'I'm just surprised that it could it be St George's Day so soon. I had not realised how quickly the time had passed. You reminded me that there is a tournament at Windsor due to take place in a matter of days. Someone I once knew will be competing.'

'Someone you cared for?' Meg asked.

Joanna bit her lip thoughtfully. A month ago she could have described Sir Roger in the smallest detail, but now his features were indistinct and the laughing brown eyes that came to mind were

Hal's. Without even realising when it had begun to happen, she had ceased thinking of him so often.

She wondered if he ever thought of her as he travelled down the country. Did he regret leaving her behind as much as she had regretted it? If he made good his losses as he had hoped, would he return to York only to find she was nowhere to be found? Once the thought had pained her physically. Now it had lessened into a dull ache and she could think of him without wanting to curl into a ball and sob.

'I thought he was,' she said slowly.

'I've never been to a tournament,' Meg said. 'Not really. There will be a tiltyard at Pickering, but I don't imagine it will be the same.'

Joanna drew her knees up and hugged them. 'York during a tournament is the most exciting place to be. There's nothing to compare with it. The colours of the banners and costumes, the roaring of the crowds as the knights fight, the scent of food, the feel of the crowds pushing to get to the front of the stands.'

She closed her eyes and inhaled deeply, recalling the smell of hot spicy rissoles and the splintering of wood on armour. A lump filled her throat at the idea of missing such fun that even the thought of Roger had not managed to conjure. She looked back towards the village at the handful of houses that made up her world now and loneliness descended on her, chilling her to the core despite the warmth of the morning sun.

'I miss the excitement,' she said quietly.

A yellow-beaked gull landed near them. It inspected the sheets with malevolent intent in its beady eye. Meg hurled a stone at it and it flew off, screeching angrily. The sound and movement roused Joanna from her reverie. She pushed herself to her feet and brushed her skirts down briskly.

As Meg stood and smoothed her skirt Joanna saw something she had not before noticed. Perhaps it was that Meg was no longer concealed beneath bulky wool. It was barely visible, and only years of living with Mary Vernon meant Joanna recognised the telltale swelling, but it was there nevertheless.

'You're pregnant!' she exclaimed.

Meg smiled faintly, her hands moving to caress her belly.

Only…

Meg's husband had been hanged two years since. Joanna struggled to dismiss the treacherous images that rose in her mind, remembering

her suspicions about Meg and Hal on first meeting. Her eyes darted towards the forge.

Meg pursed her lips. She turned abruptly and
walked to the house, head down. Joanna chased
after her.

'Meg, I'm sorry,' she said.

Meg's face was grey. Joanna motioned her to
the chair by the door where the breeze cooled the
room and fetched a cup of milk.

'I'm sorry,' she repeated. 'It's none of my business.'

'I'm not ashamed,' Meg said bullishly. She sipped
the milk. The colour returned to her cheeks. 'It's
three months or so by my reckoning,' she offered.
She chewed a fingernail. 'It isn't *his*. Master Danby's, I mean,' she said.

'I didn't say it was,' Joanna protested, but Meg
waved a hand to silence her.

'But you thought it, didn't you? I saw how you
first looked at me. Don't you know me better than
that now? Don't you know Hal?'

Joanna hung her head. 'Forgive me, please. It
was unjust of me to ever think it.'

Meg smiled. 'The father is John Coates, the
miller's son. He's kind to me. We'll marry after
the harvest.'

'And do you love him?' Joanna asked.

Meg shrugged. 'I like him enough that it makes no difference. A woman needs a man to provide for her and it would have been foolish to grow old pining for what I could never have.'

Joanna nodded. Meg had reached the conclusion with much better grace than she had done.

Meg's eyes drifted to an unseen past. 'My husband was a brute. I don't regret his passing. When Master Danby first brought me here he said it was to make amends for his part in the affair. I hoped he had a purpose other than employing me, but he never so much as looked at me in that way. I've never seen him cast any sort of look at any woman, before you.'

Joanna smiled faintly, unsure what to say to the woman who admitted her desire for Hal so frankly. She stored the 'before you' in her mind. A glowing coal to dwell on later.

'I'm going to go ask Hal to take me to market.' She poured a mug of ale. 'This should sweeten his mood.'

Joanna made her way to the forge, deep in thought. Meg's tale had been disconcertingly similar to her own story in which Hal appeared again in the role of saviour of an abandoned woman. Though in Meg's case he had done it to soften his own feelings of guilt.

Hal did not answer when she knocked on the door. She thumped again and when there was still no response she cautiously lifted the latch and entered. The heat was stifling. Hal was standing with his back to the door. He had removed his tunic and sweat ran in rivulets down his back, his shirt clinging to his body. He worked silently, unaware of her presence, tapping the bar of glowing metal, flattening and turning it as it lengthened into a sword blade.

As she stood, back to the door watching in fascination, Hal swore. He began to hammer harder, turning the blade over and over until, with a roar of frustration, he lifted the hammer high and brought it down hard on the anvil beside the blade.

Joanna gasped at the sudden ferocity.

Hal stiffened and turned.

'How long have you been watching?' he asked furiously.

'Not long…' Joanna faltered. She reached for the door latch. 'I'll go.'

'No, don't. I've lost my way with this piece.' Hal lowered his hammer and rubbed his eyes wearily. 'Why are you here?'

Joanna held out the ale. 'It's hot today. I thought you might be thirsty.'

He stared at the mug uncertainly before taking

it. He raised it to his lips, but paused and his eyes filled with suspicion. 'You haven't visited me here since your first day. Why now?'

'I have a request to ask you,' Joanna admitted. 'I want you to take me to the market next week. There are things I need.'

Hal's mouth turned down. 'I should have guessed it was not my company you craved.' He drained the mug and put it on the anvil beside the blade that was now dulling from glowing yellow to reddish orange. 'I'm sorry, but I can't spare the time now.'

Joanna's heart sank. 'Not even a morning?' she asked.

'I said no!' Hal folded his arms and glared at the anvil. His dark hair flamed in the glow of the furnace. 'If I don't work we don't eat and I have barely enough time for my own undertaking as it is. You must understand that! I'm afraid your errands will have to wait.'

His jaw was set. Even as he spoke his eyes drifted back to the discarded blade. It was clear where his attention laid. She realised as she thought it that she was missing Hal's company more after a few days than Roger's after weeks.

'I've barely seen you for days,' Joanna said softly.

Hal gestured angrily to the anvil. 'Don't you see what I'm trying to do here? I spend every waking moment working and every sleeping moment dreaming of what to create, but everything I do falls short of what I want.'

Joanna reached a hand out to his arm, acutely aware of the firm muscles beneath her fingers. 'You have months before you have to be back in York. You'll succeed before then.'

'And if I don't?' Hal twisted away and Joanna whipped her hand back. 'If I'm not accepted into the guild everything I've done over the past months has been for nothing.'

'Everything?' Joanna lifted her chin. Her cheeks began to burn, not from the heat of the furnace alone. She took a step towards him. 'You said I only came here today because I wanted something and pretended your pride was wounded. That may be the case, but I'm only here at all because you wanted the advantages I bring.'

A moment before she had considered caressing him to ease his worries. Now she wanted to do nothing more than slap him. Maybe then she would break through his indifference.

'Forgive my intrusion, I shall not disturb you further,' she muttered.

She wrenched the door open and stumbled out into the brightness.

'I didn't mean it that way,' Hal shouted from the doorway.

She marched back to the house, ignoring the voice that repeatedly called her name. She had no inclination to let him see the effect his words had on her. The wind gusted around her, stinging her eyes where tears sprung.

Hal had dashed her hopes of having one day that was different from usual, but worse than that had been his casual dismissal of their marriage. Even after weeks of living together, sharing bed and body, her only value to Hal was her usefulness. She had known when she married him that his work was his priority, but she felt a sudden loneliness. Her eyes filled again as she realised the tragedy of her situation. Here was another man who she meant nothing to and she had the distressing suspicion that was beginning to matter far too much.

She wiped her hand across her face and stared towards the hills. If she could not have the diversion of a market to look forward to, she would have the solitude of the moors. Back in the house Meg was waiting.

'He said no,' Joanna said, angry at the way her

voice betrayed her feelings. She ran to the bedroom, snatched up her bag and returned. 'I want to be alone for a while. I'll be back soon.'

She left before Meg could reply, heading out of the village along the road that led to the moors and walked until her legs were protesting, each step calming her mood. A pile of rocks stood a little way from the road so she crossed the spongy ground and sat down, leaning back against one. She removed her cap and shook out her hair. There was no one here to see her after all.

She pulled the scraps of parchment from her bag and spread them before her. She had intended to complete a sketch, but now they brought her no joy. The sun was warm even on the exposed moor and Joanna yawned. She should set off back soon, but it was peaceful and there was little to tempt her home. She rolled the parchments again. She was so drowsy and the scent of the endless heather was calming. She'd just close her eyes for a short while…

Hal's second attempt to forge the sword blade had been met with more success. He had followed that by completing the ornamentation on two decorative locks and keys for the abbot of Rievaulx who would pay well and promptly. If he could only ensure the rest of his weapon was as fine as those his place in the guild would be almost ensured.

He had been unable to stop reliving his conversation with Joanna and though the afternoon was not spent he had lost the inclination to continue. His heart had clenched with pleasure when he'd seen her, coupled with an unsettling self-consciousness. To discover that she had only visited because she wanted a favour had been bitterly disheartening. His frustration was not her fault and her angry accusation had hit the target with the accuracy of a lance striking his breastplate.

He tidied his tools and left the forge, glancing towards the riverbank as he walked back to the house, but she wasn't there. The kitchen was empty and no food was cooking. He strolled into the bedroom, smiling to himself in anticipation of making amends for his earlier thoughtless words with a kiss.

Joanna's disappointment at not being able to visit the market was understandable and Hal's conscience prodded him uncomfortably at his refusal. She had caught him at an unfortunate moment and he had been rude and cold from the outset.

The bedroom was empty, too. Grumpily he

pulled on a fresh tunic. He had not expected to find the house empty. He had become so accustomed to the sound of Joanna's humming and the shy smile that she greeted him with that its absence was unsettling. His stomach turned over as he straightened the counterpane, running his hand over the side Joanna slept on, and decided to go in search.

He walked back outside where he noticed the sheets on the bushes and ran his fingers along one. Dry.

Disconcerted, he hurried to Meg Parry's house and rapped on the door. Meg's puzzlement at seeing him was answer enough before he had even asked if Joanna was there.

'She was upset,' Meg told him, accusation in her voice.

'We quarrelled,' Hal explained ruefully.

'Upset before she spoke to you, I mean.' Meg folded her arms. 'We'd been talking about St George's Day. She was telling me about the tournaments and how she missed them. She looked like she was trying not to cry.'

A knife twisted in Hal's guts. He tried to think back to before he had spoken to her so harshly. Had he seen signs of her sadness when she entered the forge but ignored them? He could guess which part of the tournament she would be missing most. And who. He pictured how she had found him: filthy with sweat, hidden away in the darkness and responsible for deserting her in the middle of nowhere. No wonder the thought of Roger was enough to reduce her to tears.

'Do you know where she is now?'

Meg pointed toward the moors. 'She left as soon as she returned from seeing you. She isn't back yet?'

Cold sweat crashed over Hal. Without another word he ran to the stable and saddled Valiant. He rode slowly, stretching in the saddle to scan the moors. If Joanna had strayed from the path he would blame himself.

A snatch of blue among grey rocks caught his eye. The slight figure was stretched at full length, one arm across her belly, the other tangled in the mass of hair that spread around her. He dismounted with a cry of alarm and ran across the moss, heart leaping to his throat at the thought at what he might find. As he neared Joanna she stretched and rubbed her eyes. She pushed herself to her elbows, staring up at Hal through sleep-bleary eyes.

Hal threw himself to her side, gripping her arms tightly.

'What did you think you were doing?' he roared.

Joanna recoiled. 'You're hurting me!'

Hal eased his grip slightly, but the thought of letting Joanna slip from his arms was unbearable.

'I came back and you were gone. Have you any idea what passed through my mind?' he said angrily.

Joanna pulled herself out of his grip.

'I don't know,' she said coldly, turning away. 'Did you fear my uncle would bar you from the guild forever if I died on the moors?'

'What!' Her words were a dagger to Hal's heart. He sat back on his heels and stared at her furiously. 'Is that what you think?'

'That's my only value after all. It's why you married me,' Joanna snapped.

'That isn't all you mean to me!' He clutched her by the arms once more and pulled her round to face him. 'I came looking because I was worried. For *you*, not my investment.'

The expression on her face was enough to show how little she believed him. Even in his despair a small spark of hope ignited. If it distressed her to think he felt nothing for her, did that mean she felt something for him?

'I may not have shown it, but I care about your well-being. I—' He broke off, the word he wanted to say too big and disturbing. He took her hands in his. 'I…care about you.'

She looked disbelieving.

'When you're sad it pains me. When I thought you might have come to harm it near killed me.' He pulled her close, enfolding her in his arms. She stood rigid, then just as Hal was about to give up hope she laid her cheek against his chest. Hal wondered if she could feel the force with which his heart tried to burst from his chest.

'I wouldn't have come to harm,' Joanna said obstinately. 'I just needed time alone. Meg told me it would soon be St George's Day and it brought back things I hadn't thought of for a while.'

'You don't have to explain,' he said tersely. His heart twisted once more. If she spoke of Roger now he felt sure it would crack in two.

Joanna stared bleakly ahead, her eyes pools of misery. Hal's irritation melted as the force of her loneliness struck him fully.

'I miss the city and the crowds. The noise and colours and the excitement.'

'I'll give you that one day,' he vowed. 'When I become a swordsmith and join the guild we'll have reason to spend time in York.'

He wished he felt as confident as he sounded.

He stood and held his hands out. 'Let's go home,' he said.

Joanna took his hands. Scraps of parchment fluttered in the wind as she stood. With a cry of dismay she broke away, catching them up and stuffing them into her bag with her back to Hal. She missed one and Hal trapped it beneath his boot. He slipped it into his pouch, intending to return it later.

Joanna sat before him as they rode slowly home. With his arms around her Hal was in no rush for the journey to end. She'd coiled her hair back up and fixed it with a handful of pins at the base of her slender neck. The twists transfixed Hal. Her neck cried out to be kissed, the knot to be unwound, but more than that he wondered how they'd look twisted into gold adorning a pommel.

Doubts crossed his mind as he remembered his discarded attempts, but he stamped them down. He leant forward and kissed the top of Joanna's head, so softly he was unsure she had felt it. Somewhere he needed to find inspiration for his work and maybe it was closer than he'd previously thought.

Chapter Sixteen

Gentle tapping on the door broke Hal's concentration. He dropped his auger and punch on to the workbench and pulled the door open, expecting to find Matthew Shaw come to collect his pitchfork.

Joanna stood there. She looked as hesitant as she had the previous day.

'If you're busy I'll go,' she said, her manner reminding Hal of a rabbit about to flee from a hawk.

'No,' Hal said quickly. He could ill afford to spare the time, but his stomach had clenched at the sight of her and the cause was more than hunger. He put an arm around her before she could leave.

'Watt, you can stop now,' he called.

They walked to the river and sat on the bank side by side. Watt ran ahead, chasing ducks. Joanna laughed at his excitement and Hal smiled instinctively at the sound he had not heard very often. It suddenly became essential to him to hear it much more frequently.

He unwrapped Joanna's cloth to find two slices of fresh cake. Two. He raised an eyebrow at Joanna who blushed.

'I hoped you would ask me to stay,' she said shyly.

Hal wolfed his cake in three bites, then lay back on the grass watching Joanna. Work called him but he ignored it. Crumbs glazed Joanna's lips and Hal's pulse began to race at the thought of slowly licking them off. She did the job herself, tongue darting deftly out. A tremor of desire ran through him. When a cloud covered the sun Hal shifted and sat up. If he did not move soon he would still be sitting watching her at nightfall.

'I have to make a delivery at Gaskell's farm this afternoon,' he said. 'It isn't far so why don't you come with me? Meg can take care of anything you still have to do in the house.'

She looked suspicious for a moment, but her face lit up.

'I'd like that.'

She joined him as he finished loading the cart. Their fingers linked as Hal helped her into the seat and climbed up beside her. Last time they had sat together here Joanna had been stiff and awkward. They'd been strangers then but now, as their legs and arms touched, she merely looked down at her hands. Her long eyelashes concealed whatever emotion her eyes showed at the closeness and Hal wished he could see into her mind to discover what his touch woke in her.

Hal picked up the reins.

'Perhaps one day I could teach you to handle a cart and horse,' he said. 'It isn't too hard if you're firm with the animal.'

Joanna turned to face him, her eyes glinting.

'I know already,' she said. 'I used to join my uncle on deliveries. Sometimes, when he'd taken a cup too much wine with his customers, I'd drive home.'

'You never told me,' Hal said, surprised.

'You never asked.' Her smile vanished as her expression darkened. 'You never asked me anything.'

It was true and he wrinkled his nose at his own stupidity. He still knew little about her and had made poor effort to discover it. He'd even resented the fact she had not come to the forge after the first day, but he had never asked her. She'd been the one to approach him and he wondered if he was wrong to assume her heart was not for winning.

'I'm asking now,' he said, passing the reins to her and enjoying the look of astonishment and delight that crossed her face.

'We've got all afternoon, tell me everything.'

They arrived back to a late afternoon that was turning colder. Joanna had driven well, guiding the carthorse with steady hands that only tightened on the reins when she spoke of the parents she'd lost and the relatives she'd gained in their place.

Hal's veins had filled with molten steel as she talked of the way Simon Vernon had made it clear her presence was an inconvenience. If he'd known her better he would have stopped the cart and folded her in his arms to comfort her. As it was he sent private thanks to the icy gusts blowing in from the sea for allowing him the excuse to pull Joanna closer and put his arms around her as she shivered.

He lifted her to the ground and she put her hands on his shoulders to steady herself. They stood silently facing each other, bodies close. The urge to kiss her was so strong Hal felt his breath catch in his throat. His hold around her waist tightened.

Joanna was the first to move. She stood on tiptoe and brushed a kiss lightly against his cheek.

'Thank you,' she said.

Hal's heart both sang and plummeted at the gesture that was intimate yet somehow sisterly. He could hardly seize her up and kiss her with the passion he wanted to after that. He took her hand and lifted it to his lips.

'Let's go to Pickering Fair,' he said impulsively.

Joanna's face glowed, then her smile dropped. 'Can you spare the time?'

A day ago Hal would have said no, but he could not banish the picture of Joanna's sorrowful face as she talked about her loneliness. He'd been content to live his own life while she settled into hers as best she could. They had been wasted weeks when he could have been trying to gain his wife's affection, but now the thought of more time spent in her company was irresistible.

'I have to work now, but yes.' He walked round to the back of the cart and put his hands on his hips as he stared at the contents. 'I'm afraid I shall have to leave you to deal with your new purchases alone.'

Joanna joined him, laughing. A lidded wicker basket gently rocked as the dozen chicks it contained cheeped indignantly. Beside it a wiry, grey dog of no discernible breed stared up mournfully and scratched an ear that obstinately refused to turn the right way out.

'Every home needs a dog,' she said, leaning forward to unknot the rope that held the dog in place. 'I couldn't let this old boy be drowned!'

'Hmm, Mistress Gaskell knows when to spin a sad tale to a soft-hearted woman,' Hal mused. 'Though a larger hound would be better suited for a farm and no fine lady would countenance an animal like this.'

Joanna paused halfway through the knot. 'Perhaps not. But I'm no fine lady,' she said.

She led the dog to the house. Hal watched her go, her small figure swaying as she walked. Had her statement contained sadness or had it been merely resignation that tinged her voice. She'd used the word *home* not *house*. Perhaps he'd laid too much significance on that, but it glowed in his memory. Hal wished he could see into her mind, or better still, her heart.

He lifted the basket of hens from the cart and carried them to the door before dealing with the horse and returning to the peace of the forge. Watt had spent the time in Hal's absence laying tools to order. He began to work on the hinge he had left off before Joanna interrupted earlier. His smallest auger was missing and he spent a frustrating amount of time searching for it before he recalled slipping it into the pouch that he wore at his waist.

He reached in and his fingers closed around something unexpected. He pulled out Joanna's fold of vellum. He'd completely forgotten he'd captured it. Joanna had been at considerable pains to capture the sheets yesterday and he itched to know what secret it held.

He turned it over thoughtfully. Temptation whispered in his ear and his fingers were halfway to unfolding it, but he bunched it in his fist, then put it to one side on the workbench. He had enough secrets of his own; let Joanna have hers. He would return this one to her as soon as he saw her again. His eyes slid to it once more. Was it a recipe she'd been writing? A list of goods she wanted to buy? Worse than that, a love note?

He held it out. 'Watt, can you take this to Mistress Danby?'

The boy took hold of it and walked to the door. 'Oh, that's pretty!' he exclaimed.

Of course he had placed no injunction on Watt not to unfold it. Watt's words were so enigmatic his resolve to allow Joanna her privacy disappeared. He took the parchment from the boy and held it up to the light of the furnace. In the glow of the flames an eagle stared back. Hal spread it out on the anvil and stared at it in astonishment. It was not merely an eagle but a sword, the bird's head a pommel and a cross guard formed of wings spread wide. He traced his fingers over the lines of feathers on the hilt.

It was beautiful and Joanna had created this? No doubt her other sheets contained similar sketches. Hal had struggled for weeks to find inspiration and all along she had these in her possession. He sighed in annoyance, but he caught himself as her earlier words came back to him.

You never asked me anything.

She was under no obligation to volunteer the information. He'd never asked why she'd been in Simon's workshop when he called to bargain for her hand. The first day she'd come to the forge she'd made tentative offers to help and he'd bullishly scorned her. The fault was entirely his.

He leaned back against the wall and stared into the flames. He could return it to her. Or…

He picked the parchment up once more. He could make this and make it well. He had the skill. It had been the idea that had eluded him. He'd work in secret and present it to her once it was completed. At that point he'd admit his knowledge of her secret and beg her pardon. He took a nail and secured the drawing to the beam of wood above the furnace.

Pickering Fair was loud and bustling, a shock to the senses after the solitude of Ravenscrag. Joanna's eyes lit up as Hal helped her down from Valiant.

'Aren't you coming with me?' she asked as he directed her to the weavers' row and took hold of Valiant's bridle.

'I have business to attend to that I need to complete today,' he said.

Her eyes narrowed suspiciously, but already the shrill music of pipes in the square and the calls of the hawkers with their wares were calling her away from him.

He watched her weave her way through the crowds until she was swallowed up, a small figure with a skip in her step. Her money was well concealed, she was modestly dressed and she was a grown woman. Even though the thought of her coming to harm was enough to cause him to break out in sweat, Hal let her go.

He had moved swiftly, completed his own errands and was waiting for her by the castle steps within the allotted hour when she returned bearing packages that would fill Valiant's panniers to overflowing. Her cheeks were flushed and Hal's face split into a grin.

'Is there anything left for anyone else to buy?' he asked.

Joanna tossed her head amiably. 'I doubt I'll be somewhere this big for months. I didn't want to miss the opportunity.'

Her voice was without resentment.

'I have something to show you,' Hal said. Taking her by the hand, he led her down the snicket beside the castle gate. The alley was silent and cool, a tempting place to stop and steal a kiss, but Hal didn't delay. He grinned to himself. Even more appealing than bundling Joanna's tempting curves into his arms was the prospect of her reaction to his surprise.

They emerged by the stables. Valiant snickered in welcome as he heard their voices. They set their packages down. In the stall beside him was a tawny-coloured palfrey. Hal stopped in front of her and waved his arm with a flourish.

Joanna's brow wrinkled in confusion.

'She's yours,' Hal announced.

The horse had been an extravagant gift he could little afford, but as Joanna's hands flew to her mouth and her eyes widened Hal decided every coin had been well spent. Long afternoons riding would be the perfect opportunity to spend increased time in her company. Without warning Joanna flung her arms around Hal's neck and kissed him full on the lips. She pulled away and blushed at her forwardness before he could trap her for longer.

'Thank you! I love her!'

Hal's heart thumped, startling him with its strength. When the word *love* left her lips a shiver had shaken his entire body. For one moment he had thought he was the recipient of her affection and realising he wasn't caused his heart to plummet to his belly. He held his hand out for the mare to sniff and avoided looking at Joanna in case she read the disappointment in his eyes.

'Her name's Rowan. She isn't too young, but she's biddable and ideal for a novice rider. I'll teach you to ride as I promised.'

Joanna held her hand out beside Hal's. Rowan snuffled at it and Joanna ran her palm across the mare's warm neck. She gazed in admiration at the horse, murmuring soft endearments beneath her breath.

Hal only had eyes for his wife.

* * *

'I'd better go rescue Watt from the geese,' Hal murmured sleepily. He clambered to his feet and helped Joanna to hers before strolling along the riverbank.

Joanna stood and brushed her skirts down briskly to rid them of the grass she had caught up as she lay across Hal's lap by the smithy. Since the day they had visited Gaskell's farm this had become a habit. Each day at noon she would venture to the smithy and bang on the door for Hal to join her to eat. Some days he needed no asking but was already outside, his eyes fixed on the path from the house waiting for her arrival. She wondered idly how different the last weeks would have been if she had done this every day.

Hal had been more content in the last week than she remembered since they had married. He still left the house at sunrise and returned late, but the evenings where he stamped around the house moodily were a distant memory.

She returned to the house and began to prepare dinner, stewing meat and kneading pastry, humming an old tune of summer she remembered from childhood. Simon the dog pushed his nose against her skirts and whined. She reached down and scratched the old animal behind his out-turned ear.

The name had been Hal's joke and for want of a better one it had stuck. The grin they exchanged whenever one of them said it more than made up for the worry of what her uncle would say should he ever encounter his namesake.

A particular design that had been refusing to leave her for days rose in her mind. She rolled the offcuts of pastry into strips, plaited and twisted them together, then pressed the design on to the crust, laughing at her foolishness. If she could not work with iron or steel she would make do with what she had.

She wondered if she had been mistaken not to tell him about her designs. A cloud passed over her mood. For all their increased closeness, and despite knocking for Hal to join her every day, she never crossed the threshold into the forge and Hal said nothing of his work, changing the subject or answering in a monotone whenever she broached the subject. It was a part of his life he seemed determined she would have no part in.

She was still pondering the decision when Hal entered the house. He came straight to her rather than going into the bedroom as usual and peered over her shoulder. His hair was wet from his customary dip in the river and Joanna pushed the pie aside before he could drip on it, trying to banish the image of Hal's body as he scrubbed his taut muscles clean.

Hal was regarding the pie intently. 'Interesting. Are the contents so unappealing it needs decoration to distract me?'

Joanna seized it up defensively and carried it to the oven. Hal came behind her, his face still serious and put his arms around her, resting his cheek against hers.

'Don't be cross with me, I'm jesting. It looks beautiful and I'm sure it will taste as good.'

She gave him a tight smile. If he only knew what she really had in mind for the design he might not be so happy. Her secret would remain just that for a little longer.

'You have flour on your face.' Hal grinned. He brushed it off with his thumb, a gesture that sent Joanna's skin fluttering. Telling him could wait.

'You're back sooner than I expected.'

'I have to go out again,' he said. He walked into the bedroom. Joanna followed him and watched as he pulled on dry clothes. 'I'm only going into the village. It's May Day tomorrow and there are things to prepare.'

'What sort of things?' Joanna asked eagerly. It

seemed incredible a day of such celebration had slipped her mind.

Hal paused by her in the doorway and kissed her forehead lightly. 'Wait and see,' he said.

Thundering beats on the door roused them from their bed as men from the villages came to claim ale from Hal as Lord Danby's representative. He allowed himself to be taken away, leaving Joanna in the hands of Meg and the other women to gather flowers and greenery from the moors and bind them into wreaths.

The women arrived on the village green at midday. Raucous, uncontrolled games were taking place amid cheers and catcalls of the onlookers already well into the ale, but stopped as they appeared.

'Crown the queen!'

The call was taken up and repeated by everyone present. Girls giggled and blushed, young men freely ogled them and Joanna felt hands in her back pushing her to the front of the crowd.

Hal appeared from among the men. He took her by the hand and turned her to face everyone. A crown of twisted greenery was placed on her head to cheers and good-natured whistles from everyone watching. Pipers began to play and dancers found their partners.

'I thought the May Queen was supposed to be a maiden,' Joanna whispered to Hal.

He held her waist tightly as he led her to the circle. 'This year I thought I'd exercise my rights to choose.'

'You can do that?'

'I can do what I like, I'm their lord's son,' he joked. He put one hand on her back, the other to her cheek and looked into her eyes. 'I cannot give you tournaments and pageants to delight you, but I wanted to give you something to remember.'

She covered her hand with his. 'You have,' she said. 'This is enough.'

She realised as she said it that she spoke the truth.

The dancing and games carried on long into the night. As the sun set Hal and the men carried brands from the forge and lit the bonfire. More barrels of ale were tapped and the ox that had been roasting all afternoon was speedily eaten.

As groups and couples began to disperse to find their own diversions Joanna sat alone by the fire, warming her hands and yawning. She'd danced until her calves burned and drunk far too much wine. Her bed called her. Hal had vanished a while before, called away by the miller, and she was becoming tired of waiting. She walked home and was halfway to the door when she noticed light coming from the forge.

Curious, she walked across the dewy grass. The door was partly open, but no sound came from within. Cautiously Joanna pushed the door wider and peeped around it.

Hal was standing by his workbench. In the dull glow of the furnace Joanna could only see his back.

'What are you doing?' she asked.

Hal jumped at her voice. He strode towards her, blocking her entry into the forge.

'What's wrong? Why won't you let me in?' she asked.

'Nothing's wrong. I'm coming now,' Hal said. His voice was guarded. He took hold of her arm and tried to turn her away.

He was so obviously hiding something. Determined to find out what Joanna twisted from his grip and pushed past him. Her blood drained slowly away, leaving her cold to the bone as she recognised her own drawing pinned to the beam above the furnace.

'That's mine!' she hissed. 'How did you get it?'

'You dropped it on the moors,' Hal said.

She remembered the day, but that had been over a week ago and he had kept it all this time! Furious, she lunged and ripped the drawing from the wall. She rounded on Hal.

'How dare you keep it,' she stormed. 'You had no right to do that.'

She pushed roughly past him and wrenched the door open, stumbling out into the darkness.

Chapter Seventeen

Hal's arms came round Joanna from behind before she had taken three steps.

'Let me go!' she spat.

'I'm not going to do that.' Hal's voice was determined. 'I understand you're angry, but you mean too much to me to let you run now.'

His words cut through the web of anger and sorrow that surrounded Joanna.

'I mean something to you?' she scoffed. 'I mean so much you shut me out of your life and keep secrets from me! Why should I believe you?'

'Let me explain,' Hal said, his lips close to her ear. He held her close, with infinite gentleness, but his arms were like iron bars and her struggles to wrench free proved useless. 'Come back inside, here's no place for an argument.'

The sound of the revelry drifted towards them across the cloud-free sky. If she continued to fight she knew absolutely Hal would let her go rather than risk public shame for either of them. She could return to the house and they would continue as they had done. A wearying future stretched ahead of them laden with secrets. Resentment. Silence. Sadness.

He'd held her close earlier when they had been dancing, a whirlwind of emotion she had not wanted to end. Something had been growing between them over the past weeks. She did not want to give that up any more than she wished to stop her heart pumping.

She stopped struggling and Hal relaxed his grip. Shrugging him off, she walked back inside the smithy, still clutching her picture tightly in her fist. Once again the heat threatened to crush what little breath she had left from her body.

Hal's eyes never wavered from the parchment in her hand. Perhaps he feared she would throw it into the flames. In a moment of spite she moved her hand towards it. Hal stepped forward, arms out in entreaty.

'Don't!' he said, a note of alarm in his voice.

'It's mine,' Joanna said sharply. 'I can do with it what I choose.'

'I know you can. Only…' Hal ran his hand back

through his hair. 'Joanna, your work is beautiful. Are all your drawings like this?'

She could not hide the smile of pride. 'Some,' she admitted. 'Some are better.'

'What did you think I was doing with it?' he asked.

Joanna bit her lip. The heat from the furnace combined with too much wine made thinking hard. She crossed to the door where it was cooler. 'I don't know.'

'Let me show you!' Hal led her to the work-bench. Her throat tightened as she stared at an iron eagle.

'I was going to return your drawing to you. I almost sent it with Watt, but I kept it because it inspired me,' Hal said ruefully. 'As soon as I saw it I knew it was what I'd been searching for. I intended no malice.'

'Your intention is beside the point.' Joanna folded her arms defensively across her body. 'This is worse. You realised what I can do, but you didn't ask me to help.'

'Should I have forced you to work here?' Hal waved a hand around the cramped forge. 'You, who grieves for the grand life of a knight's lady? It pains me enough that you have to work in my house with only Meg to help, but to expect you to labour in these conditions? That's too low even for me!'

'You presumed so much to know what I *didn't* want that you never stopped to think what I might have wanted to do!' Joanna snapped. She took a deep breath and forced herself to regain control of her emotions. 'Working for my uncle gave me the greatest contentment I had. I steal every moment I can to draw. I may not be able to wield a hammer or beat a wheel, as you told me so coldly, but I can etch and chase the metal.'

'You never told me any of this,' Hal said. 'Why not?'

Joanna looked at the floor. 'When I first offered to help you made it clear you didn't want me here so I didn't see why I should tell you. Later I was worried you might be angry that I hadn't told you.'

'I could never be angry with you!' Hal exclaimed. 'I'm hurt you kept it a secret, but angry? Not at all.'

Joanna examined the figurine on the bench to save looking into the eyes that smouldered with the intensity of the furnace. It was cruder than her picture, but even though it was unfinished the craftsmanship was evident. Pride fluttered in Joanna's breast that her work could turn into something so fine.

She crossed to the furnace, braving the stifling heat, parchment in hand. Hal made no move to stop her though his shoulders and jaw tensed and his eyes followed her closely, his visible unhappiness razing her conscience. He inclined his head towards her. He was not granting her permission as much as acknowledging her right to do as she wished and in that moment she felt an overwhelming sense of affection towards him. She took an adze from the workbench and held the point deep in the glowing coals.

'It wasn't finished,' she said quietly. She made half-a-dozen quick strokes with the sooty tip of the tool and the bird sprang to life. She held the paper out for Hal to see and saw for the first time how her hand shook. 'Now it's complete.'

Hal reached for the parchment. Joanna expected him to take it from her, but instead he closed both his hands over hers. His touch burned into her skin even in the heat of the room.

'You shouldn't have kept it from me,' Joanna said, simply. 'If you had asked I would gladly have shared everything with you, but you only wanted my work. You didn't want *me*.' Her voice was little more than a whisper. Speaking the words aloud was enough to squeeze the breath from her lungs and the blood from her heart.

'Not want you!' Hal's eyes widened with surprise. 'Do you have any idea of the power you exert over me, Joanna?' He took her face in between his hands and held her gaze. 'You don't, do you? For days now a single work or kindly glance in my direction has been enough to make the moon shine as bright as the sun.'

Joanna stared back into Hal's eyes, rimmed with red, surrounded by dark circles and filled with a whirlpool of conflicting emotions—hope, anxiety, remorse. Her knees went weak. Her attraction to him was becoming harder to ignore and the need to be in his arms flared inside her. She laced the fingers of her free hand through his.

The anxiety in Hal's eyes was replaced instantly with joy and something Joanna recognised as desire. He broke into a wide smile that caused his eyes to smoulder with more intensity than before.

She put her hand to his cheek and tugged him into a kiss. His lips found hers, not gentle as she had expected, but hard and urgent. She wrapped her arms around Hal's neck to prevent herself falling and felt his hands come around her body, fingers spreading wide as they roved across her back and waist.

She met his kiss with a passion that caught her unawares. Not since the first morning of their marriage had his lips been so demanding, so frantic with desire that it left her reeling.

Hal pushed her back against the wall with a violence that knocked the breath from her body. She wrapped her arms around his back as his legs parted hers, his hardness pushing against her. She tugged his tunic upwards so she could run her fingers over his chest and he growled. The sound reached inside her like a fist twisting her insides into a knot from heart to groin. She scraped her fingernails down the length of his spine before bringing them round to skim across his nipples. He broke away, fixing her with eyes that burned.

His voice was hoarse. 'When you touch me like that it tips me over the edge of madness. I want you so much it hurts beyond endurance. I'm cautioning you, if you carry on touching me that way I'll take you here and now. I won't be able to stop.'

Joanna licked her lips and swallowed. She slid her hand down between their bodies, feeling the proof of his words. She brushed her hand against the hardness she felt and lifted her face. Hal was watching her intently, his eyes drunk with lust. She recognised in his expression the desire that filled herself.

'Then don't stop,' she murmured.

Hal's lips were on hers before she had finished

speaking. His hands roved across her body, lifting her skirts, pushing aside the shift beneath. His fingers began moving against her, stroking, teasing. She cried out through his kiss as an overwhelming need enveloped her. The familiar pressure began to build deep inside her belly. She sighed in pleasure, pushing her hips forward. A wave of pleasure shot through her as Hal's touch became firmer. She brushed her fingers through the dark down of his chest to stroke the firm muscles. Her hands continued downwards to take hold of him by the waist. She felt herself sagging against the wall, but Hal's other hand tightened around her back, holding her upright. His lips found her neck, nipping gently at the flesh beneath her ear with his teeth. When he took her earlobe between his lips she sighed and pulled him closer.

Hal's stroke was faster now. Every movement of his thumb sent greater crests of pleasure through Joanna until the pressure burst, splitting her body in two and she cried aloud. She sagged as molten steel encased her limbs, but Hal had not finished with her.

He held her against the wall, his chest hard against hers as he tugged his britches downwards. With trembling hands Joanna reached down, her hand closing around him. Hal moaned with pleasure, his hips grinding against Joanna as he closed his hand over hers. He plunged into her, sending coils of heat pounding through Joanna's body. With the full length of his body he crushed her against the wall. His fingers tightened in her hair and she locked her arms around his back, refusing to let him draw back until at last, driving deep inside her, he gave a guttural cry that echoed around the forge. His arms closed around her and they slid to the floor, limbs tangled together in a heap of exhaustion.

They slept. For how long he did not know, but when Hal woke it was not yet light. Joanna was in his arms, his entire frame enveloping hers, their legs entangled. He shook his head in disbelief. What they had done had an urgency that he had not experienced before and Joanna had been his equal in it, revelling in the fire that consumed them both. It had been a revelation; so similar to every time before but far beyond a simple coupling. Holding her as she slept, he knew without question his heart would be hers if she ever desired it.

Joanna sighed and nuzzled against Hal's shoulder. The slight crease in the centre of her forehead was smoothed away by sleep leaving her looking free of cares. Hal was still staring at the lines at the corners of her mouth when her eyes opened and met his. She stretched her arms and looked around in surprise, then blushed fiercely.

'I know I never promised you a life of luxury, but I should be ashamed of myself, making you sleep on the floor of a smithy,' Hal said wryly.

He would have bit back the words instantly if he could. Why draw attention to the inadequacy of what he could offer her? If she turned away his world would end.

Joanna stroked a hand along the length of Hal's arm, then slipped it under the open neck of his shirt. 'I'll sleep anywhere as long as I'm with you,' she whispered.

Hal lifted her chin, his throat seizing with joy. 'I've been such a fool,' he whispered. 'I've mismanaged everything. I wanted to give you a home and security, but I brought you here with no thought to what would make you happy. Can you ever forgive me?'

'I forgive you,' Joanna said. She frowned. 'But there can be no more deception. If I am to live as your wife I want to play a role in every part of your life.'

'Gladly!' Hal drew her towards him so they were lying chest to chest. She smiled up at him and a worm of worry burrowed into his heart as he thought of what he hadn't told her. Later. Not now.

He gestured around the forge where the glow of the furnace was beginning to dim. 'We'll work here together if that's what you want to do. I'll find someone to help Meg in the house. I want you here beside me. Always.'

His thumbs softly traced the line of her cheek-bones.

'I want that, too,' she answered.

Hal kissed her, slowly.

Joanna rolled on to her side to better reach him. He was already hard as she brushed her hips against his and he groaned. His lips parted hers, his tongue demanding entry as a proxy for the other admittance he was already aching for.

'Again?' She smiled. She ran a finger lightly across Hal's chest, sending bursts of white-hot pleasure racing through him.

'Why not?' he growled. 'I wanted you then and I want you now.'

'Here, though?' Joanna glanced towards the door where a purple tinge had begun to change the sky from black. 'It's getting light, someone will find us.'

Hal exhaled loudly. 'Very well, I would be a

poor husband if I refused such a demand and I've been one of those long enough!' He threw his arms about Joanna's waist and looked deep into her eyes. 'We'd better go now. The mere thought of you is too much to resist and I mean to have you soon, whether here, our bed or the kitchen table!'

A thrill raced through him at the idea. Perhaps one day, he promised himself. From the look in Joanna's eye he could almost believe she read his thoughts. Stifling their whispers and trembling with anticipation they ran hand in hand to the house. Hal was half out of his tunic as he flung open the door to their bedchamber and tumbled on to the mattress, pulling Joanna with him.

When, in years to come, he thought back to the early months of their marriage, those first few hours glowed in his memory like the slowly rising sun at daybreak.

Hal's life with Joanna was entirely divided into the time before and the time after May Day. He had feared the events of the night would turn out to have been entirely brought about by the wine they'd both drunk and in the light of day and sobriety he would find her cold and distant as she had once been. The idea of Joanna once again compliantly submitting to his attentions as no more than a dutiful wife chilled his blood.

He needn't have worried. Joanna's passion every time since had been astonishing. That she had come to him eagerly after a quarrel of such violence had been unexpected in itself, but to find her willing in his arms time after time was nothing short of staggering.

When once she had lain silently, now she drove him on whenever he began to plant kisses from her neck to her breasts. When his hands and mouth travelled further down she cried out with abandon and clutched at Hal tightly enough that her fingernails sent darts of delicious pain through his back. He didn't mind. He'd wear the marks she left proudly; proof that his wife was no longer the stranger he'd married. Long after Joanna slipped into a deep satisfied sleep, a smile of contentment on her lips, Hal would lie awake, determined to capture each memory in case she awoke one day changed.

He glanced over to where she sat now, head bent over her work, and his pulse started to race. A month afterwards Hal could barely imagine the time when Joanna hadn't been beside him in the forge. Not every day—his work for the farmers and villagers who sought his trade did not require much ornamentation—but often she would be there, working at the end of the bench closest to the light.

He walked to her and kissed the nape of her neck, imagining he could still smell fragrance from the flower wreath she had worn on May Day. She smiled up at him.

'What was that for?'

He kissed her lips this time. 'No reason,' he replied, embracing her. Her arms came around his waist. He knew without question that he had committed to spending the rest of his life ensuring she never regretted her marriage for a single day. It seemed incredible that by keeping his work from her he had come so close to jeopardising what he had not even realised he wanted so badly.

There was an insistent scratching at the door. Simon the dog was demanding to be let in. Hal eased his arm free and opened the door. Simon ambled across the room and curled on the floor beside Joanna in the space Hal had vacated. He turned his rheumy eyes on Hal, daring Hal to try reclaiming his territory. Hal scratched the old grey muzzle. Of all the companions Joanna could have chosen, this ugly mix of goodness-knew-what ancestry would have been the last he'd expected. But why not another unwanted being with no place in the world? He'd given sanctuary to enough of those in his time…

The secret he had not yet shared with Joanna danced treacherously in his mind. He'd put off telling her for too long already. He could picture her eyes filled with scorn, pity, coldness—who knew what? The thought of her turning away from him in anger or disdain sent him into a panic of unreasonable intensity and his resolve to tell her the truth wavered.

It could wait a few days longer.

'Let's go out,' he said. 'It's time you had another riding lesson.'

They rode slowly towards Wharram Danby in the warm June sun, an easy path suitable for a novice. Joanna was a quick learner, able and willing to follow Hal's instructions. He watched with admiration as she trotted in a wide circle around him.

Long days in the sun had streaked her already fair hair and strands of white gold mingled with the corn. The wind and sun had planted roses in her pale cheeks, making her blue eyes as vivid as the sea.

She saw Hal watching and her smile deepened as she came alongside him. 'What are you thinking?'

Hal took her hand in his. 'Poetry,' he said. 'I'm

composing a ballad for you. Perhaps another calling beckons me.'

Joanna leaned across her saddle to bat at his arm with a laugh and something behind her caught Hal's eye. In the distance a rider was climbing the ridge at full speed. Hal's hand tightened and Joanna twisted to follow his gaze.

'Is it someone from Wharram? Do you think something's wrong?' she asked.

'I don't know. Wait here,' Hal instructed. He set off at a gallop.

They rode towards each other, the figure growing larger as it climbed the winding path. A knot of lead began to grow in Hal's belly, small at first but growing steadily. By the time the rider was close enough to recognise he felt his entire body was in danger of being dragged to the ground by the weight on his chest. His hands tightened on the reins as he urged Valiant forward. The rider hailed him.

'Greetings, Hal. This is a fortunate meeting!'

Hal didn't dismount, but sat in the saddle, eyes boring into the twin pair of the rider opposite. He gritted his teeth and smiled warmly, though he felt like doing nothing less.

'Good day to you, Roger,' he said.

Chapter Eighteen

'You've made good time to get from Windsor since St George's Day.'

Hal forced cordiality into his voice. In response Roger spat on to the ground.

'I didn't get to Windsor. This useless beast threw a shoe in Lincoln.' He dug his heels into the flanks of his horse and pulled roughly on the reins as it edged forward. Hal winced in sympathy for the animal.

'I had to wait two days for a farrier. I was too late arriving at Leicester to compete.' Roger turned angry eyes on his brother, wheeling the horse close enough that Hal caught the trace of wine on his breath. 'I've had nothing but ill fortune since leaving York!' he exclaimed angrily.

'Why are you here?' Hal asked suspiciously.

'Is that any way to greet your brother?' Roger asked.

Hal's conscience gave a twinge. Roger had rarely called at Ravenscrag when he had lived at Wharram Danby. He made no secret that he found Hal's home sparse of comforts.

'My apologies. Is there something I can do for you?' he said.

'My horse's shoe,' Roger said. His voice became wheedling. 'I could not afford to match all four when he threw it. Besides, no one is as skilled as you.'

'Or as cheap?' Hal raised an eyebrow cynically.

Roger pouted. 'Why not? We're family after all. I risked everything to win glory for our name. We share each other's fortune, good and bad.'

Hal observed his brother discreetly. With his fur-collared cloak, new boots and hat with feather he certainly didn't look like his luck had been against him. He could surely afford to pay for the work. However, the cost of four shoes would be a small price to pay for Roger to leave.

'I'll do your work,' he said. He nodded and began to turn Valiant to return home.

'There was another reason for me coming to see you,' Roger called.

Hal turned back. 'What?'

'I have a message from Father. He invites you to dine at Wharram Danby in a fortnight to celebrate my return. You and your wife.' Roger grinned slyly at Hal, whose fists clenched in response. 'So you did marry her after all.'

Roger's tone when he mentioned Joanna left Hal in no doubt that she was a third reason for his visit in herself.

'Yes, I did.' He smiled.

'Excellent news, why don't we go meet your wife now and I can congratulate her myself?' Roger replied.

'I don't think now is the best time,' Hal said, lifting his jaw.

'Oh, why not?' Roger said. 'I've worked up a thirst and we're closer to Ravenscrag than Wharram. I'm sure you will provide me with hospitality.'

Hal pursed his lips thoughtfully. He had already dismissed the faint hope that he could keep his brother's presence from her when he returned to her. She would ask who he had been speaking to, expecting news from Wharram. They would meet sooner or later if Roger was staying at home so Hal might as well face whatever would happen now. More importantly, he'd promised her no more secrets and did not intend to heap new deceptions on top of those he had already committed.

'Very well,' he said, 'I'll give you some ale before you leave.' From the smell of his brother he suspected it would not be the first cup of the day. He turned Valiant around and began to trot back home. Roger came alongside.

'So tell me, is marriage to Joanna everything you hoped it would be? Should I take the fact that you aren't hard at work at this moment as a sign you accomplished what you needed to, or have you given up hope of joining the guild?'

'My marriage is none of your business,' Hal said through gritted teeth. Since childhood Roger had known exactly how to provoke him. He could feel the anger rising in him and fought to keep his breathing steady. 'If you've come here to pry you can turn back now, the laws of hospitality be hanged! Joanna's happy. We both are.'

Roger wrinkled his nose disbelievingly. 'Of course. I'm happy for you both. I'm surprised to see you out of your forge, that's all. Something remarkable must have happened to drag you away from your work. You used to be so dedicated.'

Hal ignored the jibe, his temper softening as he thought of Joanna. It was the truth. Since his marriage, and especially since the night at the forge, the long hours he had spent shut away had begun to grow fewer.

'I am still dedicated and still determined to join

the guild,' he said. 'Circumstances change, however.'

'Do people really change so much?' Roger asked. The two brothers were silent, the air between them heating in the stare they exchanged.

'Let's move,' Hal said. 'I've left Joanna long enough alone.'

'Do you feel you have to keep a close eye on her?' Roger said, raising an eyebrow. 'What do you think might happen if you don't?'

Visions of himself doing extreme violence to Roger flashed through Hal's mind.

'She's learning to ride on an unfamiliar horse and I don't want her thrown,' Hal said calmly. 'Other than that I have no need to fear.'

Hal hoped fervently it was true. He had believed when they married that Joanna's love would die naturally and that Roger's absence would hasten the end of her feelings. He and Joanna had spent so little time together truly being happy and the idea that Roger's presence might rekindle her previous affection cut him deeply.

Shame flooded him: he had no reason to doubt Joanna's fidelity and to even entertain the idea was an insult she did not deserve. He hammered the thought into submission before he allowed it to consume him while inwardly cursing the timing of Roger's arrival.

They rode fast. Their brotherly rivalry always gave an edge to their rides but knowing this would be Joanna's first glimpse of Roger in months drove Hal to push Valiant to his limits. Roger's horse was younger, but had ridden further. Hal was fresher and reached the flat land where he had left Joanna a dozen lengths ahead of his brother.

Joanna was trotting Rowan in wide circles when they approached and even his anxiety could not quell the thump of desire in Hal's heart as he watched her. She sat relaxed in the saddle, her mastery of the animal becoming more confident by the day. She tossed her head back, her long braid whipping over her shoulder, and laughed as she saw Hal approaching.

'I think I can go faster...'

Her voice trailed away as she spotted the other rider whose face was now clearly recognisable. Hal's heart began to pound and nausea washed over him. Joanna's reaction would decide his future, his happiness, everything that mattered. The roses drained from Joanna's cheeks leaving her face the colour of ash. Her mouth opened, but no words came out and she swayed slightly in the saddle, causing Hal to fear she was about to faint. Hal dismounted quickly and strode to her side, taking hold of the reins just above her hands.

'Are you all right?' he asked.

Her eyes were fixed on Roger. She nodded slowly and Hal wondered if she had even heard his words.

'If you're feeling faint I can lead Rowan and we can ride together.'

At last Joanna tore her gaze away and looked at Hal. Her skin was regaining its colour and she appeared to be in control of her emotions. So much so that Hal still had no idea whether Roger's appearance was welcome of not.

'Did you know it was him when you left me here?' she whispered urgently. Her voice was hoarse.

'Not until I got closer. I'm sorry, if I could have broken the news to you more gently I would have.'

Roger had drawn his horse to a halt and dismounted, throwing his leg casually across the saddle. He walked towards Hal and Joanna with a swagger in his step that made Hal's blood rise.

'Hello, Joanna, it's wonderful to see you,' he said. 'I could never have dreamed our paths would cross again in such a manner.'

He moved forward as if he intended to embrace

her. Joanna's lips pressed together, turning white. She held out an arm, stiffly at full length.

'Sir Roger, how nice to see you again. However, I must insist you address me properly. I'm Mistress Danby now, as you must know.'

Roger blinked in surprise as he reached for her hand and bent low over it. Hal suppressed a smile. He wondered how his brother would find Joanna since their last encounter. Looking at her now, sitting aloft on the mare while both men stood at her feet, he thought she had the air of a queen greeting her subjects.

'May I compliment you on your riding, Mistress Danby?' Roger said. 'I see you have learned a new skill since we last met.'

Joanna lifted her chin. The pink in her cheeks deepened to crimson and her eyes flashed.

'I've learned many things,' she said curtly. 'Hal, I assume you must have things to discuss with your brother. We should return home.' She smiled at him with a good degree more warmth than she had Roger.

'That reminds me,' Roger said. 'I stopped in York and chanced to meet the Master of the Guild. He gave me something for you.' He passed a letter to Hal, who read it swiftly.

'The guild has been asked to provide a prize

of a sword for the champion at the Lammas Day joust. They are accepting entries from petitioners within and outside the guild.'

Joanna clutched hold of his arm tightly, her eyes lighting with excitement, and for a moment there was no one else on the moor for Hal.

'Oh, Hal, you have to enter!' she exclaimed.

Hal covered her hand with his. Visions flashed before him of his entry winning, himself triumphant before the guild, of Joanna by his side. He looked at his wife, her shapely neck rising from the collar of her gown, her hair coiled into loops and braids of gold. Inspiration hit him. He pictured the sword's grip a slender but shapely female form, the pommel a head with Joanna's face adorning it.

'We'll start planning tomorrow,' Joanna said.

Therein lay the problem. He wanted this to be his task alone, a demonstration of his regard for her for the world to see and a gift to her.

'Of course.' He smiled reluctantly.

Joanna's forehead wrinkled and a flash of hurt filled her eyes. She gave a flick of the reins and began to trot in the direction of Ravenscrag.

The men watched her go, then followed slowly behind. Roger gave a low whistle followed by the wolfish smile that had enticed so many women into his arms. And bed.

'You've changed her, Hal. She never used to be so fiery.'

'It was always there for anyone who cared to look for it rather than demanding submission,' Hal answered.

'Now I almost regret giving her up.' Roger laughed.

Hal whipped a hand out and seized his brother by the wrist. 'You will leave her alone!' He spat the words through clenched teeth. 'You did enough harm to Joanna's heart and I will not allow you to play games with her. If you make any attempt to come between us you will never set foot in my house again.'

Hal released Roger's arm. The knight rubbed it tenderly. 'I'm only jesting,' he said petulantly. 'I wouldn't deliberately try to steal her from you. We're not adolescents any longer.'

He returned to his horse and mounted it. As he came alongside Hal he leaned over and muttered out of the corner of his mouth, 'Though if she should come of her own accord that would be none of my doing. How well do you trust your wife and how highly do you rate your charms?'

He galloped ahead and overtook Joanna. Hal's

stomach plummeted to his boots. He hoped he had done enough to secure Joanna's affections, but he suspected he had done too little for too long. He dug his heels in to Valiant's flanks and chased after his brother and his wife.

Joanna succeeded in keeping her equilibrium while they rode back to Ravenscrag. She focused on Rowan, guiding the palfrey as Hal had taught her and paying no attention to the two men who rode alongside her: the man she had worshipped for so long and the man she was coming to love with an intensity that was frightening and in whose arms she had discovered passion she had never dreamed existed.

She took herself into the smaller chamber with her sewing while they talked. She breathed a little easier when she heard the door shut and their voices carrying down to the forge. When she was sure they had left she dropped the dress she was making into her lap and buried her face in her hands.

She'd woken that morning with an unpleasant queasiness in her belly that had not eased all day. Had she been more fanciful she might have considered it a sense of foreboding, though the real reason she suspected was not something she wished to dwell on.

Why hadn't she anticipated such a thing happening? Roger returned to Wharram Danby every summer before going to the Lammas Day tournament. She should have realised they would meet again at some point. If it came to that, Ravenscrag was part of the estate he would inherit. He could come here whenever he wished whether she or Hal wanted him to or not.

And did she want him to?

The sight of Roger riding with the easy confidence she remembered from the tournaments had made her heart leap to her throat, but the desire was crushed beneath memories of the way he had abandoned her. She had not known whether she wanted to throw herself into his arms or seize his dagger and run him through.

'Not now,' she whispered to the empty room. 'Not now I'm happy with Hal.'

She dropped her sewing and began to pace around the room. Hal's face had left her in no doubt what his choice would be. Her veins filled with ice at the anger she had seen in his eyes and his coolness towards her regarding the guild's task.

Did Hal think she still wanted Roger after all

they had done together? She was Hal's wife and as such was beyond Roger's touch and he was beyond hers. More than that, even if she could, she no longer wanted to. His sudden appearance had sent a violent tremor surging through her body, but she recognised it as instinctive lust with no love behind it. With luck his visit would be short and he would leave soon and things would return to normal.

The door slammed. She wiped her sleeve hastily across her eyes, sat back on her stool and picked up her sewing. She was bent over it when the door opened and Hal came in.

He was alone. He began bustling around the room, shuffling bits of paper, straightening chairs. And never looking at Joanna.

At no time since May Day had he entered the room without greeting her with a kiss or caress.

'Whoever shoed Roger's horse didn't know what they were doing, it's amazing he didn't break his neck between Lincoln and Wharram Danby,' Hal said.

Joanna kept her voice even and her eyes on her sewing. The needle flicking in and out rapidly, the line perfectly straight and even; a mockery of her stomach, which from the way she felt must have been knotting and coiling as she sat there. Hal stopped in front of her. She lifted her eyes to meet his face. His expression was hard, more reminiscent of the surly man she had first known than the loving husband she had grown used to.

'We've been invited to dine at Wharram before Roger leaves for the Lammas tournament.' The tone of his voice made the hairs on Joanna's neck lift.

'That will be…nice,' she said uncertainly. A knife twisted in her already churning belly. Dining with Lord Danby alone would be a pleasure, but to have to sit alongside Lady Danby and Roger was more than she could bear the thought of.

Hal narrowed his eyes before continuing. 'We can ride over. I think you'll be capable of a journey that far by then. We'll have to practise, of course. Not tomorrow, I have to finish casting Beckett's axe head and there is an appointment I need to keep. In fact, there is something I want to discuss with you; a matter I've been meaning to raise.'

His words washed over Joanna. Her mind kept returning to what was to come. She would have to endure the visit for Hal's sake. He would expect courtesy towards his family. She nodded distractedly in agreement, barely hearing what Hal was saying. He broke off abruptly and she glanced up in puzzlement.

'Of course, if you have other things to think

about I shall leave you to your dressmaking,' he said, his voice bitter.

'I'm sorry, my mind was elsewhere,' Joanna said. 'Please tell me what you were saying.'

Hal frowned. 'I think not,' he said gruffly, crossing his arms. 'It can wait whereas my work cannot. I shall leave you to your thoughts.'

He swept out of the room, banging the door behind him. Joanna had jumped to her feet, but sagged down on to the stool again as she heard the door outside slam. She frowned in bewilderment. He'd only been talking about his work, hadn't he? She stiffened in shock as some of his words finally penetrated. He'd been starting to tell her something important and she'd ignored him, lost in thoughts of…

She moaned softly to herself, wincing at her inattentiveness.

She picked up her needle and thread and began to work again. The day had started so well and since Roger's appearance everything had soured. She wished fervently that the next two weeks would pass quickly and Roger would be gone soon after.

Hal left early as usual the following morning on his private business. He had not spoken of it again and indeed had rebuffed any attempt Joanna had made to broach the subject the previous night. Nor would he discuss his plans for the guild's prize. Clearly he was not intending to discuss either matter with her.

She watched him leave, then dressed slowly and made herself a cup of warm honeyed wine to drink. The sickness she had felt the previous day had not diminished in the night, another matter to cause her apprehension. She sat at the table, chin in her arms, staring glumly at the wall.

The source of Hal's mood was clear and resentment welled up. She had given him no grounds to suspect her of any wrongdoing, or even wrong thoughts, yet he looked at her as if she had been the one to invite Roger in the first place. When he returned tonight she would sit him down and tell him as much.

She cleared her cup away, swept the floor and began to brush the cobwebs from the corners of the roof, taking her irritation out on the dust and spiders when there was a knock on the door. Wiping her hands on her apron, she crossed the room and opened the door. She stared at the visitor in dismay.

It was Roger.

Chapter Nineteen

'Hal isn't here.' Joanna's fingers tightened on the doorframe. Her stomach gave a lurch and sweat rolled up her back.

Roger smiled. He still wore his charm as easily as he would a cloak, though he did not look as he did in her memory. His eyes were redder and his face seemed fatter beneath the closely trimmed beard. When once she would have vowed he was the better-looking brother, the balance was firmly tipped in Hal's favour. The unpleasant glint in his eye was something she had forgotten completely.

'Has he gone far? When will he return?'

Joanna frowned. 'I'm not sure. He's usually gone for most of the day.'

'You don't know where he's gone, do you?' Roger mused.

'No,' Joanna admitted. She regarded him suspiciously. 'Do you?'

Roger shrugged. 'My brother's affairs are his own business, not mine. How strange of him not to tell you, but he always was secretive.'

Joanna narrowed her eyes at the inflection he placed on the word *affair*. 'Would you like to leave a message?'

Roger pushed the door wider and slipped inside. He pulled a stool from the table and stretched out his legs. Perhaps by design, perhaps unintentionally, he barred the doorway. He grinned up at Joanna, revealing his teeth. The hairs on the back of Joanna's neck began to prickle. Why hadn't she said Hal would return at any minute?

'It's been a long time since we were alone, Joanna. It's good to have a chance to talk.'

Joanna folded her arms across her belly. 'We have nothing to talk about.'

Roger pouted. 'Don't be so unfriendly. I've ridden a long way. At the very least you could give me something to drink.'

Joanna's hand trembled as she poured the ale. She held the drink out at arm's length. Roger took it from her and with his other hand seized her wrist.

'Come join me,' he laughed.

'Let go!' Joanna cried, pulling away.

'I just want to talk to you,' Roger said. He stood

and tightened his grip on Joanna's wrist, twisting until she had no option but to come within his reach or risk dislocating her hand. 'Now, that's better, isn't it?'

'You're hurting me!' she gasped.

Roger eased his hands to her upper arms, his fingers digging into the flesh just enough to hint at the pain he could inflict if she displeased him.

'I didn't mean to hurt you, but you wouldn't keep still,' Roger soothed, stroking her hair.

Joanna remembered the kisses he had demanded from her, the caresses always bordering on pain. Hal's had never hurt her, not even when his touch had been something she yielded submissively to rather than craved.

'Why did you come here?' Joanna asked. She felt something pressing against her skirts and looked down to see Simon the dog standing close. The scruffy mongrel bared his teeth at Roger.

'Because I wanted to see you again.' Roger looked down at her, leering openly. 'Why don't you give me a kiss?' Roger cajoled. 'Like the friends we used to be? I'd like that. I'm sure you would, too.'

'No, I wouldn't!' The nausea in Joanna's belly began to worsen. 'I think you should leave now,' she said firmly. 'I'll tell Hal you came.'

'Are you sure?' Roger smiled.

He reached forward and brushed the hair from Joanna's cheek, then rubbed his thumb over it. It was a gesture he had done so many times affectionately, but now Joanna recoiled from his touch. He lunged forward suddenly, locking her within his arms. Before she could protest he was kissing her, his lips forcing hers apart, tongue smothering hers. It was over before she could make a sound but not before she recognised the quickening of her pulse. Roger leaned back with a charming smile.

'What exactly will you tell Hal?' His smile slid into a smirk. 'He knows you love me. He'd believe you were all too willing to fall into my arms.'

'No, he wouldn't,' Joanna insisted. She could hear the uncertainty in her voice and hoped Roger couldn't.

Her stomach clenched and cold sweat washed over her. She wrenched herself free and ran outside where she dropped to her knees. She dug her hands in the grass and her stomach emptied itself violently. She looked up to find Roger staring at her, his eyes filled with concern—the first time she had seen such an emotion.

'I didn't mean to upset you so much, I was jesting,' he blustered.

'Just leave me alone.' Joanna wiped a hand across her mouth. She struggled to her feet and turned away so Roger could not see her expression.

'Why were you sick?' Roger demanded, his eyes narrowing.

The creeping suspicion she had been nursing for days rushed to the front of her mind and she moaned softly. Roger pulled her round to face him.

'Tell me, are you with child?' His voice was accusatory.

'I don't know. Perhaps.'

Roger growled and kicked the wall. Joanna flinched.

'I hate the thought of another man taking you. Does my brother know?'

'I haven't told anyone. It's too early to be sure.'

'You're wise to wait before telling Hal. He will need all his time to think about his work, not the worry of a child.'

Joanna nodded. Hal had never talked of children other than when he had said they could be prevented and when they made love he took great pains to pull back before he spent himself. Her cheeks flamed as she remembered the hot, fierce night of lovemaking in the forge and how she had refused to let him free. This was her fault. Nothing must distract him from what he had to do, even if it seemed she was not to be included in his plans. She stifled a sob at the thought of him working without her.

Roger held his arms out wide to encompass their surroundings, curling his lip. 'Oh, Joanna, this is what you've been brought to? You look so pale and tired. I wish I could ease your burden.'

'My burdens are your doing,' Joanna said through clenched teeth.

Roger tossed his hair back and shot her another look of pity. He tucked a stray hair behind Joanna's ear, his fingers lingering on her cheek.

'You can't be happy with a man who leaves you alone all day long. Who doesn't care enough even to tell you where he goes'

Joanna raised her chin. 'I'm happy with my husband, and if where he goes is important he'll tell me,' she said. 'Now go.'

'I'll see you again soon,' Roger said. He bowed and walked away.

Joanna sat doing nothing for a very long time. Simon whined softly and pushed his muzzle into her hands. She scratched his head and closed her eyes wearily. Roger's words came back to her and she hugged her knees as misery overwhelmed her.

He'd said Hal didn't care for her, but he must have been mistaken. He was a good man and she cared more deeply for him than she had ever expected to. The weeks since May Day had been the happiest she'd known, but was that simply because Hal had realised her worth as an instrument to achieving his ambition? Once he achieved that would his affection diminish or would the possible child she carried be enough to secure it?

When Hal returned she greeted him as usual but the memory of Roger's hands on her made her wince as he bent to kiss her. She involuntarily stiffened and hurt flashed in Hal's eyes. She reached a hand out hesitantly, but withdrew it before she had touched him.

'Have you been busy today?' Hal asked.

Joanna hesitated, then shook her head slowly. 'Not really.'

Hal turned to hang his cloak on the peg. 'Meg is going to need some help in the house now she's carrying a child,' he said, his voice unnaturally light. 'It would be kind if you would help her in the house for the time being.'

'Won't you want me to assist you with your work for the tournament?' Joanna asked.

Hal moved to the table and cut a slice of bread.

'I think I'll be able to manage. Meg's need is greater,' he said.

Joanna lowered her head so Hal wouldn't see the tears that sprang to her eyes. This was what she had feared after his reluctance to discuss his intention yesterday.

'Of course. That sounds the best thing to do,' she lied.

Roger had guessed correctly, she would not tell Hal of his visit. Why would Hal ever believe she had not encouraged him? If there had been any lingering desire for Roger it had died the moment he kissed her. Her eyes pricked at the thought of him touching her, his lips on hers with bruising force, and of what else he might have done.

From then on it was little wonder the sickness in her belly was a constant presence, just as Roger's words remained seared into her mind.

Hal watched from the doorway as Joanna slipped her new gown over her head, her body moving sinuously as she eased the heavy folds of cloth downwards. She smoothed the skirt and sighed heavily.

'What's wrong?' Hal asked.

'The fit isn't right, it's too tight,' Joanna replied. She pulled at the neckline where Hal could see it dug into the top of her breasts, full and creamy and temptingly kissable.

'You must have cut the cloth wrong after measuring it,' Hal said.

Joanna stared at her hands. 'I suppose I must have,' she said quietly. She loosened the laces and wriggled to ease the gown.

Hal frowned. Once he would have offered to assist her, after taking the opportunity to ease her out of the dress first, but as the day of the visit to Wharram had grown closer Joanna had become more withdrawn.

They still made love at night but Joanna's reluctance was clear. When her lips touched his bare flesh or her fingers began to stroke his body Hal was able to forget his anxiety, but afterwards the suspicions he had harboured early in their marriage returned to haunt his nights. Roger's name stood between them like a wall and each day they did not speak it another stone was added.

'I have to go away again tomorrow,' he said, watching carefully for any reaction.

He still had not told her where he went. She had shown no interest in where he had been when he had returned the last time. He had come so close to telling her, but had missed his opportunity. Since Roger's arrival he was not prepared to risk the recriminations that would surely follow. Once he came back from York he vowed they would discuss it.

Joanna nodded absently and carried on adjusting her bodice. Her eyes were shadowed with purple, hinting that her sleep must also be suffering, and the pinched expression she wore more frequently tugged at Hal's heart.

'I won't be back late. I'll need to prepare to leave for York.'

Joanna was staring intently at something in front of her. She picked up her marriage brooch from the clutter of pins and scarves and ran a finger over the crude curls of metal as she pinned it to her bodice. Hal's fingers itched to slip his hands around her waist and help her fix it, but he resisted the urge. He'd make her another, finer brooch once he returned from the guild. Even more than presenting his work he was looking forward to Joanna working beside him once more. If she still wanted to, of course. If she still wanted him.

He could not bear to lose her.

He came up behind her. She glanced over her shoulder at him with a smile before returning her attention to the small mirror.

'You're beautiful,' he said, impulsively putting

his arms around her and leaning his cheek against her mass of hair.

Joanna stiffened. Perhaps he had merely surprised her, but to feel her recoil was a punch to the guts. The muscles in Hal's arms tightened in response and he moved away to dress himself. When he felt able to trust himself he turned back to her, face as calm as he could manage.

'Come on, let's get this over with.'

He tried to blot out Joanna's cheeks turning pale, the sight of which threatened to unman him.

By the time they arrived at Wharram Manor Joanna's face was grey and drawn. The knowing look Roger gave Hal, one eyebrow raised behind Joanna's back as she passed, was enough to start Hal's fists clenching in annoyance.

'Allow me to escort you inside,' Roger said smoothly.

Joanna smiled graciously. 'Of course.'

Hal suppressed the stab of jealousy that speared his heart as Joanna slipped her arm into Roger's. He fell beside Lady Danby, holding his arm out for her to take.

The meal was one of the most uncomfortable Hal could remember. Fortunately no one else seemed aware of his mood. Roger dominated the room, talking loudly of his successes in the tournaments he had managed to attend before his misfortune—a detail that took far less prominence than he had recounted to Hal.

Joanna ate sparingly and sat quietly, pushing her food around the plate. Lord Danby talked loudly and in intimate detail of his efforts at breeding sheep, causing the first bloom of colour in Joanna's cheeks Hal had seen for days as she hid a smile.

'When Roger brings his bride here I hope you will refrain from such topics,' Lady Danby said sharply.

'It's a little premature to be thinking of bringing her here.' Roger smiled.

'You met with success with Sir Robin's daughter?' Hal narrowed his eyes at his brother.

'A date is not yet settled, though her father is keen we don't leave it too long,' Roger replied.

There was a clatter as Joanna placed her knife on the table. Hal shot her a sideways glance, but her eyes were fixed intently on her plate. The information was clearly a surprise and from the way her lip trembled slightly Hal took it that it was unwelcome. Further proof, he thought grimly, that she still harboured feelings for him.

'You look ill, Mistress Danby. Are you finding

life on the moors arduous?' Lady Danby asked as she gestured for the serving girl to refill Joanna's cup.

Something of the defiant Joanna Hal had grown to love flashed in her eyes as she replied.

'Not at all, though we have both been busy. That is to be expected, of course, when Hal has been working so hard on his work for the guild.'

'How fortunate he has a wife who can aid him so ably.' Lady Danby smiled insincerely at Hal.

Joanna dropped her eyes. 'How indeed,' she murmured.

Her unspoken reproach tore into Hal. She had readily accepted his suggestion of helping Meg and he had been able to work on his sword, for which he was grateful, but he missed her company in the forge. Tomorrow night he would take her there and reveal his surprise.

There was an uncomfortable silence, broken eventually by Lord Danby.

'Do you feel confident?' he asked.

Hal toyed with his goblet. 'I think I stand a good chance of succeeding, even though it is earlier than the year I was given.'

Joanna gave a slight smile that did not reach her eyes. 'I'm sure you will,' she said, her voice low.

'We must hope Roger will meet with equal success,' Lady Danby added.

'Naturally.' Roger eyed Hal maliciously, then turned a charming smile on Joanna. 'We all have to play to our strengths and, after all, mine is on the field, not in the forge.'

He tilted his cup to her. She smiled faintly and Roger lifted an eyebrow at Hal.

'Now your horse is well shod you should have no problems staying mounted at the tilt,' Hal said smoothly. He refilled Roger's goblet and raised his own in salute.

'Yes, you did a good job, you're an excellent smith. If only I had a worthy opponent to practise against.' Roger sighed. 'This part of England is sadly so lacking in noblemen.'

The comment wasn't particularly barbed, certainly no worse than any of the jibes the brothers had tossed at each other over the years, but Hal felt his jaw clench.

'It's still light outside. Allow me to offer my services, poor as they are,' he growled. There was steel in his voice.

Roger stood and pushed his chair back. 'It would be a pleasure. Lance or sword?'

'Sword,' Hal said. 'There's no point working the horses now.'

Both Joanna and Lady Danby began to protest, but Lord Danby waved a hand. 'No, let them go,' he said amiably. 'I see no harm in it, they've often practised together.'

Hal marched from the room, reflecting that had his father been able to see the expressions on his sons' faces he might have thought otherwise. Joanna caught him by the arm as he headed to the courtyard. He snapped his head round and she recoiled in alarm.

'You don't have to fight Roger,' she said. 'He was goading you.'

Hal smiled grimly. 'I know I don't have to, but I want to and I intend to win.'

Joanna's face creased with anxiety. 'I don't want you to get hurt,' she said.

His spirits lifted at her concern, but her next words sent them plummeting again.

'How can you hope to win against such a seasoned knight?'

Hal's guts twisted at the comparison. Of course she would champion Roger. 'I thank you for your confidence in my abilities,' he said bitterly.

She gasped in shock. Hal stormed off before she could reply, or before her lips twisted in surprise could break his heart even further. He hurried to the courtyard, determination renewed to face his brother and win.

Eyeing each other grimly, they strapped on padded surcoats and took wooden swords from the servant who stood in attendance. They both bowed to Lord Danby and the two ladies who stood either side of him, then made their way to the square.

Roger began to edge around, twisting his sword about his wrist. He made a few experimental thrusts forward. Hal stepped around, allowing Roger to set the pace, and caught each blow before it could hit. Whatever Joanna believed, the sword was not Roger's best event. He was lunging with far too much vigour and little sense of a plan. Hal parried his thrusts in a leisurely fashion, enjoying the annoyance in Roger's eyes.

'Aren't you going to fight me properly?' Roger panted. It was early in the bout to be showing obvious signs of exerting himself, Hal noticed. He lunged forward, knocking Roger's blade aside with a clatter that resounded around the courtyard, and then quickly stepped out of reach.

'We're only sparring,' he said calmly.

'But this is your chance to show Joanna you could have been the knight she wanted,' Roger said mockingly.

'Do you think you can say anything about Joanna that can affect me?' Hal said. He had barely broken a sweat while Roger was red in the face, yet his heart threatened to burst. He concentrated on steadying his heartbeat as he twisted around.

'I don't remember her being so withdrawn,' Roger said through heavy breaths. For someone who had been competing for months he was woefully out of condition.

'If you think you can goad me into a false move you're mistaken,' Hal answered, 'and there's nothing wrong with Joanna.'

Roger paused, giving Hal the chance to land a blow that his brother barely managed to avoid.

'Are you sure?' Despite the near miss Roger grinned slyly. 'She's so pale.'

Hal's throat caught. Roger was right. They edged round, feet scuffing in the dirt. Roger laughed and made another vicious jab forward.

'You won't keep her,' Roger taunted. 'I can see it in her eyes, she's not truly yours. I know it and you know it. How long before she goes elsewhere craving affection?'

Hal advanced with a series of powerful strokes that pounded Roger backwards.

'From you?' Hal spat. Fire coursed through his

limbs. 'You don't care about her. You may want her, but that's where it ends.'

Roger smirked. 'The crucial difference is she loves me. She doesn't love you and never will.'

Hal lowered his blade as Roger's words cut deep. For months his feelings for Joanna had become overpowering. He had dared to believe she returned his affection, but that had been with Roger absent. The time between May Day and Roger's arrival now appeared nothing more than a brief interval that could never have lasted.

He could admit defeat and await the slow death of the life they had started to build together or he could fight for her. With a roar he raised his sword aloft and rounded on Roger. With renewed determination he lunged forward, raining blows down on his startled opponent until Roger stumbled backwards and his sword flew from his hand.

Hal lowered his blade and nodded at his brother.

'Stay away from my wife,' he commanded.

He walked to where the three onlookers stood, bowed to his father and Lady Danby and took hold of Joanna by the arm. She gazed up at him apprehensively.

'Come on,' he said. 'We're going home.'

Chapter Twenty

The journey to Ravenscrag had never seemed so short. They rode fast, Joanna watching Hal with desire she could barely suppress. Since the day he had returned from wherever he went and told her he no longer needed her help there had been a distance between them, but tonight she watched the fire light within him once more. His eyes had blazed with passion as he had led her by the arm away from the courtyard, sending thrills of excitement through her.

As he lifted her down from Rowan she pushed herself against his chest, lifting her face and brushing her lips against his. His eyes widened in surprise and his kiss came with a fierceness she was not expecting. She threw her arms about his neck. He swung Joanna into his arms and carried her through the house to their bedchamber.

Hal pulled Joanna down to the bed. She followed eagerly. Her fingers brushed his chest and he moaned. She tugged at his clothes, loosening his tunic. Hal guided her hands about his waist, pressing her fingers into the flesh as he unlaced her dress and slipped it downwards. Hal's fingers began to stroke her belly and he ran his lips along the curve of her neck. Joanna's head swam. She arched her back from the bed to welcome his touch, her head spinning with need.

A long time later she lay in his arms, head resting on his chest, and listened to the steady rhythm of his heart keeping time with her own. Roger must have been mistaken. Hal did want her, how else could she explain the tightness of his embrace or the fierceness of his kisses? His face flitted in her mind briefly, indistinct as a wraith and as welcome. She banished it and smiled at her husband.

'You fought so well tonight,' she murmured. 'You have such skill.'

She felt rather than saw Hal's mood change. His muscles stiffened where previously they had been soft beside her.

'My skill. That explains your enthusiasm tonight,' he muttered, his voice taut. 'I don't want to be a knight and I never did. You need to realise that and stop wishing I was some—' He broke off. 'Some*thing* else,' he finished.

'I don't,' she whispered, but he seemed not to hear her.

He rolled on to his back and folded his arms across his chest, a barrier impossible to break through.

'The day after tomorrow I'll go to York and present my work to your uncle and his men. I'll find my success in my own way. The way I know best, and I'll do it alone.'

Joanna stared at the shafts of moonlight in silence.

Alone.

If Hal succeeded she would be of no further use to him. He'd already shut her out of the forge. Would that be the end of his regard for her? She did not want to think what would become of her and her child if that was the case, but worse, she could not bear to lose him knowing she had fallen so deeply in love.

Hal paced rapidly around the bedchamber as he dressed, not for the first time reminding Joanna of some powerful animal caged against its will. She watched him from the bed, barely needing to feign the weariness she had told him would keep her there for longer than usual. The last weeks had been easier and she no longer felt nausea at every turn, but now at times her limbs felt as heavy as lead. The ride of the night before, and what they had done on their return, had left her exhausted.

Hal pulled the tunic on and ran a hand through his hair. He locked eyes with Joanna, causing a shiver to caress her body. He came to sit on the edge of the bed and reached for her hand, rubbing his thumb gently across her palm.

'Meg won't be able to come today. Are you certain you're going to be all right?' he asked.

At the concern in his voice, Joanna's throat tightened. She threaded her fingers through his. Beneath the covers her free hand shifted surreptitiously to her belly. Her suspicions could no longer be denied, yet she had still not told Hal she was carrying his child.

'I'm just tired. I haven't been sleeping well,' she answered.

The relief on his face was clear. He sprang from the bed and continued dressing.

'Good. I won't be gone as long today.' A furrow appeared between Hal's eyes. 'I can barely spare the time as it is. I have so much to do before I leave for York tomorrow.'

The corner of Joanna's mouth twitched at the

sight of him so anxious. She pushed herself on her elbows.

'I'm sure it will be perfect. Whatever you have made.'

She tried to keep the resentment from her voice, but failed. Since Hal had begun work on his new piece for the contest he had gently, kindly and most definitely hinted Joanna was no longer welcome in the forge. She did not mind, in truth. Since the summer had arrived in full force the heat had come close to making her faint and she was glad to be out of the stifling room.

It was what the change symbolised that burned into her heart with such agony. Since hearing of the contest Hal had been a man obsessed with his work. As in the early days of their marriage he barely spent daylight hours outside his forge. Then she had welcomed his absence, but now she missed him more than she thought possible. She had her secret, Hal had his and each day they did not share them was a day they grew further apart.

Today she intended to discover one of them for herself. Whatever she might find, she decided she would rather know.

As soon as Hal left Joanna climbed from the bed and dressed. She picked up her cloak before deciding against it. The day was already warm and stuffy. She made her way to the stable and saddled Rowan. The mare snickered amiably in greeting. Her conscience stabbed, but she silenced it.

'If he won't tell me, I'll have to find out for myself,' she told Rowan.

Simon waddled from the house, barked expectantly and rubbed against her legs. She scratched his ears and carried him back into the house.

'You can't come with me,' she said, 'I'm going riding.'

'Joanna, good morning. Where are you going at such an early hour?'

She jumped at the voice behind her and turned, her heart sinking.

Roger was standing beside Rowan.

'Hal isn't here,' Joanna said flatly. She leaned past him and took the reins.

'I know Hal isn't here,' Roger said. 'I came to see you.'

'I can't talk to you now,' she said.

She glanced towards the hills. Her plan relied on her leaving now. She could not hope to keep pace with Hal, and doing so would mean more chance of being seen in any case, but she knew the direction he rode in. She had watched him depart and return enough times now to be fairly sure his destination was always the same. Once he reached the furthest hill the road forked to the coast or inland towards Guisborough. As long as she saw which way Hal turned she felt sure she would find him.

She took a step past Roger. 'I want you to go.'

'I have to talk to you.' Roger lunged forward and seized her by the arms. His breath was hot on her face with the trace of brandy. 'I was watching you last night and couldn't sleep for thinking of you.'

'Why are you telling me this?' Joanna asked harshly. She tried to pull away, but he would not let go.

'I have to,' Roger answered, gripping tighter. 'The power you have over me is so intoxicating I lose control of myself.'

Months ago she would have given anything to hear these words. Now, coming after days of Hal's remoteness, they seemed a mockery.

'What is wrong with you?' Roger asked in astonishment.

'Everything is wrong.' She was alarmed to feel her eyes fill with tears. She could not, would not, cry in front of Roger. She glared at him. Her legs gave way, only Roger's tight grip preventing her from sagging to the ground as sadness enveloped her.

'It shouldn't be you saying that. It should be him.'

'Do you mean Hal?' Roger asked.

She gave a sob at his name. 'I can't help it. I love him.' White-hot fire filled her chest. It was the first time she had admitted the words aloud. 'I love him,' she repeated quietly.

'You can't love him! You didn't even want to marry him. A bastard who spends his days hefting ploughshares and horseshoes. You deserve better than that.'

Roger's fingers crept from her arms to her waist, tightening uncomfortably on either side of her spine. He dropped his head and stared into her eyes, leaving no doubt who he thought she deserved. His eyes were as deep brown as Hal's, but where Hal's contained flecks of jewel green and honey, Roger's were charred sugar and contained none of the warmth that thrilled her.

'He doesn't even know about your child, does he?' Roger scoffed.

'Take your hands off me now!' Joanna growled.

Roger raised his hands with exaggerated care and stepped backwards.

'You're glorious! Why did I never see it before?' His eyes narrowed and he smirked. 'I should never have listened to Hal when he told me to leave you. He can be so persuasive, though.'

'Hal told you to leave me?' Joanna whispered in disbelief. She sagged weakly against the doorframe and stared at Roger. He had to be lying.

'Didn't he tell you that?' Roger raised his eyebrows with exaggerated surprise. 'Why do you think I broke with you? He told me that as I could not afford to keep you how you deserved I should let him take my place. That you were of more use to him than me.'

Joanna's legs began to shake.

Roger slipped a hand behind her neck, lifting her hair, and leaned in close. He brushed her cheek with his fingertips and his lip twitched into a smile, not of fondness but of covetousness.

'The man you think you love deceived you and he'll keep on doing it. We both made a mistake. I should never have rejected you and you should never have accepted Hal's hand, but we don't have to live with that forever. I'm not going to stay in England much longer. I'm going abroad to fight, maybe for one year, possibly longer. I'll win my fortune that way, I'm sure of it. Come with me and live under my protection. I'll take care of you.'

'You're talking nonsense,' Joanna said. 'I am married and you will soon have a wife.'

Roger flung his arms wide in exasperation. 'Do

I have to spell it out? I'm not asking you to be my wife, I want you to be my mistress.'

Joanna stumbled back, her stomach revolting. Disgust and anger flooded her. 'How can you suggest such a thing?' she spat. 'Do you take me for a whore who will run to any man who asks?'

Roger's lip curled. 'You were quick enough to jump into marriage—and bed—with the first man who made you an offer. Why not me again?'

Joanna flung herself at Roger with a cry of fury. 'Quick! I didn't want to get married, but I was given no choice!'

Roger seized her by the arms and pushed her back. She hit the stable door, jarring her neck painfully. Brushing the hair back from her face, she stared at him with hate in her eyes.

Roger moved towards her.

'Don't touch me!' Her throat was too dry and her stomach twisted with sickness and hunger. 'I wasted months when I could have been loving Hal.'

'Don't be a fool, Joanna. I'll be leaving for York tomorrow. Until then you know where I am if you change your mind.' Roger laughed softly.

Joanna spat an oath at him. She stalked towards Rowan on shaking legs and mounted, wheeling the palfrey around. She eyed Roger with contempt. 'Whether or not Hal loves me I will never be your mistress. You sicken me!'

Her head ached with an insistent pounding in her temples and the need for a cooling breeze was impossible to ignore. She hoped she had not been delayed too long to follow Hal. If she had been in two minds whether to follow him, Roger's revelation had decided her.

Her stomach twisted into knots as she rode further from home. The small figure in the distance turned right, heading inland. Joanna followed, increasing her speed to a canter. She gripped the reins tightly and glanced around nervously. She had ridden alone, but not so fast, and certainly not so far. She passed occasional travellers on foot or driving carts, but the road was quiet and there were few buildings that might indicate Hal's destination.

When the road split again Hal turned further inland. Joanna paused and raised herself in the saddle. He was galloping to where a cluster of houses, barns and fields—sparsely scattered and not large enough to deserve the description of village—huddled in a shallow valley.

The road became a path, rutted and stony. As she approached the first building Joanna slowed her pace. Her skin prickled with anticipation and she bit her dry lips, wishing she had thought to bring something to drink.

Valiant, standing alone, came as a shock to her. He was tethered to a post by a low bridge, his nose deep in a bucket of oats. Joanna dismounted and patted his neck. He whinnied in greeting and allowed her to take a handful for Rowan who she tethered alongside.

Where was Hal? He had arrived long before she had and was doubtless inside one of the buildings, but which one? No door stood conveniently open. There was no smithy where he might be working. All the inhabitants were seemingly engaged in their own tasks. Joanna exhaled in frustration. She had not considered what she would do when she arrived and Hal's whereabouts were not clear.

She left Rowan beside Valiant and walked along the road through the hamlet. Curious eyes followed her. She pulled her hood forward despite the heat. An old woman sat on a stool, legs stretched out in the heat.

Curtsying, Joanna asked, 'Please, do you know who that horse belongs to?'

The woman grunted and fixed Joanna with shrewd blue eyes that seemed to read everything Joanna would keep hidden. Finally she cocked a thumb towards the furthest building.

It was a low cottage, set against the small stream that wound lazily through the valley. Beyond it the ever-present heather covered the hill that rose up and away. Joanna's knees trembled as she walked towards it, steeling herself for whatever she might find within.

Her step faltered when she realised she could hear voices: one familiar and one new, and it was the new voice that reached inside her like a fist and tightened around her heart.

It was the voice of a child.

Joanna walked towards the building, concealing herself around the corner, following the voices. Her mouth dropped open at the sight of the girl as she ambled up and down the hill in front of the man following her. She was no more than three years old and with unruly black hair tumbling into her eyes there was no mistaking her parentage.

Any lingering doubts Joanna might have had vanished as she watched the girl's face light up at the sight of her father. Hal bent and caught the child, swinging her high in a wide circle, their identical raven curls flying out behind them. Her shrieks of excitement split the air, ripping into Joanna like a knife. She clutched on to the wall, digging her nails into the stones.

There was worse to come. As Hal lowered the

girl and they walked together down the hill, the door opened and a woman came out. She was tall and slender, her dark hair neatly wound beneath a plain cap. She bent to her knees and the girl let go of Hal's hand and ran to where the woman waited open armed. The woman said something to Hal who laughed in response, deep-throated and warm. His reply was too low for Joanna to discern, but the woman and child laughed as well.

Joanna's stomach clenched. A hot sweat began at the back of her neck, creeping across her scalp and down her back. Her heart tightened in her chest, squeezing the air from her body. A loud thumping filled her ear, rhythmic and rapid. She realised it was her heartbeat.

The girl broke away and skipped to the stream where she began throwing pebbles into the water. Hal and the woman stood side by side, watching. The scene was one of such contentment that Joanna had to force down the wail of loneliness that rose in her throat. She gave a soft moan as nausea enveloped her and she sank to her knees retching and thankful she had eaten nothing all morning.

A sob burst from her and she clasped her hands across her mouth to silence it. The pain that overwhelmed her must be how Roger's mother had felt. At that moment Joanna forgave Lady Danby all her sour words towards Hal. She pushed herself to her feet and leaned against the wall of the house. Hal and the woman were walking back towards the house, swinging the squealing girl between them.

Her eyes blurred. She wiped the tears away roughly with her sleeve. Why should this discovery shock her? The child was clearly older than their marriage. A marriage she had entered into knowing she was a means to an end for Hal and not expecting, or wanting, his love. Hal himself was the product of such a tryst. Hadn't he even hinted it to her when he said he would not make his father's mistakes? Bitterly she wondered if he had ever intended to share his secret with her or if there would have been excuses and reasons to delay even further.

Hal glanced in her direction and their eyes met. His smile vanished. Joanna threw herself back around the corner, breath catching in her throat. She had to leave. There was nothing to keep her here in any case.

Chapter Twenty-One

'Joanna! Stop!'

Joanna froze and turned around. Hal was running towards her, his face twisted in surprise. He seized her by the arms. 'How did you find me?'

'I followed you,' she muttered. 'On Rowan.' She gestured needlessly to the horse, then burst into tears, arms limp at her side as sobs racked her body.

'On horseback? You rode alone?' Hal's eyes widened with worry and Joanna felt an unwanted rush of affection that his first concern had been her welfare. She hammered it down.

The painful knot in her head tightened and she swayed alarmingly. She felt herself pulled into Hal's arms. For one sweet moment she forgot what she had seen and everything Roger had told her. Her body moulded itself to his and she closed her eyes, drinking in Hal's warm, musky scent.

'I'm sorry. I didn't mean to distress you,' Hal soothed. He brushed the hair from her face where it stuck to the tracks of her tears and enveloped her tighter in a caress at once so fierce and gentle that her heart cracked. She leaned against his chest, dizzy with confusion as her longing for him and her anger at him fought for supremacy.

'Why have you come here? Is something wrong?' Hal demanded urgently. 'Are you hurt?'

Joanna stiffened in his arms. A high-pitched laugh erupted from her at the irony of his questions and she clapped her hands across her mouth in surprise. Hal's brow wrinkled in confusion.

'Hurt?' she murmured. 'Yes, I'm hurt. I'm hurt beyond imagining and I cannot conceive of the physician who can heal my wounds.'

Hal uttered a low cry and his arms tightened once more around her. He buried his face in her hair. 'Tell me what happened. Did someone harm you? Give me a name and I swear they will regret it.'

She had planned to shout and confront him with her knowledge, but her heart cooled into a hard ball of lead that lay heavy in her chest and exhausted her. She took a slow, ragged breath that tore at her dry throat and pushed his arms away from her body, stepping back out of his embrace.

How could she have thought her anger had diminished, or that she would be able to contain it? At the memory of Hal laughing with his child and woman jealousy rushed through her like molten iron in her veins. She advanced towards him, her legs trembling with anger, her voice rising in pitch until it sounded unfamiliar in her ears.

'The name you seek is your own, Henry Danby. I know everything you've been keeping from me. I know about your mistress.'

The colour drained from Hal's face, leaving it grey beneath the tanned skin. His voice was uncharacteristically deep when he spoke and Joanna could hear the fury bubbling just below the surface.

'Leaving aside your deceit in following me, what do you believe you saw?'

'I saw what there was to see!'

'I want to hear it from your lips,' Hal said quietly.

'A child! A woman!' Joanna trembled as she spat each word out. 'You have a family, Hal.'

'No!' Hal stepped towards her and reached for her arm, then drew his hand back. He ran his hands through his hair, his expression changed from belligerent to wretched.

'Is that the sort of man you think me?'

She shook him off. 'A man keeping a mistress is commonplace after all. Your father kept his when he took a wife he did not want, why shouldn't you? Do you deny it?'

'I deny it completely,' Hal snarled. He passed a hand across his eyes. 'It's because of what my father did that I would never do the same. Do you think I would inflict my life on another?'

'You're lying.'

She threw his hand off roughly. Her heart thundered in her chest, threatening to burst free. A cart trundled across the bridge. Joanna and Hal faced each other, the silence thick between them until it had passed beyond earshot. Hal was staring at her with an intensity that made her stomach churn.

'The resemblance is so strong that child could not belong to anyone else! Who else could she be but your daughter?' Joanna demanded.

Hal turned abruptly away. He walked a dozen paces, his shoulders tense. When he turned back his cheeks were flushed and his lips a thin line of anger.

'Am I really the only one who could have produced a child with those features?' he asked. He folded his arms and glowered at the ground. Joanna gasped in shock at the venom in his voice.

'I hoped by now you would trust me more, but it seems I was too optimistic.'

'You ask for my trust after proving yourself capable of keeping such a secret from me!' Joanna said incredulously.

He raised his eyebrows and gave a sigh, then nodded and spread his hands wide in a gesture of acknowledgement.

'I am her guardian and I pay for her keep, but the child, unless I am very much mistaken, is not mine. She's Roger's.'

'Why should I believe you?' she said. 'You've lied to me, kept secrets from me all through our marriage.'

His face twisted into a grimace of distaste and despair.

'I don't deny I've kept things from you, things I should have shared long before now, but it's the truth. Her mother's name was Katherine. Kitty. She was my lover for more than a year. I would have married her.' His eyes were filled with a sorrow greater than Joanna had witnessed before.

'I intended to, until my brother seduced her and she tried to pass her swelling belly off as my doing. Fortunately I can count and my apprenticeship had taken me away for long enough for that to be impossible.'

'But you still visit the woman who was unfaithful to you?' Joanna asked.

A shadow crossed Hal's face. To Joanna's shock his eyes glistened.

'Do you still love her so much?'

Hal ran a hand through his hair, then passed it across his eyes.

'Do you?' she demanded, hating herself, hating that she pushed him to answer.

Hal blinked and the hint of tears was gone. He stared back at Joanna with heavy eyes. His face took on a softness that cracked her heart in two.

'Kitty died bringing Anna into the world. The woman you saw is a nursemaid, a respectable woman who I pay to raise the girl. My brother—the fine, honourable knight you admire so much—refused to acknowledge the child as his. As far as he cared the baby could have been exposed on the moors at birth. He doesn't even know where she lives. Just as I always have, I took on the responsibility of cleaning up the havoc he leaves behind him.'

Roger's revelation about Hal's role in their relationship flashed through Joanna's mind. After the enormity of what she had discovered here she had almost forgotten she intended to confront him with that, but she flooded once more with rage.

'Is that why you forced him to leave me? Was it revenge for stealing your lover that made you determined to take me from him?'

'What are you talking about?'

Joanna crossed her arms and regarded Hal coldly, though inside she was burning.

'You told Roger to break off our betrothal. He told me so himself.'

Her hands shook so she balled them into fists. She bit the inside of her lip until the pain overcame her hurt.

'Tell me the truth,' she hissed.

Hal stared at her for an age. Silence surrounded them, blocking out all sounds of the ordinary world they stood outside.

'Yes, I did,' he admitted. 'And I don't regret it. Haven't you listened to what I've been telling you here? Isn't the evidence before your eyes enough? You aren't the first woman Roger has seduced and you won't be the last. Oh, I know you were a virgin, but sooner or later Roger would have talked you into bed and you would have been ruined.'

'You didn't know that,' Joanna cried, though his words were terribly plausible. 'If he had known of our betrothal he would have returned for me, whatever you had told him to do.'

'He did know!' Hal spat the words out.

Tears welled in Joanna's eyes. 'You're lying! He never got my letter, there wasn't time for it to reach him!'

Hal's expression darkened. 'Roger knew about our marriage before he left York. I told him the night your uncle put the idea to me and he told me to do as I wished. He never intended to marry you once he discovered you would not inherit from Simon.'

Hal stared coldly at Joanna as she heard the final confirmation she needed. He folded his arms and lifted his chin.

'As we're sharing our confidences, when did my brother tell you this information?'

'This morning,' Joanna admitted. 'He came to the house soon after you left.'

'Did he?' Hal muttered. His dark eyes flashed with suspicion. 'And was that his first visit?'

Joanna's cheeks flamed, remembering the previous visit she had kept from Hal. Her fingers moved to her lips as she remembered the kiss Roger had forced upon her that for one, brief instant she had not regretted.

Hal's lips twisted scornfully. 'I thought not. You accused me of infidelity, but perhaps you should consider your own conduct!'

Joanna launched herself at him with a cry of

fury. Hal seized her by the wrists, still gentler than Roger's grip had been, and held her at length until she stopped struggling.

'Here is not the place for this,' he said quietly.

She lifted her gaze and met his eye defiantly.

'Where is? All I've heard today are lies and secrets. How many more are there?'

'Perhaps you should tell me that, seeing as you appear to have kept plenty of your own,' Hal said with a grimace. He let go of her wrists. 'What else did you and Roger discuss this morning?'

Joanna's hands moved unconsciously to her belly, cradling the baby growing within and remembering Roger's sneering accusation. Hal's face twisted as his eyes followed her movement. She was not showing signs yet, but understanding blossomed in his eyes.

'I see,' he said, his voice utterly devoid of emotion. 'Go home, Joanna. There's no purpose to carrying on this conversation now. I have not finished my business here yet. Aside from everything else I shall have to explain why I left so hurriedly just now. I'll be back this evening and we can speak later.'

He took hold of Valiant's bridle and unhitched it from the post.

'If you think Roger will make you happy then

go with him. I'm tired of living with the knowledge that you would prefer another man to me in your bed and life. I won't stand in your path.'

He walked back to the cottage, his head down and shoulders set.

Joanna mounted Rowan and blindly started towards Ravenscrag, not knowing how she would endure the pain that threatened to consume her.

By the time she reached the stones Joanna's head was pounding insistently. She dismounted and walked across the spongy ground. So many thoughts assailed her that she could not unpick a single one without causing others to shift like a pile of rocks poised to fall and crush her.

The ugly words that had passed between her and Hal replayed themselves, none more painful than the devastatingly quiet two he had uttered when she had unwittingly revealed her pregnancy. It had not been how she intended him to find out, but if Joanna had needed proof of Hal's indifference towards her this was it.

I see.

And he had told her to go home as if what she had told him was of no consequence. His suggestion that she might wish to go with Roger was a knife in her heart. She had believed he cared for her, but he would give her up in a heartbeat even though she was carrying his child.

Roger's vile suggestion reared up, turning her stomach. His certainty that Hal would not believe she had been unwilling had been correct. The accusation struck her and her cheeks flamed once more, but worse still was the thought that Hal believed she still cared for Roger. How could Hal even think for a moment she could contemplate such a thing after Roger's treatment of her?

She put her head in her hands. Because she had never told him what Roger had done when he'd visited.

The unfairness of her accusations against Hal struck her and she squirmed. What did it matter now that Hal had prevented her marriage? He had been right to do it; Roger cared nothing for her and never had. She had failed to win Hal's heart, too.

The moss was soft and she was exhausted. Rowan stood patiently by the road, grazing. The breeze she had craved blasted her, colder than she had expected, and she regretted leaving her cloak behind. She sat down and leaned back against the largest rock and closed her eyes, drinking in the sweet scent of heather. She'd rest just for a while before thinking what to do.

* * *

When she next opened her eyes the sun had almost sunk beneath the horizon, casting long shadows before her. Clouds were gathering over the sea, promising a storm to thin the heavy air. She looked to where Rowan stood, but the horse was gone. She called, but there was no sign of the mare. Hoping desperately that Rowan would have the sense to return home, she realised she had no choice but to walk back to Ravenscrag. Joanna's stomach growled, tightening painfully. With all that had occurred she had eaten and drunk nothing all day. No wonder her legs shook and she felt lightheaded.

A short way beyond the stones the beck trickled over the edge of a small gully. Her dry mouth ached at the thought of cool water. She pushed herself to her feet and crossed the spongy moss. Water oozed over her boot as her foot sank into a hidden pool to the calf. Wrinkling her nose, she pulled her foot out. The moss was a darker green band that lay between her and the beck. Beyond it lay darker clumps of tangled heather and grass. Probably a better way to cross. She edged closer, took a step back, swung her arms and jumped across the moss.

The landing she expected never happened. Her

feet carried on through and beyond the heather, deeper by far than she had anticipated. She flailed her arms wildly, but was unable to prevent herself sliding down into the gully that was much closer than she had realised. Heather whipped her face, a bough caught her temple, sharp pains that stung and sent flashes of light bursting behind her eyes. She came to rest half over the edge, her legs scraping painfully against the bushes that grew out over the edge.

With her hands clutching at woody stems of heather Joanna twisted herself on to her front. She tried to climb back up, but her feet skidded against the slippery moss and she slid further down, only coming to a halt by digging her fingers deep into the bushes.

She lay face down on the heather, panting, shivering and dizzy with shock until blackness closed over her.

Hal had watched Joanna ride away and said nothing. Every impulse in his body insisted he follow after her, but he ignored them. He put his arms around Valiant's neck and leaned into the horse's warm coat, giving himself up to the emotions and despair he had mastered while Joanna was in his presence. He was unsure how long he stood there before he was in sufficient command of himself to go back inside the cottage and even then he took little joy from the rest of the visit.

He could barely comprehend how the day had ended up with such bitter words and revelations. His outrage at discovering Joanna had followed him, the guilt of his deception and discovery of his part in Roger's leaving her all paled into insignificance at the sheer despair her unwitting revelation had caused to fill his heart.

'Is the lady coming in?' Anna asked. Hal shook his head sadly. He could barely look at the child.

Unless he had misunderstood her gesture Joanna was carrying a baby. But whose? His eyes watered and he blinked violently to clear them. Four years ago the discovery of Kitty's infidelity had been heartbreaking, but it was nothing compared to discovering Joanna's, which ripped into him with the pain of a dozen swords.

He knew Roger's methods of old and could scarcely blame Joanna for allowing herself to be beguiled by the words he would have whispered and the lies he would have spun. Joanna might be unfaithful and despite all his hopes still in love with another man, but she was his wife. And he loved her.

Terror surged inside him, slapping him from his stupor.

'I have to go home,' he said. He knew he would not catch up with her on the journey, but he would make sure she did not leave before he told her so.

He arrived back at the stable to find the door closed and Rowan standing patiently by her stall, still with saddle and bridle. Annoyed, Hal led both horses inside. As he brushed them down his mood changed to worry. Joanna knew better than to leave the palfrey in such a state, so to leave her like that was a clear indication of her emotional state. He finished quickly and returned to the cottage.

Hal sensed it was empty as soon as he walked through the door. He moved from room to room, looking for signs of where Joanna might be. He poured himself a cup of wine and sat at the table, intending waiting for her to return, but her absence filled the house and he paced the empty rooms restlessly. He drained his cup and looked out of the window. The sun was level with the bottom of the frame, indicating it would soon be sinking below the hills.

Joanna should have been here by now. If she was trying to punish him by causing him to worry she had succeeded admirably. A feeling of unease pulled at Hal. He walked to the forge. Watt jumped, startled from his doze by the forge, causing iron nails to scatter across the floor.

'Has Mistress Danby been here?' Hal asked.

Watt shook his head, yawning. 'You said I wasn't to let her in if she came, but she didn't.'

'Run along to ask your mother if she's there,' Hal instructed.

If she was, a confrontation on Meg's doorstep was not something he wished to provoke. Better Watt go. He propped the door open and while he waited he unfolded the bundle on the workbench. The sword was good. Excellent, if truth were told. The blade was well balanced and sharp. The roses that balanced each end of the quillon bore no faults and the pommel was the finest work he had done. A slender figure, head erect and adorned with a circlet inlaid with coloured glass. It fitted his hand as perfectly as Joanna fitted his arms.

Watt ambled back in. 'Mother hasn't seen Mistress Danby all day,' he said.

Hal took a deep breath, forcing himself to think logically. Joanna often went walking to the stones when she wanted to be alone with her thoughts, but returned before the sun started to set. Could he have ridden right past and not noticed? It seemed unlikely, but at this point he would try any possibility.

He saddled Valiant again and rode to the stones, eyes watchful for Joanna returning, but he saw no one. He reached them at dusk. The moss by the largest rock was scuffed and slightly flattened where a body might have stretched out, leaning back, but it was damp with gathering dew, so if she had been here it had not been recently.

With increased unease Hal galloped back to Ravenscrag. He hurried into the house, calling Joanna's name, trying to keep the panic from his voice. There was no answer.

He ran back to the forge.

'Go from house to house,' he instructed Watt. 'I want everyone who can to be out searching for her.'

'It's getting dark,' Watt protested.

Hal rounded on him. 'That's *why* I want everyone out!' The boy jumped in alarm.

'I'm sorry,' Hal said. 'I can't sit by and do nothing, knowing she is out there alone.'

He paced anxiously around the village green while his neighbours assembled, told them of his plight and begged their assistance. Joanna had made herself popular in the village and help was readily offered. It crossed Hal's mind briefly that perhaps the afternoon's drama had been a ploy and Joanna was even now with Roger. He remembered the suggestion he had spat at Joanna and further shame filled him. If she took him at his word Hal would never be able to live with himself, but he'd willingly relinquish her to Roger if it meant she was safe, not lost, or worse.

His stomach twisted as he took the miller's son to one side. 'Send a message to Wharram Danby and inform them, too. If she isn't there...' his throat seized '...if she isn't there ask my father to send aid.'

As he watched the men walk off in every direction, lanterns and torches aloft, he felt a soft pressure on his foot. Simon the dog whined softly.

'Are you missing your mistress?' Hal asked, bending to scratch the dog's muzzle. 'Me, too.' He scooped Simon into his arms and ran to Valiant, folding the small dog inside his cloak. 'Let's go find her.'

Chapter Twenty-Two

Black clouds had gathered overhead and the air smelled of rain. Hal rode until he passed the furthest searchers on foot, dismounting once he reached the brow of the hill. He put Simon on the ground and walked the horse alongside, searching in a wide arc across the dimly lit landscape. It took a little less than an hour before he reached the stones and he had cried her name unceasingly until his throat was raw.

He leaned against the largest stone where he was convinced she had sat and closed his eyes in despair. Rain began to fall, cooling him, but adding to his anxiety. If he did not find her soon it would become increasingly unlikely she would be discovered before morning. He shouted her name and listened for the answer he knew would not come. He circled the rocks, Simon at his heels, calling out, pausing for a reply, then moving in ever-widening spirals. His feet squelched through bog water and he gave a grunt of revulsion as he pulled them free.

Hal called her name once more. There was a moan on the edge of his hearing, so soft he wondered if he had imagined it, but enough to set his heart racing.

'Joanna!' he bellowed once more. 'I can't see you,' he called. 'I'm here, but I need to know where you are.' He stood silently, counting his heartbeats. Finally from where the heather clumps were darkest there came a wordless moan.

Simon whimpered excitedly and raced arthritically back and forth across the muddy moss. Hal gave a sob of relief and followed, sinking in to his calves as he took long strides, peering ahead.

'Hal?' Joanna croaked. Her voice was closer now. 'I slipped. Rowan ran off.'

Hal paused, raised one foot and lowered it. He could make out the sound of water—a stream gurgling over the gully. He began to edge forward instead until he felt the ground tilt. He blinked to let his eyes adjust to the gloom. Simon was nuzzling at what Hal would have dismissed for a twisted clump of heather but for the pale mass of hair tangled down one side. She was lying on her stomach. Hal half-slid down to where she lay, running his hand over her damp dress. He rolled her over, his blood chilling at the sight of her face drained of colour save for scratches and a gash to her temple. Now he had her, relief and panic flooded through him. He eased himself to his knees and helped Joanna upright.

'Can you walk?' he asked brusquely. She nodded, but swayed alarmingly in his arms.

'My head hurts. I'm so tired.' Joanna sighed. She clutched anxiously at her belly, cradling it in a manner that Hal could not mistake for any other gesture. 'My baby!'

She said nothing more, slipping to her knees and into a faint.

My baby. Not ours.

Hal could not think about that now though, the only thing that mattered was taking Joanna to shelter. The bank was steep and more than once Hal's feet slipped, each time his blood pounding in case Joanna or her child suffered harm. Exhausted, he laid her on the flatter ground, dropping on to his back beside her. Joanna lay still, eyes closed. Simon snuffled her and licked her hand. She sighed, but did not open her eyes. Hal peered at her in the gloom. Her forehead was crusted with blood at the temple, but her heart beat evenly beneath Hal's palm, giving him hope.

Now the ground was more stable he could lift her easily. He held her close as he made his way back to Valiant. She was so light, her hands ice cold. Somehow he contrived to hold her and the dog in front of him on the horse.

By the time they reached Ravenscrag it was raining hard. Joanna was stirring from her faint, but shivering and not fully conscious. The bed-chamber was chilly; no place for anyone who had been lying on the dark moors for so long. Hal turned back and carried her to the forge. Ignoring the protests of Meg and the women who had gathered, he laid her down by the furnace and de-manded blankets and mead be brought.

'As soon as it is light send a message to my father. Ask him to send for the physician,' he told Meg. Most likely there would be no need but why take the chance?

Once they were alone again Hal tenderly eased Joanna out of her damp, filthy dress and lay back against the wall, cradling her in his arms. She sighed and her eyelids flickered open, though her eyes were unfocused. She tried to speak but no words came, only a hoarse, unintelligible whisper. Hal held the bottle of mead to Joanna's lips, tipping the liquid into her mouth.

'Don't try to speak,' he told her. 'Rest now. I'll be here when you wake.'

He reached for her cold hand and enclosed it within his, holding it long after her body had gone limp and she slid into a deep sleep. He wrapped the covers tighter around them both and settled back. He closed his eyes and remembered the last time they had lain here together and what they had done before and after. It had been the first suspicion Hal had that Joanna's feelings towards him were anything more than fondness, her actions more than duty. He realised now how little he had appreciated that. He cast his mind back and realised with shame he had never actually told Joanna he loved her. He vowed that when she woke he would tell her every day.

The first sign that all was not well was when Hal awoke with a searing heat on his chest. Joanna's cheek was pressed against him, hot to the touch. He sat up, alarmed at the way her body flopped against him. He eased himself free of their covers and pushed the forge door open, letting light flood in. Still she did not wake.

Panic chilled him. He carried her back to the house and laid her on their bed, not leaving go of her hand until he heard the cart that signalled the arrival of the physician. He was not alone. Roger followed into the room.

'Get out,' Hal growled, his blood rising until he felt as hot as Joanna did. 'You're not welcome in my house any longer.'

Roger backed out at the venom in his voice. Hal slammed the door. He paced around the bedchamber as the physician examined Joanna.

'She has suffered from the cold. I do not believe she has drunk or eaten for many hours,' the physician said. 'Now she has a fever, which is good. It will restore the balance of her humours. If this breaks, perhaps within three days or four, all will be well. Any longer than that I cannot vouch for her recovery.'

He put a cup of bitter-smelling liquid to her lips.

Hal seized the physician's wrist. 'She is with child,' he said. A chill coursed down his spine and curled like fingers of ice around his belly. He forced tears back.

The physician shrugged. 'Then we must hope

the fever breaks sooner rather than later. This will do the child no harm. Give her broth or small beer if she will take it.'

He administered his draught, gathered up his belongings and left.

Hal followed him out. Roger was at the table, drinking.

'Why are you still here?' Hal snarled. 'I warned you to stay away from my wife and yesterday I find you've been visiting her behind my back.'

'Whatever she told you, it was all done in jest!' Roger said.

'Jest! Was it not enough that you took Kitty from me, but you had to seduce Joanna, too?' Hal spat.

'I did not seduce her,' Roger exclaimed. 'Joanna is innocent of any wrongdoing. I did not expect her to agree and she did not.'

Hal's blood turned to ice. Visions of events too terrible to contemplate flashed before his eyes. 'She was unwilling?'

'Yes.' Roger held his hands up in supplication. 'Completely so. What I did was wrong, I admit it.'

Hal swung a punch that collided with his brother's jaw, knocking him to the floor. Roger scrambled to his feet. Hal readied himself for Roger's return blow, dodged aside and drove both fists heavily into his stomach.

'I understand, you're angry,' Roger panted, hands out in supplication.

Hal lunged forward, grabbing his brother round the waist and bore him to the ground.

'Angry does not begin to cover what I feel,' he roared. 'You told her I had forced you to give her up against your will. You twisted facts and turned them to poison.' He drove his knee into Roger's belly, pinning him down. 'I accused her of infidelity. Of willingly lying with you and now I find it was rape!'

Roger's eyes bulged and his mouth dropped open. 'No! Never. What makes you think that?'

He wiped a trickle of bloody saliva from his lip. 'Yes, I visited Joanna. I wanted to see if she still had feelings for me, but it was nothing more than a kiss, I swear, and that I took from her unwillingly.'

'A kiss! She is carrying a child!'

Roger gave a curt laugh. 'And you think that's mine? You're an imbecile, Hal. You're so consumed with jealousy and self-pity. She's carrying your child, Hal. She told me so weeks ago.'

'I've always taken care regarding that,' Hal said.

Hadn't he? His heart lurched as he recalled May Day and the morning afterwards where there had been no thoughts of prevention. No thoughts of anything else but his urgent need for Joanna and hers for him.

'But she told you, not me,' Hal muttered, agony piercing his heart.

'She didn't want to tell me,' Roger said. 'I saw her vomiting and guessed. I forced her to admit it.'

Roger shielded his face with his hands, anticipating a further beating, but Hal sat motionless. His brother's words rang true in his ears. His hands dropped to his sides.

'She told me nothing,' he admitted.

Roger sneered. 'And you didn't guess yourself? You didn't see how pale she's become? How tired she is? Why do you think she kept it from you?'

Remorse filled Hal. He had noticed, but had not bothered to ask, preferring instead to throw his attentions into his work. His anger at Roger faded, replaced with an all-consuming guilt and fury at his own negligence.

'I beg your pardon,' he said quietly, standing up. 'I wronged you.'

'It isn't mine you should be begging.' Roger stood and walked stiffly to the door. Hand on the frame, he glanced over his shoulder. 'If you've lost Joanna, it is none of my doing. You need to seek elsewhere for the blame. Yourself, perhaps. Yesterday I came to tell Joanna I'm leaving the country. She was distressed. I don't know why, but it was not my doing, I swear. I asked her to go away with me, but she refused.'

'Then why did you come back today?' Hal asked.

'Father sent me with the cart to see if you were ready to leave for York.'

'I'm not going to York,' Hal said quietly.

Roger gaped at him. 'But the guild is expecting you.'

'The guild can be hanged,' Hal said. 'I'm not leaving Joanna's side.'

Roger rolled his eyes. 'You're a fool,' he said.

Hal folded his arms and squared his shoulders. 'I've been a fool too long,' he said. 'I've put my work first too many times. Go to York; enjoy your tournament. I wish you well, but I'm going to be with my wife.'

He returned to the bedchamber and took Joanna's hand. Her skin was pale, her hands hot and clammy to touch.

For three days he stayed with her. He sponged her brow and throat when she burned and wrapped her in furs when she shivered. He refused all Meg's offers to take his place. The food and drink that passed his lips went unnoticed. He might as well have been consuming dust for all he cared.

Sometimes Joanna sighed, her voice a croak. Mostly she lay silently and still. In the lonely nights Hal stared at the sword he had asked Watt to bring to his bedchamber. Joanna's sword. He'd show her it when she woke. The thought that she might not wake made him double over in agony so real and physical that he could not bear to contemplate it. Instead he remembered the days he had spent crafting and coaxing Joanna's form from the metal, of the early mornings slipping from the bed when he should have stayed with the warm, living woman, and he wrinkled his nose at his stupidity. None of it meant anything if Joanna was not by his side to share it.

Joanna was lying on something soft. Her limbs felt stiff and heavy but the pain in her temple had gone. It was still dark, but an orange glow shone behind her eyelids. Was she still on the moors or somewhere else? It didn't feel like the heather where Hal had found her and which had been her last clear memory. She took a deep breath that hurt her throat and immediately a pressure tightened around her hand, as though it was being squeezed in a vice. She heard her name spoken through a thick sob and forced her eyelids open. Candlelight explained the orange glow. Hal was bending over her, clutching her hand in his.

'You bloody fool,' he cried. 'What were you thinking? I warned you not to venture too far.'

Tears would have racked her body if she'd had the energy to sustain them. As it was, one violent sob was enough to send her into convulsions of shivering in his arms. She turned her face away from him.

Hal eased his hands beneath and around her body.

'It's myself I'm angry with, not you,' he said. 'Furious. Terrified. You could have died. I could have lost you.'

Something dripped on to Joanna's cheek. To her amazement Hal was weeping. Joanna's own eyes began to blur. After the harsh words between them it seemed incredible she was now held so tightly and tenderly in his arms. Even through her anger, ripples of desire coursed through her. She buried her face in his neck and said nothing.

'After we quarrelled I thought you were trying to punish me,' Hal said, his voice steadier. 'I should have come to find you immediately, but I didn't.'

'I didn't intend to go off the path. I was going to set off home, but I heard the stream.' Joanna licked her lips, which were still dry. Her belly felt shrunken with hunger. 'I haven't drunk anything since this morning and I was thirsty.'

'This morning?' Hal's arms stiffened around her. He pulled away and regarded her intently. 'Joanna, I found you three days ago.'

She opened her mouth to argue, but then she peered closer at Hal. The stubble of his beard had grown fuller than the absence of a few hours would explain and his eyes were dark, sunken circles. His shirt hung open at the neck, crumpled and carelessly worn. From his appearance it could have been him lying on the moors, not her.

Hal brought her a mug of wine and she drank it, warmth spreading through her. He fed her sweet cake as he described in a voice thick with emotion how she had lain insensible, in and out of waking and in a fever.

'I never left your side.'

'But you should be in York by now!' Joanna struggled to sit up. Hal eased himself closer and put a finger to her lips.

'York doesn't matter. How could I leave you,

even for an instant, until I knew you were safe?' he asked incredulously.

'But the guild! It's all you've ever wanted,' Joanna protested. Guilt racked her, that she had been the cause of his failure. 'It's everything you've worked for. It's why...'

Her stomach writhed. 'It's why you married me.'

Hal drew his legs up and lay with Joanna on the bed. His chest was firm beneath her, his powerful arms locked tightly around her. She lay back in his embrace, not wanting to be anywhere else.

'There's something I want more,' Hal said. 'Something I've wanted for so long now I can't even remember when I started wanting it. Needing it.' He rolled on to his side and put his hand to Joanna's cheek. 'Needing *you*. Nothing matters unless you are with me.'

'You gave up your chance for me?' Joanna asked.

'There will be other chances,' Hal said, shrugging. He smiled suddenly. 'As for giving it up for you, I'm more confident than ever that I'll succeed because of you.'

He reached below the bed, pulled out a bundle and laid it across Joanna's lap. As he unrolled it she was transported back to the dismal inn where they had sat so long ago as angry, grieving strangers.

'Look,' Hal instructed softly.

Joanna studied the sword that lay before her. Tears blurred her vision as she recognised herself in the figure.

Hal gazed at her, his eyes burning with desire. 'I couldn't let you into the forge. I wanted it to be a surprise. To make you understand how much you mean to me. How you've inspired me.'

Joanna started to speak, but the emotions assailing her choked her words so instead she simply ran a finger gently across the pommel.

'It kills me to know I will only ever be a pale imitation of what you want,' Hal said quietly.

'You're no imitation! How can you think that?' The suspicions Hal had aired in their fight came back to her in a rush, bringing her voice with them. 'I don't want Roger. I haven't wanted him for so long. What you think I've done isn't true.'

Joanna clutched at Hal's arm and stared into his eyes, frantically willing him to believe her.

'I know. Roger told me what he asked you to do and that you refused him.'

'Is that why you came to find me?' Joanna asked.

Hal took her hand and raised it to his lips, sending waves of desire surging through Joanna. 'I didn't find out until after I brought you home. I came looking for you because I love you.'

Her heart sang at the words she had so longed to hear. 'Say that again,' she whispered.

Instead of speaking he dipped his head and kissed her, slowly and fully, leaving her breathless. Joanna closed her eyes, giving herself over completely to the sensation and not opening them until Hal pulled gently away. He took her face between his hands.

'I've been such a fool. Jealous and inattentive. I could hardly censure you if you *had* run to him for companionship. I've kept secrets and shut you out. I should have trusted you to understand about Kitty and told you everything from the start.'

'Why didn't you tell me that Roger knew we were to marry?' Joanna asked.

'Because I knew you loved him. I thought hiding his knowledge of our marriage would cause you less pain,' Hal said. 'Can you forgive me? I swear to you, there are no more secrets.'

'Can I trust you?' Joanna asked.

'Completely,' Hal answered. 'I was scared you would hate me if you found out what I'd been hiding, but nothing I could reveal would be as terrible as losing you.'

She stared deep into his dark eyes, seeing the sincerity in them.

'Then I forgive you if you will forgive me.' Joanna said seriously. 'I've kept secrets of my own, but that has to stop, for both of us. No more secrets.'

'No more,' he agreed, bending to kiss her.

She laced her fingers through Hal's and guided their hands to her belly, trembling slightly as she prepared to reveal her remaining secret.

'I'm carrying your child.'

She eyed him cautiously, terrified that after everything that had happened he would be angry or disappointed but Hal's smile of joy melted any doubts she had that her child was wanted.

'I know. I guessed. For a while I believed…' His cheeks coloured and he looked away. 'Never mind what I believed.'

He stroked his hand over the flatness of her stomach. 'I love you,' he repeated.

He smiled, sending Joanna's heart racing with desire. 'I should have told you as soon as I knew, then perhaps half this nonsense might have been avoided. I vow that I'll speak those words every day I live. I love you, Joanna, and my heart will be yours as long as you want it.'

She slid her arms around his neck, pressing herself close until there was no space between them. The powerful need for him filled her, obliterating all other sensations, and a rush of desire took her breath away. She wrapped her arms tightly around him, feeling the heat rising from him. Her entire body pulsed with longing.

'I want it now and forever,' she breathed. 'I love you.'

Hal wrapped his arms around Joanna as tightly as hers were around him. His feet twined themselves between hers until their limbs were tangled together.

'Be my wife properly, Joanna.'

'What does that entail?' she asked.

Hal's lips curled into a grin containing the promise of pleasures to come. Joanna saw her own desire mirrored in his eyes. She pressed herself closer to his body, raw desire pulsing through her. She ran a fingernail down the side of Hal's neck, delighting in the groan of passion that erupted from him.

'Why don't we find out together?' he breathed.

Joanna smiled coyly.

'I like that idea.'

She raised her head, tilting her lips to meet Hal's and preparing to lose herself in the love she knew would be hers as long as ever she wanted it.

* * * * *

If you enjoyed this story, you won't want to miss these other great reads from Elisabeth Hobbes

A WAGER FOR THE WIDOW
FALLING FOR HER CAPTOR